Horace Viel-Castel, Charles Bousfield

Memoirs

a chronicle of the principal events, political and social, during the reign of Napoleon

III, from 1851 to 1854 - Vol. 1

Horace Viel-Castel, Charles Bousfield

Memoirs
a chronicle of the principal events, political and social, during the reign of Napoleon III, from 1851 to 1854 - Vol. 1

ISBN/EAN: 9783337350031

Printed in Europe, USA, Canada, Australia, Japan

Cover: Foto ©Andreas Hilbeck / pixelio.de

More available books at **www.hansebooks.com**

MEMOIRS

OF

PRINCE ADAM CZARTORYSKI,

AND

His Correspondence with the Emperor Alexander I.

WITH DOCUMENTS RELATIVE TO THE PRINCE'S NEGOTIATIONS WITH

PITT, FOX, AND BROUGHAM,

AND AN ACCOUNT OF HIS CONVERSATIONS WITH

LORD PALMERSTON

AND OTHER ENGLISH STATESMEN DURING HIS STAY IN LONDON IN 1832.

Two Vols., Demy 8vo.

EDITED BY

ADAM GIELGUD.

REMINGTON & CO., Henrietta Street, Covent Garden.

MEMOIRS OF
COUNT HORACE DE VIEL CASTEL

A Chronicle of the Principal Events, Political and Social,

during the Reign of

NAPOLEON III

FROM 1851 TO 1864

INCLUDING

THE COUP D'ÉTAT—MARRIAGE OF THE EMPEROR TO MADEMOISELLE DE
MONTIJO—VISIT OF QUEEN VICTORIA AND PRINCE ALBERT TO PARIS—
CIRCUMSTANCES CONNECTED WITH THE CRIMEAN AND FRANCO-AUSTRIAN
WARS AND THE ITALIAN REVOLUTION

AND

EPISODES AND ANECDOTES OF THE IMPERIAL FAMILY AND COURT

Translated and Edited by

CHARLES BOUSFIELD

TWO VOLUMES

VOL I

SECOND EDITION

REMINGTON AND CO PUBLISHERS
HENRIETTA STREET COVENT GARDEN

1888

NOTE BY ENGLISH EDITOR.

In translating and editing these Memoirs it has been deemed advisable to omit much, but everything of real interest, whether personal, social, or political, has been carefully retained.

Count Horace de Viel Castel's official position, and his close and intimate relations with members of the Imperial Family and Court, gave him exceptional opportunities of observing and noting all that is recorded in the following pages.

CONTENTS.

CHAPTER I.

1851.

CHAPTER II.

1851 (continued).

CHAPTER III.

1851 (continued).

CHAPTER IV.

1851 (*continued*).

CHAPTER V.

1852.

CHAPTER VI.

1852 (*continued*).

CHAPTER VII.

1853.

CHAPTER VIII.

1853 *(continued)*.

CHAPTER IX.

1854.

CHAPTER X.

1855.

CHAPTER XI.

1855 *(continued)*.

CHAPTER XII.

1856.

CHAPTER I.

1851.

January 29th.—I dined to-day with Princess Mathilde (Demidoff), the daughter of Jérôme Bonaparte. The

VOL. I.   B

other guests were Madame Bresson, wife of our old
ambassador; Mons. de Guitaud, her brother, second
Secretary at Madrid; the Marchioness de Contades,
daughter of General de Castellane, commandant at
Lyons ; Mons. Chaix d'Estange, of the bar, and Count
de Nieuwerkerke, Director-General of Museums.
The conversation, which was extremely animated and
witty, turned chiefly upon Madame Piscatory, General
Foy's daughter, a blue-stocking of very pronounced
type, who handles Egyptian history with remarkable
audacity, and even pretends to an intimate acquaintance with the Assyrians themselves. This learned
person, it seems, is fully conversant with the ancient
mythology of the Nile and the internal economy of the
Pharaohs; in fact, she is mad on antiquity.   On her
hand, which is incessantly displayed above her head,
may be seen the royal signet of I know not which
Egyptian monarch, whose mummified remains were
discovered in one of the pyramids, while another of her
peculiarities is to insist upon her fanatical followers
admiring the beauty of her daughter's Egyptian
muscles.

After this lady the Marchioness of Caraman—
Cesarine de Bearn—had the honour to appear before
our Areopagus.   She is another blue-stocking of the
first water, who is devoted to modern languages and the
guitar.   I knew her when she was an affected coquette,
and have seen her smoking cigarettes at Princess
Metchersky's.   Poor Elim Metchersky was very fasci-
nated with her, and she was nothing loth to receive his
attentions; but his mode of courtship was not suffi-

ciently spirited for her taste, and they quarrelled; she would not forgive his want of enterprise. About this time—that is to say in 1834—she used to accept bouquets of camellias from Elim and boxes of the same flowers from Tanneguy Duchâtel, who was afterwards Minister of the Interior. Chaix d'Estange complained to us a good deal about the pressure that was being put upon him by Prince de Canino, formerly President of the Roman Republic, to induce him to undertake his case against Viscount d'Arlincourt. We all endeavoured to dissuade him from lending his services to that coarse, vulgar Republican, except Princess Mathilde, and she could not help admitting three things with regard to Canino, namely, that he had been a bad son, and was now a bad father and a bad husband.

January 31st.—Went to an evening party at the Louvre. The music good; Seligman, violoncello; Dancla, violin; Ponchard and Geraldy, vocalists. I talked a good deal with General Perrot, who commands the National Guard in the Seine district. He was very civil and friendly in his manner, and I like him extremely; a brave and resolute soldier, who is delighted to be rid of Changarnier.

The President is the object of a fresh outburst of popular indignation. The National Assembly having nominated a Commission to examine and report upon the St. Cloud Stud, the Commissioners were proceeding across the park belonging to the palace, which is now being occupied by the President, when they were stopped by a keeper, who objected to this fragment of the National Sovereignty going to the stables through one of the private walks. The Commissioners resented the interference, and in pompous and stentorian tones exclaimed — "We are the representatives of the people." To which startling assertion of authority the keeper replied, with perfect equanimity, "All the more reason." Indignation of these august individuals, of course, and an appeal to the authorities. How the affair will end I cannot say, but we live in an age when trifling causes lead to great results. Poor France !

February 1st.—Dined at Princess Mathilde's, Rue de Courcelles. Met at dinner a Sicilian Princess, whose name I forget, and Viscount de Saint-Mars, Colonel of the Dragoon Regiment now in Paris. He is the husband of the Viscountess de Saint-Mars who writes novels and newspaper stories under the name of Countess Dash ; the mistress by turns of Roger de Beauvoir, Elim Metchersky, and Alexandre Dumas. This lady left France six years ago to marry the Hospodar of Wallachia's son, and returned two years afterwards in melancholy case, abandoned by husbands and lovers alike. On coming back she used every imaginable device to regain her old position as journalist. A regular Bohemian, Countess Dash writes to live, and to have the means of frequenting public dances, spending on extravagant costumes more money than it would take to keep a dozen honest women. Pleasures of the dissolute order have a special attraction for her, nor is she very fastidious about whom she sups with after the masque at the Opera is over. She

is a clever enough woman, but no longer young, being
close on forty-six, a fact which she regrets chiefly
because she is no longer able, as formerly, to pick and
choose her admirers. Count de Rochefort, who has
just been made Colonel of Cuirassiers, was one of her
early adorers.

After dinner several people came in, amongst others
Count de Flamarens, an aristocratic dandy of thirty
years' standing, who still pursues the tender passion,
and dresses with all the resources of art, but a kind-
hearted man withal. For more than fifteen years he
was avowedly on the most intimate terms with the
Marchioness de la Chataigneraie, whose husband has
just been made Prince de Pons. The Marchioness
was as silly as an owl, but just the kind of little gossip
to retain her sway. After the Count came General
Exelmans, an amiable man, but very old and deaf;
still devoted, however, to the Princesses of the Imperial
house of Bonaparte; then his son, an officer in the
Navy, and aide-de-camp to the Minister of Marine;
also Mons. and Madame Berger, male and female
préfets of the City of Paris. The male one entered
the room like a knight of the middle-ages, only in
place of a hawk he bore his wife on his wrist. This
Berger has all the moral and physical characteristics
of a vulgar bourgeois—spiteful, foppish, and self-
sufficient, resorting to all sorts of antics to bring himself into notice.

Princess Mathilde, Guitaud, and I stayed until the
last, and had half-an-hour's cosy chat about everything and everybody. Nieuwerkerke, having other

visits to pay, had left early. In the course of conversation we talked a good deal about French diplomatists—a topic, perhaps, of no great importance, considering that one-third of them are fops, another third blockheads, and the remainder have only just passable qualities enough to make them useful. Two anecdotes, however, with regard to them are worth recording.

Baron de Lagrenée, who had been brought up at St. Acheul and was backed by the influence of that clerical establishment, was attached to the French Embassy at St. Petersburg in 1830. At that time a Bible was always prominently displayed on his table, a rosary hung on his chimney-piece, and a scapular decorated his breast; in 1831, however, he became a Free Thinker, and at the present date he is a representative of the people and a pompous Orleanist. It was in Princess Mathilde's drawing-room, about the time of the Ivan conspiracy, that he told Mons. Baroche, in the hearing of everybody, that the would-be assassin was in the pay of Louis Napoleon's financial agent. Never shall I forget the Princess's indignation, her heightened colour, the tears in her eyes, and the tone of scorn and anger in which she addressed the insolent rascal; she looked magnificent, and every inch a princess. But, to continue, this Lagrenée was sent on a special mission to China, and started at the head of an expedition for the purpose of concluding a commercial treaty with the Celestial Empire. His diplomatic efforts I need not dwell upon; we all know how fruitless they were. He had, however—and small blame to him, for nowadays everybody has the epidemic—a great weakness for decorations. His mission having come to an end, it only remained for him to set sail home, but he became possessed of the idea that it would be a splendid thing for his country if he returned a bigger buffoon than he left. He accordingly went in search of the Imperial Commissary, Lin, and begged he would procure for him the order of the " Crystal Button," which he would be delighted, he said, to wear as a souvenir of his Chinese friends. Lin, being a man of sense, told him that the thing would be impossible; first of all, because it would offend the susceptibilities of the Chinese, who had no institutions at all corresponding to our European orders, and, furthermore, that the " Crystal Button " was a distinctive mark of mandarin rank, and could only be obtained by passing an examination in Chinese literature, which, of course, our ambassador was unable to do. Lagrenée insisted, and declared that he would not leave without the "button," even if he had to wear it like a Chinaman, on his navel. In fact he prolonged his stay for six months, which piece of obstinacy cost the estimates another million and a half of francs. Lin, like a prudent Chinaman, now looked about for the means of ridding his country of so importunate a guest, and this is how he did it. Among the yellow race justices of the peace wear as their badge of office a collar of glass beads, and this collar was offered to and accepted by Lagrenée, who, satisfied with the gift, agreed to leave Canton forthwith. He did so, and a few months afterwards was demonstrating to the wonder-stricken Parisians how proud France ought to be to possess a Chinese J.P. among her Ministers for the small cost of 1,500,000 francs.

The second anecdote relates to Baron de Bourgoing, our plenipotentiary in Spain, one of the most astounding ninnies I can offer as a specimen of the species. With the manners and address of a fashionable abbé he combines a pretentious good nature and affectation of sincerity which stamp him at once as a knave. "Sir," said he one day to Guitaud, at the ambassador's palace in Madrid, "it would be an excellent thing if Spain could be induced to give some proof of the friendship she entertains for the French Republic, and so cement between the two nations an alliance which Nature herself seems to have projected. Go and ask the director of the museum for authority to take a cast of the mastodon in his collection, and tell him that in return he shall have the Legion of Honour." He added: "If I am not mistaken it is by such amenities that the policy of Louis XIV. should be perpetuated." Guitaud, who knew no more about mastodons than about natural history generally, delivered his message. But the director, in no very cordial manner, replied: "We have not got a mastodon, sir, but we have an anoplotherium, at least a skeleton of one." And he led him to the fossil remains of an enormous decayed-looking beast which was held together by wires. "And," continued he, "you may tell the French ambassador that anoplotherium skeletons do not lend themselves to moulding; that it would be a barbarous act to attempt it, and one to which His Majesty Charles V. would never consent." Guitaud retired in confusion, and thus ended the proposition by which Bourgoing hoped to re-establish the policy of Louis XIV., from which it may be inferred that French diplomacy at the present day is of a very brilliant order indeed. After 1848 we sent a fiddler to Naples, a melodramatic writer to Lisbon, a professor of languages to Frankfort, and to Berlin the son of an astronomer, a barrister of questionable repute, who passed his time in running after actresses and playing dominoes. *Risum teneatis.*

February 2nd.—I heard no news this evening at Mons. Baroche's. There were a number of foresighted people there who had apparently come to keep themselves informed of any insurrectionary movements. Persigny and Flavigny were also present in most affable mood.

At Baron Gustave de Roman's (the editor of a semi-Legitimist newspaper published at Montpellier) it was reported that Mons. Guizot had had an interview with the Orleans Princes the previous week at Clairmont, and that he had been entrusted with the task of negotiating with the Count de Chambord a fusion of the different Bourbon interests—any further delay in which, Mons. Guizot might have told them all, would certainly hand France over to the empire. These fusions, alliances, and political intrigues are little better than drawing-room cabals. Fatality marks the advent of the second empire, and the wisest course in the midst of a people without faith, energy, or rectitude is to anticipate nothing. Personal interests are alone dominant. The Republic is like a poor creature on the point of child-birth, and everybody wishes to propitiate the fates by acting sponsor to the baby. We shall all have to pay for the sugar-plums at the christening!

February 4th.—What will be the result of the proposed increase to the President's salary, notice of which was given yesterday? If the people were consulted it would be voted by acclamation. A genuine Republican, Huguenin the sculptor, tells me that such is his interpretation of the popular feeling; indeed, he added that, although he voted for Cavaignac on December 10th, he, and many who think with him, would now vote for Louis Napoleon.

Up to now I have been unable to form any accurate opinion of that prince's character, and I cannot determine whether he is a calm and resolute opportunist or a man who is swayed by doubt. He refused the throne when it was offered him by General Changarnier, and now wants a prorogation, which is after all only the stepping-stone to it. I recognize one great quality in him—he has courage; one great political virtue, reticence. Not one of his friends at the Elysée is in his confidence, for he opens his mind to no one; at the same time he is informed of every step his enemies take against him. He has proof of his cousin Jérôme's intrigues, of Changarnier's duplicity, and of the orders issued by that general to the Paris garrison to fire upon him whenever he attempts to leave the Elysée for the Tuileries. This order was communicated to him by the Count de Saint-Mars, who had himself received it.

Dejected and almost dull before the official world, he becomes animated and unconstrained in private life. I saw him last summer at St. Cloud, and again during the winter at his cousin Princess Mathilde's; he was no longer the President, but a charming and well-bred companion. He is not without *finesse* and cunning; as regards his disinterestedness, I do not believe he sets so little store upon the permanence of his power as he pretends in his Presidential messages. He is ambitious and a firm believer in his destiny, which from childhood he has asserted will one day make him ruler of France. Unfortunately for him, although he is acquainted with the principal actors in the political drama, he knows nothing of those who play the minor parts. The Government, and especially the diplomatic section, is in the hands of men who are ready to turn their coats at the first reversal of fortune. The Army is sounder. The diplomatists are either Orleanist in sentiment or, what amounts to the same thing, under the influence of those who, even if Bonapartist in name, are mere pawns in the hands of the Orleanist faction. The President has to use too many tools which have been fashioned by other hands and for other purposes. At the present time new situations require new men. What is the use of all these diplomatic flunkeys belonging to the dethroned *régime* of 1848 as Ministers and active agents of the present Administration? These men are everlastingly pestering the Governments to which they are accredited to obtain for them some high order, and when they have got it they apply for removal, in order that they may solicit fresh distinctions elsewhere. Such diplomatists remind me very forcibly of the temporary altars of rough canvas erected at religious *fêtes* in country districts, on which are displayed all the old-fashioned knick-knacks and tawdry collections of the village.

I dined at the Marchioness of Guadalcazar's. She is a grandee of Spain of the first-class and an old coquette of sixty, who endeavours to act the part of a young girl, fancies herself what she never was, very beautiful, and dances the minuet, cachucha, and bolero—a sensible enough woman if she would only admit to being more than twenty, and not try to obtain [the character of being a trifle disreputable. It was she who was sent by Ferdinand VIII. to Louis XVIII. to solicit the intervention of the French Army in 1823. The other guests were my brother Louis, director of the political branch of the Foreign Office; Mons. de Bois-le-Comte, at one time ambassador in Switzerland; and Mons. de Bretonne, trustee of the St. Geneviève Library. The latter, a learned dreamer, half Voltairian, half Dolt, talked fairly about subjects he did not understand. He is the author of an historical work, and translated "Don Quixote" to please her Excellency the Marchioness, with whom he is still on tender terms in this doubtful year of grace 1851.

During the course of a very agreeable dinner politics were largely discussed, and the two diplomatists, who are not very well disposed towards the present Government, expressed themselves in high terms of the pamphlet by Thuriot de la Rozière (an ex-diplomatist of their own kidney, and now a member of the Assembly), in which he contrasts the policy of the Assembly with that of the President, very much to the latter's disadvantage.

I am vastly afraid my brother will compromise his position. He avows his Orleanist proclivities too openly, and every Sunday breakfasts and talks politics with Viscount de Flavigny, the brother of Countess d'Agoult (Daniel Stern). The Viscount has been Legitimist and Orleanist by turns; what he is now I do not know. The members of this diminutive senate and breakfast party are, besides my brother and Flavigny, Gabriac, an old diplomatist with clerical tendencies, Bois-le-Comte, and a few occasionals of the same persuasion. They conduct themselves like thieves at a fair, taking care always to have one of their number in the crowd, in order to get the office and means of escape in case of need. These gentlemen of Flavigny's breakfast table hold the world in their grasp like little Charlemagnes; but what I admire in them most is the skill with which they have allotted to each other their several tasks. My brother occupies the diplomatic post, and is answerable for foreign affairs; Flavigny, as a member of the Assembly, the Home Office; Bois-le-Comte is a sort of insurance policy, in case the Legitimist party should ever come into power; and Gabriac, the leader of the saints, brings the support of the Church. These four almost unknown personages, therefore, form a sort of Council after the manner of the Ten at Venice. Being very much in request in society, they forage about everywhere, and, like bees, make their honey on Sunday with the ingatherings of the week.

February 5th.—The President's salary is to be refused, at least so the Coalition have determined. Mons. Molé was in favour of postponing the discussion until a responsible Ministry was definitely formed, but the other leaders, being more impatient of delay, preferred to settle the matter without adjournment, and there and then vetoed the grant, although aware that opinion out of doors was against such a course. Thiers, Odilon Barrot, Emile de Girardin, Victor Hugo, Larochejaquelein and Co. are like so many frogs croaking at the approach of bad weather.

The newspapers have just arrived, and my worst fears are confirmed; the grant has been refused. What a charming opportunity to jump on the Government! Coalitions will not be wanting, and both Orleanists and Legitimists, how they will crow!

The more I consider the matter the more preposterous does what is called parliamentary government seem to be; it might just as well be called government by dissolution or demoralization.

Having an abominable influenza, I am going to devote this evening to re-reading the history of the decline and fall of Rome.

During the three hours that I have been reading I might have been perusing the history of my own time. We have, alas, all the vices of Rome, and will not take

warning by the example of her fall. We have the two
pretenders, and we have the barbarians; not on our
confines it is true, but here in the very midst of us,
and, as in Rome, each party appeals to them for aid
against his adversary.

What sort of men are our leaders! Wretches who
merely play with revolution for purposes of their own,
having neither conviction nor faith in anything but
themselves. Chateaubriand and his royalists brought
about the events of 1830; Thiers and the middle class
those of 1848. Saddest of all sights is to see these
Members of Parliament travelling merrily towards
destruction. The barbarians are here only waiting
for their opportunity, and then will be sadder havoc
than when the Huns and the Vandals ravaged the
Roman Empire.

Lamartine, to flatter the populace, condescended to
write that "a French crowd was remarkable for its
respect for public monuments and works of art."
Formerly kings only had their flatterers, but now the
very mud of the streets must have its laureate.
Respect for works of art, indeed! Why, when I first
went to the Louvre I saw pictures from the galleries
at Neuilly and the Palais-Royal cut, hacked, and dis-
figured; statues mutilated and broken; lovely porcelain vases, onyx and crystal cups, and books, drawings, and manuscripts treated in the same way. Monsieur de Lamartine, you lied knowingly; the people
are robbers, and every successful revolt, since glorified
in your writings, was achieved by persons who looked
to disorder for means of larceny. It can never be

repeated too often that public writers were insincere in praising the rebels of 1848 and 1830. In the latter year these honest citizens stole a million and a half francs worth of jewels and other valuable property from the Louvre, without counting the sack of the Tuileries. In 1848 the Tuileries was again plundered, as well as the Palais-Royal, which was also set on fire. Neuilly and Mons. de Rothschild's house were rifled, and contributions were levied at different private houses. At Lord Henry Seymour's, for example, where I happened to be at the time, valuable arms and 1,000 francs in money were forcibly demanded. At the Tuileries diamonds and precious stones were fought for at the point of the knife, and prostitutes inhabiting the lowest slums were expected on occasions to dress themselves in silk.

Surely, the Huns and the Vandals were not equal to this rabble.

February 6th.—There is a good deal of excitement this morning about a dinner given by the great Lamoricière to Messieurs Molé, Thiers, Baze, and other members of the Coalition belonging to the left-centre. The revision of the Constitution was the principal subject discussed, and there was a general agreement as to the desirability of doing away with the Presidency of the Republic, and substituting for it a Directory composed of five members. We shall be drifting, in that case, towards a Convention. Can nothing instruct men, nothing in the past or present serve to enlighten them? Is this progress? A Directory, forsooth! Just a repetition of what was most shameless and revolting in the Revolution of 1789. Five niggardly and insignificant Barrases quarrelling and disputing among themselves. Rome, Rome, art thou returned to us? Are the soldiery again to put up to public auction the chief offices of State? They tell me that General Changarnier was at the dinner.

February 7th.—The President's *soirée* yesterday was the most successful of the season; everyone made a point of protesting, by his presence, against the hostile vote of the Chamber. For the first time since the present *régime* came into power the Opposition has become unpopular. On all sides one hears of subscriptions being offered to make up the grant refused by the Assembly. Lyons, it is stated, offers 300,000 francs, Limoges 120,000, the Eure district 180,000, and the different trades bodies in Paris are putting their names down for considerable sums.

The President ought tactfully to refuse these donations, and so enhance his popularity.

February 11th.—The President has sent a communication to the *Moniteur*, thanking those who have contributed to the public subscription being raised for him, but declining to accept it. The letter is brief, but dignified, and will have an excellent effect. The list of those who voted against the grant is published this morning; it includes Orleanists, Legitimists, and Democrats, the strangest and dirtiest coalition on record. Jules and Ferdinand de Lasteyrie, my two cousins, are in the list. Jules, the grandson of Lafayette on his mother's side, was an ardent

Democrat until his marriage with Mdlle. de Jarnac, of Rohan Chabot, the sister of Jarnac, our ambassador in London previous to 1848; since then he has espoused the Orleanist cause, and his wife, they say, is dowered by the younger Bourbon branch. Ferdinand is a capital and intelligent fellow, but wrong-headed; the kind of man who acts foolishly without intention. His mother and mine were sisters. His father, one of the most violent Jacobins of modern times, had been a priest, and left the Church in order to marry; he had no religious belief whatever, and died eighteen months ago, over eighty years of age, in the principles of some low form of Voltairian faith. He was another example of a charming simple-minded man. Ferdinand has two natures, one aristocratic, which he carefully hides from the Chamber and his constituency, but gives full vent to in the security of his own room, where he studies his genealogy, touches up his coat of arms, and cherishes the memory of his ancestors; the other is that of the citizen Lasteyrie, and is meant for the public. His speeches in the Assembly, though wanting in depth, are fairly smart, and are greatly admired by the female relations who congregate at his house to hear them rehearsed.

Ferdinand arrived from America two days ago, full of disgust for American Republicans, who he declares are the rudest and most arrogant noodles in the world. His wife is a pretty little American, badly brought up and spoiled, but very kind-hearted.

My cousin has two sorts of visiting cards; on those for Liberals and his constituents he simply puts Ferdinand Lasteyrie ; for the aristocratic world—Count F. de Lasteyrie.

This evening there was a concert at Princess Mathilde's, where I heard Seligman, Mdlle. Masson, and Dupont. As usual a good many people were present, and the diplomatic corps crowded the rooms. Kisseleff, the Russian ambassador, and I chatted together for some time, and amused ourselves by quizzing the ladies. The dress and appearance of the Turkish ambassadress were very striking. When most of the guests were gone, and the circle was narrowed to a few intimates, we discussed the speech which Montalembert had delivered on the grant question, and all expressed our approval of it except the Princess. I felt very much pained, I admit, at her injustice, for the more attached I become to her the more I desire that she may show fairness, impartiality, and broad and noble views.

The Bonapartes have but one faith and recognize but one power, namely, that which was bequeathed by the first Napoleon. In their eyes there never lived but one great man, Napoleon. Charlemagne and Louis XIV. were as nothing in comparison. You may question religious ideas, religion, or even the Almighty Himself, but you may not question the god of their idolatry. They do not pretend, it is true, that he was born without sin, but in their eyes he certainly lived sinless. No spot can be found on that particular sun. Such Napoleon worship is wrong, and can only lead to misfortunes.

CHAPTER II.

1851 (*continued*).

BARON HUMBOLDT AND THE MARQUIS DE CUSTINE — THE
BEY OF TRIPOLI AND ENGLISH JEALOUSY—THE MARQUIS
OF ROCCA GIOVINE — RUSSIA AND CONSTANTINOPLE —
MONSIEUR AND MADAME GUDIN—THE ANNIVERSARY OF
FEBRUARY 24TH; THE AUTHOR'S ACCOUNT OF THE FIGHT
ON THE BOULEVARD DES CAPUCINES—PRINCESS MATHILDE
AND PRINCE DEMIDOFF—THE CZAR NICHOLAS'S OPINION
OF DEMIDOFF—TANNEGUY DUCHÂTEL, LOVE AND LOTTERY
— SUSANNE — THE CARNIVAL — FRENCH VULGARITY —
GALLANTRY AND SOCIETY — THE DUCHESS OF SUTHER-
LAND AT THE LOUVRE—LAVALETTE AND HIS DIPLOMATIC
CAREER — SCHOELCHER, CHARLES BLANC, AND LEDRU-
ROLLIN—DOCTOR BELHOMME'S MADHOUSE.

MONS. DE NIEUWERKERKE, senior, has been to the
Louvre to see his son, who is just now suffering from
fever. I had a long talk with him upon a variety of
topics, and he told me the following anecdote about
the Marquis de Custine, the author of "Travels in
Russia," a *roué* who is still tolerated in society because
of his wealth. Before his marriage with Mdlle.

de Courtomer (who died quite young, with great forti-
tude, but of a broken heart) the Marquis de Custine
paid his addresses to Mdlle. de Duras, whose mother
was the authoress of " Ourika " and other works. The
young lady listened to his suit, and the engagement
was about to be announced when one morning there
happened to assemble in the Duchess de Duras' drawing-room, besides the young lovers themselves, Count
de Nieuwerkerke, Baron Humboldt, and one or two
intimate friends of the family. Baron Humboldt pretended that he could read character from handwriting,
and this gift, which had been proved by frequent ex-
periments, chanced to form the subject of conversation.
" Come, now," said the Duchess, suddenly taking a
letter from her waist-band, " let us see, Baron, if you
can read by the handwriting in this letter the character
of the writer." Humboldt, like a learned German,
collected himself, examined the epistle, and began to
expatiate upon the formation, general appearance, and
peculiarities of the letters. He then proceeded to
demonstrate that the person who had written them
was an extraordinary being, of whimsical tastes,
corrupt imagination, and devoid of all moral sense.
He in fact drew a most abominable picture in spite of
the Duchess de Duras' endeavour to stop him, for the
writer of the letter was no other than the Marquis
de Custine himself. The engagement was in consequence broken off. Custine, who subsequently married
Mdlle. de Courtomer, turned out an indescribable
scoundrel, and Baron Humboldt's divination proved
correct.

February 19*th*.—Viscount de l'Epine has been to see me. He tells me that previous to 1848, when Marshal Soult was in office, a friend of his who had spent many years in Africa, in the neighbourhood of Tripoli, established very friendly relations with some desert tribes, who agreed for a small periodical tribute to guarantee the safety of caravans going between Timbuctoo and Constantine. This would have been of enormous advantage to France, as it would have enabled her to open up a direct communication with the central part of Africa.

Marshal Soult espoused the idea very warmly, and had even gone so far as to send presents to the chiefs of the tribes, and to the Bey of Tripoli, when Guizot put an end to the matter by asserting that England would take umbrage at it. The British Government got wind of the negotiations, and set to work to frustrate the understanding between the Bey of Tripoli and the French. A rival was found in Constantinople, who, furnished with a firman of investiture from the Sultan, landed in Africa and made war upon the Bey. The latter defended himself with such vigour and bravery that in despair of overcoming him he was invited to a conference. Thither he repaired in good faith, and was assassinated. That is the way French policy was conducted and English agents worked.

It is our everlasting timidity which fosters the pride and arrogance of the English Cabinet. Shades of Louis XVI. and Napoleon, what are you about?

I dined this evening with Tarrall, an English doctor

who has married a rich Italian lady and retired from practice, and devotes himself to pictures and art criticism. We were a large party, consisting of some English people who were unknown to me, Prince Canino, his son-in-law, the Marquis Rocca Giovine, a sallow-faced little Roman, with good features and the voice of an eunuch, whose pretty wife seems likely to lead her husband as she pleases, and unless I am mistaken has already been scratched by Cupid's darts; Ricardo, brother of the English banker, a charming fellow, whom I like extremely; Rizza Bey, secretary of the Ottoman embassy; Nieuwerkerke, a Russian gentleman, and a limited number of lesser stars.

After dinner, which was good and well served, some of the men stayed to smoke in an adjoining room. I was among the number, and extraordinary to relate, we were five smokers of five different nationalities: an Italian, a Turk, a Russian, a Frenchman, and an Englishman. Rizza Bey talked to me a good deal about Turkey, and very much surprised me by the confiding manner in which he remarked, pointing to the Russian, "Why do we not understand each other better with such an enemy at our gates?" These poor Turks wish to persuade us that Russia is an enemy to be feared, and that Constantinople in its power would mean a constant menace to Europe. I verily believe that the English alone dread such a contingency. Our policy should be to prevent England from laying hands on Egypt, and to exclude her from any possessions on the Mediterranean littoral.

February 20th.—The Marquis of Hertford and
Richard Wallace came to the Louvre, and I accompanied them through the modern Sculpture Galleries.
The Marquis is anxious to obtain the cast of a small
Promethean group of figures. I am very fond of
Wallace, and was pleased to see him again. He is a
delightful companion, possessing an intelligent knowledge of art, and many is the time that we have made
excursions together to sales of curios.

In the evening I dined with Gudin, the marine
painter, at his pretty Beaujon house. The dinner was
in every respect excellent, but he and his wife have a
stiff and formal way of receiving you, which does not
put you at your ease. They are the sort of people
who, without any desire to do so, would be constantly
offending your susceptibilities if you allowed them to
do so. Madame Gudin, a brawny Scotchwoman, without
much intelligence, is a niece of the Duke of Wellington, of which fact her husband is not a little proud.
Both husband and wife live in most extravagant style.

February 24th.—To-day's anniversary has been
dull and spiritless in spite of the magnificent weather,
which has usually a cheering effect upon the Parisian
temperament. A *Te Deum* was performed at Notre
Dame, and there has also been some singing of the
" Marseillaise," and sporting of immortelles in the
button-holes of a few loungers. Lagrange, the hero
of the fight on the Boulevard des Capucines, addressed an unenthusiastic crowd in front of Notre
Dame, but the celebration of the Republic's third
birthday was, generally speaking, a *fiasco.* On the

evening of the engagement on the Boulevard I happened to be at the Café de Paris, and seeing a demonstration led by Lagrange go by I was foolish enough to follow to see what would happen. The insurrectionary mob was principally composed of a few hundred agitators, carrying torches and a red flag, but among them were thirty or forty men, evidently armed, and one or two in the officers' uniform of the National Guard. At the top of the garden belonging to the Foreign Office their progress was stopped by a battalion of infantry. Someone in the insurgent ranks fired a shot, and the soldiers replied with a volley. For a minute I felt paralyzed, and when I recovered myself the Boulevard, which a moment before had been all noise and excitement, was as still as a desert; the military stood quietly under arms, the torches were extinguished, and the wounded were dragging themselves into the side streets to die. Others were lying lifeless on the paths, and the leaders had gone to fetch carts on which to convey the victims' bodies through the streets of Paris.

The next day the people assembled in the streets. I was at the Tuileries with my battalion of National Guards, which had been furnished with cartridges, and seemed well disposed, and there was plenty of artillery besides. The King reviewed us, and then went off; the troops were dismissed, and in the midst of general stupefaction the Republic was proclaimed.

March 3rd.—Baroness de Reding's funeral took place to-day. That lady had had the care of Princess Mathilde from childhood, and had since acted as her lady companion. The Princess is in great distress, for the loss is an irreparable one. It was from the Baroness that I learned the story of the Princess's marriage with Demidoff, and his cruel and heartless treatment of her, and how at Florence he made love to the Duchess de Dino before her face. She also told me how the Princess had begged her husband on her knees not to allow the Emperor Nicholas, when he came to Florence, to be a witness of the vile conduct that polluted their married life. The first words the Emperor said to her when he arrived were : " You do not know what a scoundrel you have married," but although already conscious of the fact for nine months past she answered : " It is not generous of your Majesty to speak in such terms of a man who is my husband." The Emperor then added more gently, " Poor child, you will know it one day, and then you will come to me for shelter. Remember that you may always count upon my sincerest friendship." The Emperor knew the man as I did ; nothing viler or more truly base could be imagined—insolent with valets, and grovelling when opposed; false, cowardly, and vicious, without a single good quality. Believing him to be capable of any secret treachery, the Emperor had him watched, and but for want of absolute proof would have sent him to cool his heels in Siberia for a libel of which he was the inspiring author. He was furthermore a pretending scholar, and got himself elected a corresponding member of the French Institute, in virtue of an important and learned work for which he supplied the funds only. I knew Demidoff's father, who possessed the same bad qualities, and was as undesirable a person as his son. He rented a country house belonging to the Countess Duchâtel at Sceaux-Penthièvre, in, I think, 1819. He had in his house a young Circassian or Tartar woman named Nédirdgka Latacheff, a sort of favourite female slave, for whom Tanneguy Duchâtel conceived a violent boyish affection.

Tanneguy and I were great friends, and when I was at school in Paris in or about 1818 always came to see me during the week. On Sundays we met again at his mother's house at Sceaux, where my eldest brother, Theodore, was *sous-préfet.*

One Thursday, when the rain kept us indoors and we were hard pressed for amusement, we passed away the time in discussing all the pretty women we knew. We were only sixteen at the time, and ended by confiding to each other by which of the fair ones we wished to be loved, but as it was necessary, in order to arrive at so desirable a consummation, first to declare our affection, and had never yet told any woman we loved her, the difficulty seemed very great.

Suddenly a sublime idea seized our young imaginations, and we proceeded to put it in execution. To make a declaration by word of mouth was impossible ; we were too inexperienced and timid for such a course. To do so in writing looked much easier, so we wrote each in turn a line of an imposing epistle, and when it was finished drew lots as to which should sign it. It fell to me to assume the part of gay deceiver. I signed—not without secret misgiving,

however—and then we proceeded to consider to whom
the letter should be sent. We agreed to place in a hat,
on separate pieces of paper, the names of twenty
young women of our acquaintance, and to leave the
rest to chance. We did so. Duchâtel plunged his
hand into the hat and took out a paper, which I
opened and read. It contained the name of Susanne
de C—, a young person three or four years older than
myself, who lived at Sceaux with her father, and was
much admired on account of her beauty. Her mother
was dead, and her father, the descendant of a very
ancient and noble family, who had been in the Church
previous to the Revolution of 1789, saw only a few
intimate acquaintances, and rarely went to Paris.
When the name of Susanne was read out Tanneguy
laughed in derision, and cried out : " Don't you wish
you may get her ! "

I would have wished, I honestly believe, not to send
the letter, but Tanneguy seized it and put it in the
post.   Then commenced a life of anguish of which I
can give no idea. I neither slept nor ate, was in
constant dread of meeting Susanne, and did all I
could to avoid her. At last I was obliged to meet
her, and one day, being left alone in her company,
I endeavoured to express my regret for having
dared to avow my feelings.   Both apology and love
were accepted notwithstanding, and our intimacy
lasted for five years. All the world got to know of
it, and as Susanne was liked and sought after, I, too,
was liked and sought after.   If she was asked out to
dinner I received an invitation also. We met several

times a week, passed the whole of Sunday together, and wrote to each other every day—such letters! Love's romances, which never seemed long enough for the expression of our heart's feelings. . . . Since our rupture I have never once seen Susanne, but she still lives in my memory as in the first bloom of early love.

March 4th.—Everywhere carriages full of masquer-aders, and crowds of idlers looking on. At night costume balls, veritable resorts of debauchery, where people speak in strange tongues and act as by right with unseemly vulgarity. Such is, in fact, the French carnival.

I dined at a *café*, spent the evening out, and returned home to the Louvre at one o'clock in the morning. Noisy and half-drunken maskers were still about, some going to revels at the taverns, others to the casinos.

The vilest costumes are those which are most popular at public dancing places. The masker who makes himself most unsightly and hideous, who com-mits a dozen indecent acts at each step, and scarcely utters a word without some disgusting allusion, is the king, the hero of the youthful merrymakers, and the women select him for the object of their most pointed coquetries. And what poetical names he invents for apostrophizing the women—fowl! camel! The men are " snouts," a face is a " mug "—in fact, all the slang of pickpockets and cut-throats is little by little brought into common use. The women of the better class are proficient in the cancan, the dance of

the lowest class of girls and tramps.   They know all
the kept women by name, and even endeavour to rob
them of their lovers.   The mud tide is rising ; where
will it stop ?

March 9th.—Dined at Princess Mathilde's ; a small
party consisting of Rotomsky and his wife, Nieuwerkerke, Madame Deprès and her daughter, the doctor,
and the Princess.   The conversation was almost exclusively restricted to stories and observations concerning society.   Poor society ! you are expected to be moral
and are so constituted that it is impossible for you to
be so.   What is the world itself but a wide arena for
the display of coquetry and intrigue, where men and
women each play their parts.   Man is esteemed for his
conquests or his knowledge of the world.   The crown of
gallantry, or the crown of ambition, is worn with equal
zest, and is as ardently and cunningly contended for.

The gift of fascination is an immense power in
women's hands, for from the Secretary of State to the
meanest rung in the official ladder all are under the
dominion of the captivator.   Fould, the late Minister
of Finance, for example, is very amenable to female
charms, and does not hide his weakness.

Every man can count in his private life, if he lives at
all in society, five or six seductions, or in other words
five or six mistresses ; but the day he marries all his
amorous past is forgotten with the love letters
he consigns to the flames, and the faded bouquets
he casts to the winds, persuading himself in honest
faith that his wife will be his private property.   But
no, society is on the look out, it entices and entraps

her; marriage has torn from her the robe of innocence, the flower of youth. She is initiated now, and
no longer the ignorant maiden, and little by little she
learns to understand in the words of love whispered
in her ear the outpourings of sensual passion. Saying
to a woman " I love you " ninety times in a hundred
simply means, in plain language, " You please me, you
appeal to my senses; share my life, or let me share
yours, until my whim is over." Poor women! poor
men! poor society! poor everybody!

March 10th.—From four to six o'clock, I was engaged in showing the Duchess of Sutherland and her
daughter over the Louvre. These two ladies called at
my office and begged me, in the absence of Nieuwerkerke, to act as their guide. The Duchess is extremely
gracious and affable, and evidently wishes to appear
so; her daughter, who is still unmarried, is pretty and
distinguished-looking, an excellent specimen indeed
of the English aristocracy.

Our Louvre is always an object of admiration to
strangers, and the magnificent restoration it is now
undergoing is to them a source of wonder and astonishment. The gallery of Apollo strikes them as being,
what in point of fact it is, the most beautiful royal
apartment in the world. The room with the seven
chimney pieces, and the large square drawing-room,
decorated by Duban, will greatly increase his reputation. The carvings in the former room are by Duret,
those in the latter by Simart.

The Duchess of Sutherland was loud in her admiration of the sculpture in the Renaissance galleries, the

Michael Angelos and others, and speaks like a woman who loves and understands the arts. Her daughter, with whom I conversed for a few moments during our somewhat extended ramble, told me this was her first visit to France; she examined the pictures by Raphael very attentively, but was positively repelled by the Egyptian sculpture. She resents, as does her mother, the immobility and stiffness of all those figures of the time of Pharaoh. In the matter of art these two ladies are by no means archæological, they like that which is perfected, which entrances by its mode of execution. They made an exception, however, in one particular instance. Two tombs of the latter part of the 15th century impressed them extremely by the simplicity as well as the marked subtilty of their execution. The Duchess remarked that in her opinion the Middle Ages had best understood and appreciated tumulary art— those grand reclining bodies, motionless, but so amply clothed in the majesty of death, smiling and at the same time full of piety.

I pointed out to her the happy admixture of life and death in the recumbent figures, each one sleeping in eternal slumber, the mortal body for ever stretched on the marble tomb, but the spirit living and in prayer. The soul springs as it were far from the human form, and the two hands, lifelike and real, are clasped in the attitude of devotion, as if to describe the spirit's immortality. Serenity and quietude are impressed on all these figures. "What," said the Duchess, "'quietude!'" and she repeated the word, seemingly astonished to find it in the French language, and then she added: "I

like that word, but thought it was exclusively Italian."
Her pronunciation alone is like some sweet music which
expresses and diffuses that which she wishes to say.

March 14*th.*—Lavalette has been appointed to the
diplomatic post at Constantinople in the same way
that he was appointed consul at Alexandria, namely,
through the influence of the *Debats* newspaper and
Véron's agency. Lavalette has two hundred thousand
francs in shares in the *Debats.* He wanted his money
out, and applied for the Constantinople post at the
same time. Some meddlesome people interposed, with
the result that his money was left in the paper; it
adopted his line of policy in opposition to the President, and the Constantinople mission was given him.
The arrangement was ratified at a big dinner which
Véron gave.

Ever the same disgraceful jobbery, immoral collu-
sion and trafficking in places, dignities, and so-called
honours. You may labour and wear yourself out,
follow the straight path, walk loyally in the prescribed
route, and act your part in life honestly, but you will
find yourself one fine day outdone by someone who
plays with marked cards and cheats you out of your
career. Figaro said truly, " Worldly knowledge is a
more valuable commodity than intelligence." The
two hundred thousand francs which Lavalette has in
the *Debats* he won at piquet.

March 16*th.*—I dined at Princess Mathilde's, and
after dinner we went to the Opera Comique and had
the President's box. The party included the Princess,

Prince de Canino, Marquis and Marchioness Rocca Giovine, Countess Ledochonska (Mdlle. de Menneval that was), General Exelmans' son, Nieuwerkerke, and myself; also Ratomsky, whom I had forgotten. The programme consisted of "Fra Diovolo," "Bonsoir, Monsieur Pantalon," and the "Dame Voilée," which were well played and sung.

Exelmans is making violent love to the Marchioness Rocca Giovine, which is very amusing. Her husband is like a schoolboy, who is afraid to say bo to a goose, but the Marchioness flirts like ten little devils in one, and heaven only knows the havoc she makes with her eyes!

March 17th.—A very extreme Republican, named Schoelcher, came to my office to-day. I have known this tribune of the people for twenty years. He has the great advantage over his compeers of being an honest man, but he allows himself to be robbed, and is simple enough to share his purse with his party. During our interview I succeeded in cajoling Schoelcher into giving the Louvre eight or ten thousand francs' worth of costumes and Mexican or American statuettes and antiquities. He asked me, with a chagrined air, if it was true that Charles Blanc and Jeanron, while the one was Director of Fine Arts and the other Director of the Museum, had allocated to themselves valuable works, consisting of ninety-nine volumes containing plates and drawings, belonging to the Louvre. When I replied in the affirmative Schoelcher looked pained, his sense of honesty revolted at having to allow that two of his own faith had com-

mitted so indelicate an act, and he expressed himself in
no very measured terms with regard to them.

Alas for poor Schoelcher! He must often have
had occasion to blush since 1848. His friends have
been mixed up in many dirty businesses. Look at the
luxury in which citizens Marrast and Ledru-Rollin
live. It is all very well for credulous people to be told
that these two great men married English heiresses,
but I know a good many things, and, amongst others,
that Madame Marrast, who is now dead, was an English
governess before her marriage, and had even undertaken the education of young men. As for Madame
Ledru-Rollin, who was the natural daughter of an
Irishman, she brought with her a dowry of 48,000
francs, but at the present time the accumulations of
her husband's capital, lent on house property in Paris,
amount to 700,000 francs—not bad!

Madame de Lamartine is also of English birth. She
wishes to pass for a fine lady, but her father was a
pastry cook in the Strand.

March 23rd.—I have spent my day in visiting the
establishment of Doctor Belhomme, where idiots,
whose friends can afford to pay largely for special
treatment, are taken care of. The house is very fine,
and is situated in the Faubourg St. Antoine; the
gardens and buildings occupy more than six acres of
land, and both the domestic service and care given to
the inmates seem excellent and well ordered.

I saw all kinds of cases, from mere monomaniacs to
actual lunatics, all frightfully sad to contemplate—
intellects destroyed or gone astray. Thinking beings

degraded to the level of beasts and machines, with souls in suspense, are a painful sight.

Ambition is a frequent cause of insanity. In one room I saw an Italian marquis, who says he is the President's cousin, and calls himself Bourbon Bonaparte. He is greatly incensed against the President for not answering his numberless letters. Pride and vanity are apparent in every word he utters, and he does not pardon the least want of respect ; his manners are refined, and his language, which is a mixture of French and Italian, most choice. He has an animated phisiognomy, but that part of the head which is occupied by the brain is very constricted. He is the victim of inordinate attacks of vanity.

Another imbecile detained me for some time explaining a discovery he pretends to have made for squaring the circle, and by inquiries concerning Madame Casier, an imaginary being for whom he entertains a strong affection, and whose mission he assured me was to release him from his place of detention. With regard to his pretended discovery he said to me, " I keep the secret, sir, from no one, and I will explain it to you in two words—the square of the circle is as 40 is to 49."

This imbecile, about fifty years of age, has the appearance of a respectable shopkeeper of the kind one sees going to the Champs Elysées to play bowls. He thinks he is in prison, but always hopes that Madame Casier will liberate him.

Another case was that of a gloomy, sad, and melancholy person inclined to mysticism, who spoke to me

incoherently and in so low a voice that at first I could
scarcely hear what he said. Then he suddenly turned
and asked me to come to his assistance against the
tyranny of his father-in-law, the Marquis de Bonneval,
who by means of a *cornet à piston* oppressed him and
kept him in private confinement. This poor idiot,
dressed in a long cloak, became more and more irritable
as he spoke; he squeezed my arm very tightly,
making fearful grimaces all the time. The keeper
warned me to get away quickly as he was about to
have one of his paroxysms of rage. I released myself
with some difficulty; he followed me to the gate which
divides the garden where he was walking from that
belonging to the other part of the establishment, and
there I separated from him.

In the part reserved for the graver cases the patients
are not men, and, unhappily for themselves, not even
animals. Some cannot speak, others can scarcely
walk; again, there are those who speak in mono-
syllables only. One is enabled, in fact, to trace in
stages the destruction of the mental and human condition. These are organizations which have become
wrecked through debauchery, or paralysis of the brain,
caused by some sudden emotion, or shock, which their
feeble natures have been unable to withstand. All,
however, die speedily, and from the same cause—brain
paralysis.

One of these unhappy beings walked incessantly
round a tree laughing to himself; he was scarcely
twenty, and had come to his present idiotic and
degraded condition through incontinence practised

from early childhood. Another, through the window of his room, replied to our inquiries about his health with the foulest imprecations.

Those who do not talk stand motionless and stare at you with a fixed and inane look, but they obey their keepers as pigs do a swineherd. This portion of the establishment is the most heartrending to visit, for even in the open air one is conscious of the odour of savage beasts, which adds to the feeling of disgust. Moreover, among these cases there is not the least vestige of intelligence or even of animal instinct. 'Tis man in a state of decomposition.

The patients on the female side were just as numerous, and in much the same condition.

In one room I saw, seated with her keeper and employed at some needlework, a young, fair creature with a defiant, and at the same time sad, sweet expression ; she scarcely replied to our questions. This young woman's madness first showed itself in an attempt to murder her husband. The peculiarity of her mental condition is that in the evening she is perfectly sane, and can be taken into town, sometimes even to the theatre, but in the morning she is depressed and under the influence of her mania. So marked is this that one would almost suppose her to be influenced by the sun's appearance above the horizon.

One aged lady, the Countess de Quelen (sister-in-law of the old Archbishop of Paris), who occupies a separate apartment, is completely idiotic. She has lately lost an imbecile son who shared her room, and is not even conscious of his absence.

This old countess, who is very proud and full of vanity, was knitting with apparent ease a quilt of complicated design. She received me as if I had come to hire her room, and said, "I don't think it will suit you. I am leaving it because I find it very inconvenient, and when my furniture is removed it will not be very attractive." She showed me her furniture and the family portraits that adorned her walls. Among them were grandfathers and grandmothers in powdered wigs, and the picture of her deceased husband in the uniform of a colonel of the National Guard. This visit was taken up in the interchange of extreme courtesies. I also went to see an idiot of good birth, a girl of twenty, who cannot speak, and passes the whole of the day, under the supervision of a nurse, in bending and folding up packs of cards.

These visits over, I went back to the drawing-room, where one of the patients joined us with his music, and for an hour played the piano and sang in the most marvellous way. He talked about music in rational language and like a real connoisseur; but when I asked him who was the doctor's wife, he replied, "The lady who has just heard me sing, Madame Pradher." After an hour's music he retired, saying that he would be always at our disposal if his playing and singing gave us the least pleasure.

My inspection terminated with the perusal of some letters written by the unfortunate inmates. In some instances the letters were a tissue of extravagances or aberrations logically and consistently followed out;

others, again, perfectly well written and sensibly
expressed, were the productions of patients who
had received from the lady principal—who possesses
a certain power of imparting knowledge—the faculty
of writing sensibly to their friends.

On leaving this unfortunate establishment I know
not what induced me to go to dine at the Marchioness
du Vallon's *table d'hôte*. Wishing to ascertain what
effect this gangrenous household had had upon the
virgin minds of her two daughters, I asked the
younger, a good musician, and a clever, interesting, and agreeable girl, with the sweetest diction and
accent possible, what she had been doing since I last
saw her. She replied in her musical voice, and timid,
girlish manner, " Learning to flirt."

I was horrified; the corruption is growing apace
amid surroundings more or less vitiated. She is
drinking in the poison, and will soon be intoxicated·
with it. Poor, dear child! she might have been so
good; but her fine, delicate, impressionable nature
has been sacrificed to the *habitues* of a *table d'hôte*,
just as in earlier times Christians were delivered up
to wild beasts in the Roman circus.

After dinner, in order to finish my day properly in
the spirit in which I had begun it, I went to the wild
beast tamer's on the Boulevard Beaumarchais. The
man is courageous, and a splendid sight to look at as
he plays with the tigers, lions, and hyenas, rolling on
the ground with them, and taking part in their
gambols, wrestling with them for pieces of raw meat,
which he finally distributes. But in spite of all their

strength and beauty the animals are a painful sight to witness in their degradation before the man, who, with his whip, keeps them in subjection like wretched curs. My experiences of the day were perfect— debasement everywhere. Poor idiots ! poor girl ! poor beasts !

CHAPTER III.

1851 (*continued*).

SCANDALOUS STORY OF COUNTESS DE NESSELRODE, MADAME
ZÉBA AND PRINCESS KALERDJY—OBSCENE WRITERS—
THEIR BANEFUL INFLUENCE—MARSHAL NARVAEZ—THE
PORTUGUESE INSURRECTION—INSIGHT INTO THE PRESI-
DENT'S INTENTIONS—THE QUEEN OF SPAIN'S LOVE
AFFAIRS—RUDENESS OF THE DUKE D'AUMALE'S AGENTS
TO PRINCESS MATHILDE—PRINCE CANINO PUBLICLY IN-
SULTED BY COUNT ROSSI'S SON—NIEUWERKERKE CHAL-
LENGED BY PIERRE BONAPARTE—REPUTATION OF THE
BONAPARTE FAMILY—POLITICAL INTRIGUERS—MAZZINI
AND MONSIEUR DE LESSEPS—MONSIEUR DE VÉRON—
THE PRESIDENT'S TOOLS—NARROW ESCAPE OF THE
BARON DE CHAMEROLLE — THE AUTHOR'S OPINION OF
THE DEMOCRACY—VICTOR HUGO—PRINCE NAPOLEON.

March 29th.—I was to-day made acquainted with a
terrible piece of scandal, reminding one of the worst
days of the Regency, and the stories of Parabère,
without their elegance and delicate aroma.

The Countess de Nesselrode arrived in Paris from
Russia about the beginning of the winter, and was
joined by a young Russian, with whom she is said to

have been on terms of intimacy before her marriage
with the Count de Nesselrode, to whom she brought a
fortune of three or four hundred thousand francs a
year. The young couple were enjoying themselves to
their heart's content, when a friendship sprang up
between the noble dame and two other Russian ladies
of aristocratic birth, Madame Zéba and Princess
Kalerdjy. These three merry ones, happily constituted and not overburdened with scruples, but
most desirous of enjoying their last days of youth,
conceived the idea of forming in common a concord of
debauchery. They divided each week into two parts,
one dedicated to the exigencies of society, the other
to performances for their own benefit, and for the
purposes of such representations selected as assistants
a troop of young fellows from the ranks of the most
licentious writers of the day. The Countess de Nesselrode put herself under the tutelage of one, the
Princess Kalerdjy of another, and Madame Zéba
seemed to languish for the assistance of the whole
assortment. Between these three ladies and their
advisers, lubricity acquired consummate proportions,
the aim of the scoundrels being to see which could
render his pupil most accomplished in wantonness.
They searched books and studied different systems of
vice until at last the degraded Marquis de S— must
have thrilled with joy at the scandal caused by his
inspired authorship. The lesson bore its fruit, and
the Countess de Nesselrode, imitating the example of
Messalina, the corrupt wife of the Emperor Claudius,
appeared on the Boulevards as a common street-

walker. Heckeren, the deputy, met her twice under that guise, reproved her for her shamelessness, and endeavoured to reclaim her, but without avail. The end of it all was that an order from the Capital recalled the Countess to Russia, and at the present moment the husband is *en route* to St. Petersburg, the wife to Moscow.

One can scarcely gauge the evil done nowadays by obscene works. I do not refer only to the more ignoble writers themselves, but to the influence their writings have had upon the literature of the nineteenth century. Hugo in " Notre Dame de Paris," Jules Janin in " l'Ane Mort," Théophile Gautier in " Mdlle. de Maupin," Madame Sand, Eugene Sue, de Musset, &c., and Dumas in his theatrical pieces, all throw into their productions the leaven of impurity.

They do not invoke that graceful, youthful, attractive love which strikes the senses like the voluptuous breath of spring, but the love which is drunken, debauched, and *blasé*, seeking, like Tiberius in his Caprian retreat, fresh vigour in disordered orgies. These writers violate the modesty of their heroines by the very effect excited in the minds of their readers, whose senses are intoxicated and inflamed by coarse materialism until they are ready to imitate all the transgressions and rites of the ancient bacchanalian revels, anxious, in fact, to wallow in the profanation of love.

April 18*th.*—I saw Marshal Narvaez this evening at Princess Mathilde's. We discussed the insurrectionary movement which has just broken out in

Portugal, under the leadership of Saldanha. Narvaez believes the Spanish Minister for Foreign Affairs is in the plot. When the latter represented Spain at the Portuguese Court, Narvaez, who was then Prime Minister at Madrid, wrote to urge him to support Thomas, the Portuguese Minister, and leader of the insurrection then on foot. The ambassador replied that it was impossible, as he was already engaged on the other side. He was recalled and exiled, but at the present moment he holds the portfolio of foreign affairs in the Ministry which replaced Narvaez's.

"The Queen of Portugal," said Marshal Narvaez, "is a woman of energy and intelligence, who *at least* supports the Minister who possesses her confidence; and she it was who made her husband, the King, put himself at the head of his troops."

The way in which Narvaez emphasized *at least* conveyed a world of reproaches to the Queen of Spain, and justly so. The intrigues of the Queen with one or the other of her lovers brought about the fall of Narvaez, who is admitted to have kept a tight hand on Spain and her dissolute Court. What will happen in his absence? Already there is an insurrection in Portugal, out of which the English will doubtless make profit and regain their influence while Spain and France bite their nails.

April 23rd.—Dined at the Princess Mathilde's with Marshal Exelmans. We went afterwards to the opera, where we had the President's box, and heard Verdi's "Hernani." Persigny came and did the affable, affecting the manners of a grand signor. To my notion he is as much like a gentleman as chicory is like coffee. Marshal Jérôme was in one of the centre boxes with Madame de Plancy and Madame de Monyon, a hideous and disreputable old wretch. Marshal Jérôme had a wicked reputation under the Empire, and is still an old rake. All the President's family, with very few exceptions, are a blackguardly set, and do him infinite harm. Gilbert des Voisins was in a stage-box with a big, coarselooking woman, with whom he is doubtless living. Des Voisins has been successively the charge of Madame de Nicolaï, Madame Manuel, the wife of the stockbroker who was killed in a duel by Beaumont, and the Duchess de Raguse. He then married Taglioni, the dancer, whom he ruined and ultimately obliged to separate from him. Despised, degraded, and penniless, he had recourse to Véron, who found him worthy of his protection. He is now rehabilitated, is a Government official at the Italian Opera, has his own box, and lives in a very pretty flat in the Rue Caumartin. Virtue has always its reward in this world!

April 28*th.*—For several days I have been so occupied with official work that I have had no time to think of my book, although I have had many things to enter up. I must, therefore, put them down as they occur to me.

Gudin, the marine painter, who married the Duke of Wellington's niece, is the most conceited and egotistical coxcomb in the world. He is larded all over with crosses, like everybody who wears orders nowadays, spends in luxury and entertainment every penny he makes, plays the noble lord, and is "at home" to the two most aristocratic quarters of Paris. He is a niggard, however, when he dares to be so, and stories of his meannesses still survive among his pupils. Under the reign of Louis-Philippe he managed to ingratiate himself in Court favour, became petted, admired, and coddled, and finally was made painter to the French Navy, with a uniform, orders to the value of two hundred thousand francs, and a studio in the Louvre. After the revolution of February this gentleman, who aspired to the level of Vandyke and Rubens, believed he would have little trouble in procuring the appointment of ambassador to London; he was laughed at, however, and the attack passed off.

He is now, however, a great painter, and something of a great man besides. The son of a Monsieur Bérand and a little milliner, who were never married, Gudin is simply the victim of the bar sinister. His mother, an excellent, but commonplace person, is still living, and entertains herself by assisting his cook. These, forsooth, are the domestic trials that cause the great lord painter's hair to whiten.

Madame Koreff, a former mistress, arranged Gudin's marriage without the knowledge of the Hay family, and he repaid her with his usual illiberality.

The President still shows the same coolness and imperturbability. He told the princess, who is changing her residence, that she was quite right to take a larger house, "For," said he, "in 1852 your present one will be too small for you, and after the prorogation you will require a suitable establishment." This man is convinced of his good fortune, which is in itself a guarantee of success. Only last year he said to the princess, "Rest assured, my dear cousin, I shall not leave France alive."

May 16th.—I dined on Tuesday last at Princess Mathilde's with Marshal Exelmans, Count de Flahaut, Morny, Guitaud, Madame Bresson, Nieuwerkerke, &c. I wanted to learn from Guitaud some details concerning the Queen of Spain's love affairs, and he related many anecdotes with reference to Miráflores, an officer of the palace, and young General Serrano, which proved that Isabel has turned her opportunities to excellent account. In order to gratify her fancy for Serrano she had recourse to her father-in-law, Don Francis, who for a money bribe promised to second her infidelities to his son. Isabel gave him sixty thousand francs, the King was exiled, and Serrano was introduced into the palace. France, becoming uneasy, however, at the way in which matters were going on in Spain, employed Serrano's services to procure General Narvaez's recall, and the latter had no sooner come back again than he exiled Serrano and brought the King back to Madrid. Since then the Queen has given free rein to her caprices, but the Phillipine islands can testify to the disenchantment of some of her tender victims who at Narvaez's orders have been sent there to reflect on the evanescence of royal favours.

Narvaez is now in France again, with an income of 300,000 francs, to pay which the Queen, having no money in her own purse, gave him a draft on Spanish credit. This successive Ministries always refused to honour, but Narvaez found a means of getting it cashed, and is now very well off. The King of Spain has also his indulgencies, in spite of what report says, and the Marchioness of Campo Alanqué at least has not failed to attract his royal notice.

May 17th.—Doctor Koreff is just dead. He was a witty, talkative, and rather inquisitive man, without religion or law, and dissolute to the last degree, giving himself readily to malpractices in his profession when required to do so. He was always short of money, and his conduct to Lady Lincoln, when he was attending her with Doctor Wolonsky, was most infamous. Her treatment by these two rascals was foul in the extreme. He is dead, however, at last, and may God have mercy on him.

For a time he was member of a club which met for conversational purposes and dined at some Paris restaurant once a month. The set was composed of Mérimée, Alfred de Musset, Eugene Lacroix, Koreff, Stendhall, Marest, and Viel Castel (myself). We were a pleasant party, talked well and much, and did not get drunk.

May 20th.—Princess Mathilde tells me that she was at the Chantilly races last Sunday, with her cousin Lady Douglas, the daughter of the Grand Duchess of Baden. The President had placed at their disposal the box he was to have occupied, and which belonged to the Duke d'Aumale. After they had been seated for a quarter of an hour the Duke's agents appeared and told the two ladies they must pack off, as his

Grace had offered his box to the official head of the state and not to Prince Louis Bonaparte. Could anything have been in worse taste?

June 7th.—Yesterday, while Prince de Canino was dining with the Vice-President at the Café d'Orsay, a young man, who declined to give his card, asked to see him. The Prince, however, sent word that he did not care to disturb himself for a person without a name. When dinner was over and the Prince was leaving with Boulay de la Meurthe, the same individual came up to them, and, accosting Canino, asked him if he was the Prince of that name. On receiving a reply in the affirmative, the young man said, spitting in his face, " Then you are a scoundrel and an assassin. I am Count Rossi's son." This morning they are to fight. Nieuwerkerke and young Exelmans are, I believe, to be the Prince's seconds. I am sorry for the former. Canino was president of the Roman assembly when Rossi was assassinated; he is a cowardly knave, but Nieuwerkerke can scarcely refuse the service he asks.

The President has just sent Lepic, his orderly officer, to beg Nieuwerkerke to act as Canino's second, but he has already left for Versailles with Exelmans, doubtless on account of the duel.

I am dining this evening with Princess Mathilde and shall learn more about it.

June 12th.—Nieuwerkerke fought Pierre Bonaparte on Monday last, and was slightly wounded in the thigh. Pierre challenged him because he refused to act as Canino's second in the Rossi duel. These sons of Lucien Bonaparte are all veritable ruffians, whose bad reputation is fully deserved. Pierre and Antoine were obliged to fly from Italy for killing a keeper who sued them for trespassing in pursuit of game. Their mother, the worst woman of her day, told them on one occasion when they wanted money "that they were resolute and strong, and should find it for themselves on the high road."

With the exception of the President and Princess Mathilde, all the family are good for nothing. Prince de Canino, who has been received in France owing to the President's kindness, is always conspiring against his cousin, and even talks about putting himself at the head of those who are opposed to him. He is in fact the most manifest blackguard it is possible to meet. One of these days, however, he will find himself in the wrong box. His son-in-law and daughter, the Marquis and Marchioness Rocca Giovine, have been obliged to leave the house they occupied with him in consequence of this duelling business, and his endeavour to set them at variance with all honest folk. Although actively engaged in conspiring against his cousin Louis, he still goes to the Elysée, but he has ceased to bow to Princess Mathilde.

On Monday evening he begged the Duchess de Crès to give him a seat in her carriage, and as they were driving along he set to work to vilify the President's government, and expressed himself so unreservedly that he alluded to certain demonstrations that were to be made against the prorogation, and ended by saying that he should lead the agitators

in the streets. The Duchess thereupon stopped her
carriage, told him that she could not listen to such
language, and would rather deprive herself of the
honour of his society than be made the *confidante* of
such projects. Canino got out, said good-bye to the
Duchess in a terrible rage, and in loud and angry
tones had the vulgarity to inform her that he had
spoken to her for the last time.

The Duchess sought an interview with the President,
and acquainted him with the schemes cherished by this
beautiful ex-member of the Roman assembly.

Some time since, when Canino was discussing Italian
affairs in Princess Mathilde's drawing-room, and in-
veighing against the Pope and the French with his
usual urbanity and Mazzini-like language, General
Baraguy d'Hilliers, losing all patience, interrupted
him, saying: " If I had found you in Rome, Prince, I
would have shot you like a dog."

Everybody is persuaded that the prorogation will
take place in spite of party intrigues and machinations.
Each side plays for its own hand, the party of order
becomes that of disorder, and since the adjournment
will take place, whether or no, people think they may
as well have the satisfaction of a little agitation. Our
politicians sacrifice the tranquillity of France on the
altar of their own ambition. Thiers, Guizot, &c., &c.,
believe themselves to be necessary to the country.
What luck if a good illness would carry them off!
Then one could cry, " God defend France ! " These
gentlemen wish to begin over again the game they
played for twenty years, and which ended in losing

the monarchy of July; they are like blind beggars
who never cease whining to the passers by: " Place
France in our hands, just one little France to do with
as we like, good kind Christian friends ! "

The dominion of vulgar pedants, the reign of professors, would be fatal to humanity. Let them return
to their school-rooms and birch their pupils.

June 23rd.—Princess Mathilde has rented the
chateau belonging to the Marquis de Custine at St.
Gratien, near Enghien, and has kindly offered me a
room as I go there twice a week. The place is
charming and most agreeable to stay at, with its
pretty surroundings and proximity to the lake. This
season the pleasures of a country life are sought with
avidity; everyone says, who knows where we shall
be next year? From one end of France to the other
1852 is awaited with the same anxiety that characterized the approach of the eleventh century, when
people thought that the year 1000 was to be the end
of the world. In those days people went to confession,
became reconciled with their enemies, showered their
wealth upon the poor and endowed religious houses, but
now they are reconciled with no one, and the fatal
moment is awaited without any effort being made to
avert the dreaded evils. One does not know in whom
to trust, and in the Government itself there are few
who inspire me with confidence. The office-holders
are so many Figaros, without faith or self-restraint,
who worship the rising sun, and sacrifice only to
success. They make one sick. Three days ago all
the Ministers dined with Véron. This noble don told

his " dancers " (as his familiars are termed) that it was obligatory to invite them, but that they were awful bores. Véron is typical of the present century; cynical, scrofulous, shameless, and puffed-up with importance, he infects all who come near him.

I have just seen a letter written by Canino's mother after Count Rossi's death. In it she says : " The last indignity I could suffer was to have an assassin for a son." This was really not wanting to the good lady with such sons as Pierre and Antoine, but the avowal is worth noting.

That Canino did not hold the knife is true, but he was in the plot. The letter from his mother is written from Italy, and is addressed to her friend Madame de Drisen.

June 25th.—There is in Paris, in reliable hands, a letter written by Mazzini to Monsieur de Lesseps, who had the care of French interests in Rome during the war. This is the tenor of it : " My dear Sir,—The French have occupied such and such positions; they have, therefore, intercepted all our communications and blockaded us. It is for you, therefore, to remedy this state of things by staying the operations of the general in command."

Lesseps, therefore, betrayed his country in Mazzini's interests.

Véron the great has a chateau at Auteuil, where he keeps open house and acts the part of a big wig in the same way that children play at mass on religious fête days. It is a piece of bombastic vanity which makes one nearly vomit. The Ministers themselves

think that they cannot dispense with the formality of
dining with the divine " Constitutional." Guisard, too,
dines at its table, the picture of a city merchant in the
character of politician. Véron has four gentlemen of
the chamber who are deputed to do the honours of the
house, as the great man himself does not condescend
to receive his guests or show them out.   These four
gentlemen are : Romieu, the ex-préfet ; Malitourne,
the journalist ; Gilbert des Voisins, the husband of
Taglioni ; and Millot, of the Treasury.   Véron occa-
sionally vouchsafes to accompany his guests (two at a
time) in the pony carriage round the park.   This is
a sign of royal favour of which they are commen-
surately proud.

After dinner they play the game of "creps," and more
people arrive : Roqueplan, of the Italian Opera, with
his mistress, Mdlle. Marquet, of the Français, and
Valdes, with the memory of his past successes, all
anxious to take part in this comedy of " Louis XIV.
Véron," who reigns in virtue and by right of the
Constitutional newspaper.

Véron lords it over the Ministry, finds good places
for his myrmidons, and also holds his court.

July 15th.—I still go every Wednesday and Saturday to the Princess Mathilde's at St. Gratien. I meet
all sorts and conditions of people there, and listen to
conversations often strange enough, were it not that
nothing is strange to one nowadays, only curious.
The Princess ignores the aristocracy, the influence of
birth, or of family traditions, except such as belong to
the Bonapartes themselves ; all is to be forgotten

save and except that great man whose acts are beyond
dispute, and in whose record it is rank treachery to
find a blot. It is a fetish worship of the most exclu-
sive kind. France is as nothing without the glory of
the Bonapartes; the royalty of bygone days merits
scarcely a passing thought; it is a crime almost to
compare Bonaparte with Charlemagne.

But Napoleon himself knew better than his succes-
sors how to estimate greatness, and longed for comparison. He imitated the great personality of the eighth
century, and loved to be called the second Charlemagne of our history. Clothed in that monarch's royal
insignia, and with his sword in hand, he wished to be
handed down to posterity. To-day, however, Charlemagne scarcely reaches to Napoleon's knees, and in
twenty years' time our Saviour himself will be forgotten
in the absorbing memory of the conqueror of Austerlitz.

Since yesterday the "revision of the constitution"
has been under discussion. Monsieur de Mornay
appears for the Orleanists, General Cavaignac for
his friends of the National, to-morrow another deputy
will plead for Louis Napoleon, and the day after
Henry V. will have his turn. Of the real interests of
France no one takes the least heed.

The President came on Friday to St. Gratien; he
was in excellent spirits and enjoyed himself hugely;
he amused himself like a child, and seemed in no
sense preoccupied. What does he want? Of what
is he dreaming? No one knows exactly. The position of affairs is more critical than it has been
since 1848.

The President affects neither his Ministry nor the Chamber; he would say as willingly as did Louis XIV., "The state is myself." He does not understand the country, and the men who are about him are of no personal value. Persigny is an old tomtit, who is not without intelligence, but has none of the qualities which make a statesman. Mocquard, a retired barrister and beau of 1822, is a man of education but nothing more. Morny, the most influential of his friends and his half-brother, is an excellent fellow but of no political significance. The President is a species of Numa Pompilius, but his guiding Egeria is his own star; he has ever been a fatalist. *Che sara, sara.*

That which the President ignores the most, and that which he is allowed to ignore, is the character of the men in his employ. At least half of them are hostile to him, and of the other moiety a great number are content to let things take their course, seeking only to secure their own interests whatever may happen. Many kinds of men are entrusted with duties who make a show of their devotion and are believed in.

The great men of to-day, like those of former times, prefer to be deceived and blinded. It is for this reason that the crown is called a "royal bandage."

July 16th.—A great dinner party was given by Baroche, Minister of Foreign Affairs, yesterday. Baraguay d'Hilliers, Oudinot, Mouchy, Prince Hohenzollern, and Véron were there. The latter is to be caricatured no longer in the *Charivari*. He has given this paper the management of a theatre and is to be allowed to sleep in peace.

The journals may attack President, National Assembly, Ministers, and Clergy, but the arch-saint Véron, no! that would be a sin. The State, moreover, pays for his repose.

A person of my acquaintance, Baron de Chamerolle, son-in-law of the Duchess d'Esclignac, was recently having a well dug on an estate of his near Montargis, and during the work two men, who had not taken proper precautions to secure the sides, were buried beneath the falling earth. After seeking for them some time one of the workmen was found dead and the other severely hurt. At once Chamerolle had the injured man carried to his house, where he was tended with care, rooms being set apart for him and his family. He also gave quarters to the family of the man who was killed, and whose funeral it was his desire to attend. But between the death and the burial a revolutionary sheet, which was printed in the village, gave out that the aristocrat did to death unhappy peasants at his pleasure, by forcing them to undertake dangerous duties, and then, when a calamity occurred, refused all succour. The people of the village, as savage and ferocious as all their class, set upon Chamerolle before he reached the cemetery, and, deciding to drown him, dragged him with that intention towards the river. Happily at that moment a gendarme arrived, and at his instance the brutes were induced to postpone their sentence; the interment was proceeded with, and Chamerolle escaped.

The next morning, however, he was besieged in his chateau on the pretence that he was doing nothing for the families of the two men, and these had actually to show themselves, and assure the mob that they were being well cared for, lodged, and fed.

The danger has been stayed for the time, but how long will the state of quiet last?

Chamerolle went to the sous-préfet to get redress, but this spiritless administrator, afraid of compromising himself, merely told him to be careful, as his district was a dangerous one. He then came to Paris and took out a summons against the village newspaper, and Léon Duval is to conduct his case.

Having arranged this matter, Chamerolle left last evening to return home, saying, as he went: "I have not the least idea what my fate will be."

Such are the times in which we live, and such is the mob we dignify with the term "the people." I would as soon see the lions and tigers of the Zoological Gardens let loose as such a mob, moved either to joy or fury. There is nothing to choose between them. Our duty is to repair that which we have all endeavoured to destroy—respect for authority, but for myself I am always prepared for the time when, like the Arabs, we shall have to go and live in tents. The dream of the our co-citizens, the Communists, is to make a clean sweep of everything: history, monuments, and arts.

What a lovely thing is philosophy, and what a debt of gratitude do we not owe to the eighteenth century! If the Voltaires, Diderots, and Holbachs, the fathers of these brutes, could but return to life, how proud they would be of their progeny !

The "reds" are ruffians, the "whites," to whichever side they belong, are idiots; and the rest are supreme nincompoops. With such materials make a great nation if you can.

July 18th.—The Assembly is beginning to get excited over the revision business. Yesterday Victor Hugo delivered himself of the most cowardly and abominable speech it was possible to listen to, and he met with frequent and angry interruptions. This man is a wretched knave, with the pride of Satan, and the heart of a rag-gatherer ; poltroon and passion-tossed at the same time, his denunciations are principally directed against the magistracy, which he told his brother-in-law, V. Foucher, he would one day crush beneath his feet.

Victor Hugo long coveted a peerage, and obtained it at last through the good offices of the Duchess of Orleans, who was cleverly persuaded by him that she was obeying the wishes of her husband in covering the poet's shoulders with the ermine mantle. Hugo was in those days not the detractor of princes, but their slave.

He was surprised *in flagrante delicto* with Madame Biard, and it was owing to the solicitations of his wife, and the influence of the Duchess of Orleans, that he was not condemned. Madame Biard, however, was sentenced to twelve months' imprisonment in expiation of the poet's love, and on her liberation was received into his own house. So much for the morality of the poet reformer.

August 11*th*.—Prince Napoleon, the son of Marshal Jérôme, has just been expelled from the Hôtel des Invalides by order of the Minister of War. His conduct has been scandalous, for, when not engaged in entertaining a lot of common street-walkers, he has opened the doors of the Hôtel to a Democratic Club. This Prince is a terrible scoundrel, who acts the same part towards the President that Philippe-Egalité did towards Louis XVI. He is a braggart and a coward, ambitious, self-sufficient, quarrelsome, and dissolute, the impersonation, in fact, of every bad quality. His father was a mischievous rascal, but he is even worse.

CHAPTER IV.

1851 *(continued)*.

August 18*th.*—I dined with Véron at Auteuil the
day before yesterday. The guests consisted of the
two Didiers, my brother Victor, Gilbert des Voisins,
Saint Ange, Romieu, Millot, and one or two others.
The dinner was very cheerful, and the conversation

sparkling. During dessert we discussed literature, both ancient and modern, but especially the poets of the 16th and 17th centuries. Each of the guests recited a verse or two of his favourite poet. Didier took de Marot; Romieu, Corneille; and someone else Marthurin Regnier. Véron, near whom I was seated, in the end agreed with me that of all our actual poets the most poetical in ideas and mode of expression, as well as in the faculty of imagination, is Alfred de Musset. The party was a curious one; politics were not touched upon in general conversation, except on one occasion, and at the expense of that very overweening person Fould (Finance Minister), who had been terribly bantered when he came to take leave of Véron a few days previously. It seems that Ministers do not disdain, when visiting Véron, also to pay their respects to Sophie, the major-domo, cook, and valet of this Sultan of the *Constitutional*, and for this purpose they are not above going to her kitchen. Véron still entertains a feeling of irritation against the President, who has not treated him with sufficient regard and courtesy in their intercourse; and he narrated to me his visit to the Count de Chambord in 1849. He expressed himself in terms of high praise of the pretender, who received him with great distinction, and spoke of the political future without reserve. "I have," the Prince said to him, "several strong guarantees in my favour; for my advent to the throne would mean universal peace, the re-establishment of good relations with the European powers, and the re-acquisition by France of her com-

plete liberty of action in matters of general and special
importance." Véron did not deny these advantages,
and said to the Prince —" Believe me, your Highness,
if you include in your programme an economical
government, the reduction of indirect taxes, if not
their total repeal, and fewer offices, you will not be
the less welcome to the nation." Véron tells me that
the Count de Chambord has a sympathetic and plea--
sant face and manner, and expresses himself well,
perhaps availing himself rather too often in conversation of set expressions. Gilbert des Voisins and
Lautour Mézeray accompanied Véron on this journey
as his aides-de-camp. Lautour, who was not then
Préfet of Algiers, thought it would be in good taste to
tickle Henry the Fifth with a few vulgar platitudes,
of Legitimist flavour, assuring the Prince of the regret
felt by France at his enforced absence. And the
descendant of Louis XIV. actually condescended
to humour these gentlemen in order to capture
their votes and interest. He coquetted with Véron,
and was amiable to Gilbert and Lautour, supposing,
no doubt, that they represented French feeling.

On his return from this visit Véron was gently
taken to task by the President for his inconsistency in
thus entering into relations with the pretender. " I
admit," said the President, " that my gratitude is
already due to you, and you will find that I am prepared to give you proof of it." This was Véron's
opportunity. He knew that Lautour was desirous of
figuring as Préfet of Algiers; the place was vacant;
he asked for it in his friend's name, and obtained it as

the recompense which Louis Napoleon offered for his fidelity. And so it was that Lautour Mézeray, on his return from Ems, with Legitimist professions still fresh on his lips, accepted the prefecture of Algiers from a Bonaparte.

August 27th.—Léon de Laborde has been made a Chevalier of the second class of the Prussian Order of Civil Merit. People are asking why and wherefore? Is it for having written books without point, or for his publications justifying his history of the Dukes of Burgundy? He is a successful intriguer and nothing more. Another of his class who ought to be held up to opprobrium is Raoul Rochette. When this gentleman had finished his book on Greek vase-painting he took a copy to the King of Prussia, who received both the academician and his work rather frigidly. As Raoul Rochette in course of time heard nothing either of diamond snuff-box or decoration of any kind he went to Baron Humboldt and confided to him his disappointment. The illustrious Prussian informed the King the same evening of the visit he had received from the French savant, and its motive. The monarch reflected for a moment, and then said to the Baron: " I will take four copies of his book ; one gives money to a man like that, not orders."

October 9th.—I resume to-day the writing of my diary, which has been interrupted owing to the negligence of my bookbinder in not furnishing me sooner with a fresh note-book.

We are now approaching what people call the crisis of 1852, and never in my experience have conspiracies been so rife. Every day the papers notify the discovery of some fresh plot, and publish in their columns revolutionary manifestoes which have been secretly formulated.

The dregs of the population are endeavouring to form themselves into another "Jacquerie," and those who are menaced by the movement are restrained by mutual jealousies from banding together to resist the common foe. Everybody studies his own individual interests, or endeavours to promote those political ends which his own narrow and selfish egotism suggest. I know few persons who are loyally and sincerely devoted to their country.

In accomplishing the rude task I have set myself in writing this book I fear that I shall have to pen many a sad page. Men and things may be found equally wanting at the supreme moment, and the lava and cinders of our national volcano will, I fear, scarcely preserve our remains for future ages, as did those of Vesuvius, Pompeii, and Herculaneum.

The men who at present serve the State are wavering and uncertain, and if they do not participate themselves in the plots that are on foot they are at least silently conscious of them. For example, in June, 1850, Monsieur de Billandel, a Legitimist from Dauphiny, went to Brussels to offer Serrurier, our first Secretary of Legation, a division to contest at the election in 1852. Serrurier refused for himself, but introduced his brother, a dismissed préfet, to the Legitimist committee. Monsieur de Billandel is the head of a vast organization which embraces eighteen departments in the South, and Messieurs Mollé, Berryer, and Changarnier recommended the brothers Serrurier to him. The diplomatist is now first Secretary to the London Embassy, and the second brother is still a candidate for a prefecture and the willing *protégé* of Princess Mathilde and an old wire-puller at the Elysée, Madame de Salvage.

Neither conspiracies nor *coups d'état* have yet come to anything, for one and the same reason, namely, that when the moment arrives for belling the cat people are too timid to act.

On the 21st of last September the *coup d'état* was all ready. On the 23rd it was uncertain, because at the critical moment the Generals, and notably Carrelet, could not be relied upon. It was, therefore, postponed. We can only trust to unexpected contingencies.

October 11*th*.—Yesterday an important meeting of the Cabinet was held at the President's house to consider the law of the 31st May. In my opinion this is the question on which the Ministry will go out. The friends of the President believe that it would be wise to return to the old law of universal suffrage. God grant that they may not be mistaken. At four o'clock to-day it was announced that the Ministry, with the exception of Fould, had resigned, and that the President had proposed the abrogation of the law of the 31st May.

October 13*th*.—The Ministerial crisis continues.

October 14*th*.—It appears to be agreed that the whole of the Cabinet will resign. For some days Emile de Girardin has been making advances to the President in

the hope of getting some minor office.   To-day everything will be decided.   The morning papers remark
that this is the anniversary of the battle of Jena.

I dined last evening at the Rue de Courcelles with
Princess Mathilde.   She seems to approve of a possible
understanding between the Republicans and the Elysée.
on the question of the revision, and she favours the
return to universal suffrage.   I ventured to remark to
old General Armandi that such respect is mere hypocrisy; the Prince can only continue to govern by
violating the Constitution.   Let him do it, therefore,
boldly and defiantly ; the country will side with the
man who acts with courage, but it will oppose him
who forms alliances with the enemies of society and
civilization.

October 29*th.*—The Ministry has been formed since
yesterday, and the names are published in the *Moniteur.*
Rentes having gone up twelve centimes as the result,
the new Administration was immediately nicknamed by
the wags the Ministry of two sous and a half.   Tur-
got's appointment to the Foreign Office causes general
astonishment.   General Saint-Arnaud, the Minister of
War, is a spendthrift, who is overwhelmed with debt,
as is General Magnan, Commander-in-Chief of the
Paris Army, whose furniture and effects are always
being seized and sold.   Lieutenant-Colonel Fleury,
orderly-officer at the Elysée, is also a prodigal, whose
debts are frequently paid by the President.   He is the
lover of the Marchioness de Contades, who ruined my
friend Coislin, and has been the mistress of many others
besides.   Of the Ministers themselves I expect no great

things; they are merely intended to blind the public to the real situation. We are approaching the critical moment. The President wished to attempt a *coup d'état*, but his adherents could not agree together, and Carlier, the Prefect of Police, overacted his part. His successor, who was appointed yesterday, is a Monsieur de Maupas, Préfet of the Haute-Garonne. I knew him as a drawing-room ballad singer.

October 31st.—The day before yesterday I dined with La Guéronnière, editor-in-chief of the *Pays* newspaper. He sounded me as to his coming over to the President's views. I had the Prince informed of the circumstance, and advised his seeing La Guéronnière, who is a man of parts and intelligence, and may be useful, if only as a set-off against Véron, who would scarcely appreciate another influential rival in the same field.

November 1st.—Princess Mathilde told me yesterday that Belmont's cross was solicited by Madame de Belmont herself. The only reason I know that he should have it is that he has had more contagious diseases than any other man living, and that it is his lawful wife who has asked for it for him. Why not give the cross to his brother-in-law, Léopold d'Ivoy, because he has killed more rabbits than any other man in France?

Laurent Jan, the most witty of our Bohemians of the press, thus hits off Lamartine and de Musset: "Lamartine," he says, "is the Marseillaise hymn played in church, and de Musset a peach growing on a thistle."

November 4th.—To-day our representatives are setting to work again after their two months' vacation. God grant that the spirit of wisdom may descend upon them and enter into them, for never did France require more the care of experienced physicians. She is in the throes of agony, and there is but one way to cure her.

During the past day or two there has been a pretty little intrigue on foot with the object of profiting by the first cause of difference between the Chamber and the President, and subjecting the latter to impeachment, in the event of which Changarnier was to have been made dictator. Immediately the news of the Ministerial changes was officially reported General Changarnier, thinking that the moment had arrived for his dictatorship, left the country and hurried to Paris. The quidnuncs assert that thereupon Carlier, the Préfet of Police, rushed off to the Elysée, and told the President that it was his duty to acquaint him with the sudden arrival in Paris of General Changarnier. Louis Napoleon replied very calmly, " That ought not to astonish you, Monsieur Carlier, as he comes in answer to a letter you wrote him four days ago." The Préfet of Police was thunderstruck at the discovery of the plot, and, not knowing what to say, retired in confusion. He then wrote and asked for another audience, but, seeing that it was impossible to regain the Prince's confidence, sent in his resignation. In whom can one trust nowadays ? Although Didier has been nominated to the prefecture of Ariége, Véron is still in the sulks. This Achilles is shut up in his tent, and expends his fury in violent denunciations of Persigny. Since the intervention of the bourgeois element in State affairs things have come to such a pass that France is led by a handful of ill-conditioned

journalists. The peerage of Louis XIV. is supplanted
by the peerage of the press, whose three grand dukes
at the present moment are : Bertin, of the *Debats*,
Véron, of the *Constitutionnel*, and Girardin, of the
Presse.

Juvenal, where art thou ?

November 5th.—I explained yesterday how it happened that Carlier lost the prefecture of police ; to-day
I must explain how Maupas got it. It was he who
discovered the cabal with Changarnier, and informed
the Prince of it. " Your Highness is being deceived,"
he said, " and I have the proof in my possession.
Here it is." He thereupon produced and showed the
Prince a copy of the letter which had been sent to the
General, urging him to repair to the capital.

The President's message was read yesterday ; it is
very comprehensive, succinct, judicious, and dispas-
sionate. It was badly received by the Right, Berryer
at their head. The coming storm is already felt
within the precincts of the Legislature. We are on
the eve of 1852.

November 6th.—La Guéronnière came yesterday to
tell me of his interview with the President. He is
enchanted with him, and very grateful to me for
bringing about the meeting. Lamartine will lose his
influence in the *Pays* and the 50,000 francs which he
draws from it annually ; but what he will feel most is
the loss of an organ in the press at the very time
when his party are preparing for so important a
matter as the opposition which is to be offered to
Louis Napoleon's re-election to the Presidency.

Lamartine is an old idiot. La Guéronnière can, and will, render immense service to the cause of law and order ; it was of the first importance to extricate him from the clutches of his patrons, Girardin and Lamartine, whom he estimates at their proper value. He said to me yesterday, " Lamartine is a man who is blinded by his conceit, who believes in no one but himself. Girardin is quite impossible to follow in his sudden changes of policy ; he has neither conscience nor political worth, and his paper, as a fighting weapon, is used up. As to ourselves, the staff of the *Pays*," added La Guéronnière, " we have no wish to play the part of Girondists—indeed, we do not possess their talent—but neither do we expect to have recourse to the scaffold in order to recover our courage. We will support the Government in its new methods, and you may rely upon my maintaining our line of policy in spite of Lamartine."

November 7th.—Events are moving at a rapid pace, and the situation is becoming more defined ; the National Assembly has declared openly against the President. The Questors have lodged a proposition to reinvest their President, Dupin, with the power of summoning as many soldiers as he judges necessary to protect the representatives, and of nominating a general to command them, and urgency is demanded. If this proposition is accepted we shall be drawn into open civil war, for Prince Napoleon will find himself face to face with extreme measures ; it would mean war to the death between himself and the Assembly. This body, with an army at its orders and a general to command it, would simply mean a repetition of the Convention—and what a Convention !

Every plot comes to my knowledge little by little. Changarnier is the leader of the Coalition, and the Count de Chambord has written to tell Berryer to support him with the Legitimist votes. The Princes of the House of Orleans have written to Admiral Baudin to the same effect. Thiers inspires the whole conspiracy, by which Changarnier is to be Military Dictator, himself President, a Civil Directory proclaimed, and Louis Napoleon incarcerated at Vincennes, after being deprived of his prerogatives one by one. Such are the objects these gentry have in view.

When the President was informed of the proposition of the Questors, he simply said : " So much the better; these gentlemen are unmasking themselves."

Lamoricière is to speak against it as being subversive of all military discipline.

The President wishes me to communicate to him my project for getting up a demonstration of the commercial interests in his favour, by means of which I hope to bring the middle classes over to his side.

November 8th.—I met Clary at dinner at Princess Mathilde's yesterday. He told me that the Assembly recoiled before the bellicose frolic of its Questors, and that Dupin sent for him and begged him to tell the President that nothing would induce him to accept the power with which it was proposed to invest him. Baze will have to pay pretty dearly for his valour. I wonder what the Coalition will invent next.

November 9th.—I dined with La Guéronnière yesterday as he wished to have a talk with me. He first of all told me how interesting he thought my letter to him of the day before yesterday, and that he had had it inserted in the *Pays* in the form of an article. He then revealed another act of treason which has been committed by a prominent official. Monsieur Leroy, ex-Préfet and principal Secretary to the Ministry of the Interior, the creature of Thiers, has had interviews with that personage, and shown him the work of his department. He has been seen very early in the morning with a portfolio of papers leaving the hôtel in the Rue St. Georges. I have had the President informed of the circumstance; he will know what measures to take.

Immediately after the division, if the abrogation of the law of the 31st May is agreed to by the Assembly, the Minister of War will ascend the tribune and inform the members that they are all prisoners. The threshing will then begin, and the good separated from the bad grain, which will be placed where it can do no harm. To support the declaration of the Minister of War, five regiments will invest the House of Representatives.

This bold project is not to be regarded as a fanciful invention of my own; it comes to me secretly from a " reliable source," and if I inscribe it in my book it is because I firmly believe in its reality. The Minister of War is quite prepared to play his part, and the Army well disposed and ready for action. Since the monstrous proposition of the Questors, military protests have been received in showers at the Elysée.

Important events are close at hand, but any crisis will be preferable to this state of inaction, which is eating into one's very vitals.

November 10*th.*—I give the text of the speech which was made yesterday by the President of the Republic to the officers of the regiments which have been recently brought to Paris, on their presentation to him by Monsieur Magnan, Commandant of the City troops :—

" Gentlemen,—In receiving the officers of the different regiments which have succeeded to garrison duty in Paris, I am glad to observe that they are animated by that soldierly spirit which has made our fame in the past and guarantees our security in the present. It is not necessary that I should speak to you of your duty or discipline. Your duty has always been performed with honour on African equally as on French soil, and your discipline has ever been maintained intact, although sometimes subjected to the severest trials. I trust that these trials may never recur ; but if the gravity of events should oblige me to have recourse to your devotion, it will not fail me I feel sure, because, as you know full well, I shall only ask of you what is in accordance with my Constitutional rights, with military honour, and with the interests of the country ; because I have placed at your head men who possess my entire confidence, and who merit yours ; because if ever the day comes when we are menaced by danger I will not act as my predecessors have done, who said to you : Lead on, I will follow ; but I will say to you : Follow me, I go first."

The proposal to repeal the law of May the 31st has been defeated in the Assembly by a majority of six. Clary is ashamed of having voted against the President. Lamartine, being ill, could not take part in the division. Altogether the Chamber have won their victory by a close shave. Baze, his adherents, and General Changarnier were seized with fear after the voting, and passed the night at the Questor's office in great agitation and with their pistols ready to hand. Thiers also passed an uneasy night at his house in the Place, or Rue, St. George. All these gentlemen and a good many besides believe they will be arrested.

There were certain grounds for this fear, for at the next meeting of the Chamber, and in the face of a hostile majority, Carlier proposed that the leaders and most turbulent members should be arrested, sent by special convoy to Havre, and there immediately embarked for South America. He demanded that Paris should be instantly placed in a state of siege, and said he would make himself answerable for whatever might happen. The whole affair could have been carried out in one night, without the assistance of the troops, and on the following day, when Paris awoke to the *coup d'état*, the prisoners would have been already under way.

The President declined the proposal, either from want of confidence in his Ministry, or because he did not think the time was yet ripe. Magnan, the Commander-in-Chief of the Paris army, is not very resolute, but they say that Saint-Arnaud, the Minister of War, is, on the contrary, very much so.

November 18*th.*—The proposition of the Questors has been rejected by 408 votes to 300. This vote postpones the solution. The President was firmly resolved not to be beaten, and had everything in readiness. The army would have marched at his word of command.

Yesterday evening, at the reception at the Elysée, the military officers congregated in large numbers, and did not disguise their antipathy to the Assembly. The Minister of the Interior has appointed me Chief Secretary of Public Museums.

December 2*nd.*—The *coup d'état* has taken place ! The Assembly and the Council of State are dissolved, and a large number of arrests have been made during the night.

Lamoricière, Changarnier, Bedau, and many others have been taken. Several members of the Assembly met together at the Palais Législatif to offer a protest, but were forced to retire. Some of the deputies and leaders of the people are said to have been wounded in endeavouring to force their way through the lines.

12.30 p.m.—I am preparing the last archway in the large gallery at the Louvre for the reception of troops. Rumours of the most contradictory kind are in circulation; according to some the Republicans are preparing to make an energetic resistance. According to others everything is quiet. We must wait till to-night.

The troops shouted " Long live the Emperor ! "

Universal suffrage is proclaimed, and the elections are to take place on the 14th. Louis Napoleon asks for a decennial term of office. Morny is Minister of the Interior and General Lavoëstine commands the National Guard.

The affair has been conducted with the greatest secrecy, and none of the persons arrested had the least suspicion of their sentence.

2.0 p.m.—Cavaignac, it is said, has been arrested.

On the boulevards at the top of the Rue Taitbout there is a crowd, and a few orators are declaiming, but there is no organization and the streets are under military guard.   The Faubourg St. Denis is quiet and so is the Faubourg Poissonnière.

3.0 p.m.—*La Patrie*, which has just been issued, contains the names of some of the arrested members.

Last night the Préfet of Police called his men together and gave them the orders for arrest, saying : " If you hesitate I have others who are ready to do the work." Two hundred members of the Assembly endeavoured to meet at the Mayoralty House of the tenth ward. They drew up and signed the President's deposition ; some were arrested.

December 3rd.—The night has been undisturbed and all the troops have been brought into barracks.

Fleury, the President's orderly officer, has been wounded in the head by a gunshot, but the wound does not prevent him from performing his duties.

It is said, but the news is false, that Thiers is confined at Ham, in the same room formerly occupied by the Prince.

Piscatory, who was conducted after his arrest to the barracks where General Forey is in command, was very abusive in his language, so much so that the General at last lost patience and said to him: "If you utter another word I will run my sword through your stomach."

December 4th.—Yesterday Mons. Baudin and Mons. Madier de Monjau* were killed behind the barricades, and Mons. Schoelcher was severely wounded.

The High Court of Justice endeavoured to hold a meeting, but was dissolved by an armed force.

La Guéronnière, who overrates his own individual importance, like the rest of the staff of the *Pays*, announces his retirement as a writer in this morning's edition; he also announces his brother's resignation of the office of sous-Préfet.

Midnight.—I have just gone through the Louvre and inspected all the posts. I have also walked along the roof with the keepers and assistants. The town is gloomy, and from time to time isolated musketry firing is heard. Nieuwerkerke came to give us news at half-past ten. There has been rough work during the day, especially for the 72nd regiment, the Colonel of which has been wounded, and Lieut.-Colonel killed. A Captain has also had his leg broken. Altogether, the troops have had about twelve killed and forty wounded. The barricades were carried in splendid style and the gendarmerie showed great zeal.

Money has been scattered in profusion, but men are asking large sums this evening—eighteen francs each—to defend the barricades. The Orleanists are at the bottom of it all. Nadaillac was, for a time,

---

* The latter was only wounded and taken prisoner. Schoelcher, who was slightly wounded, was subsequently able to leave France.

arrested.   He was shouting that the President should
perish by his hand alone, and that the National Guard
ought to be called out.   He was subsequently released.
Eighteen well-dressed individuals, among a group who
were firing on the troops at the corner of the Rue de
Richelieu, were arrested and taken to the Tuileries.
Nieuwerkerke has gone to find out their names.

Generals Cavaignac, Changarnier, and Lamoricière will
be brought before a court-martial if evidence of conspiracy can be proved against them.   Falloux has been
set at liberty and has been to leave his card on the
President.   Berryer is on parole at his country house.

Severe measures will be taken to-morrow, cannon
will be used, and the most stringent orders have been
issued.   All who are found with arms in their hand
will be shot.   Soldiers will search all the houses in
the insurgent quarters, and everyone who cannot prove
that he inhabits the house where he is found will be
shot.   Persons will also be put to death who bear
about their persons the marks of gunpowder.   The
provinces are quiet, and General Castellane, in a
despatch dated from Lyons at midday, says he will
answer for his division.

Amiens wished the army to unite with the National
Guard in support of the Prince's pronunciamento.   The
Préfet and Mayor, who protested, are deposed, and
Bernard, an ex-Deputy, who is very energetic and
devoted to the President, has been sent there as extra-
ordinary commissioner.

The middle classes in Paris look sour at the idea of
having to vote openly ; their cowardice is better accom-

modated by a secret ballot.   They do not wish to compromise themselves, and are always the same stupid, craven-hearted, vain race, hiding themselves in times of danger, and in times of peace longing for the influence they are incapable of retaining.

December 7th.—The foreign powers are very satisfied with the President's action, and Lord Palmerston has written him a congratulatory letter.   Some of the English papers, and the *Independance Belge* and *Courrier de Gand*, are prohibited from entering France in consequence of the revolutionary tone of their articles.

The great English newspaper, the *Times*, is also hostile, which is not to be wondered at, being very Phillipist in its tendencies and largely influenced by the Orleanist faction.

There were at Montmartre cemetery yesterday the corpses of twenty-eight respectably-dressed men, whose hands or faces bore traces of gunpowder.   Two stockbrokers' associates were shot, after being captured in the act of firing on the troops.

I received the following account of the *coup d'état* from Colonel l'Espinasse's own lips :—

"On the 30th of November last the War Minister sent for me and said, 'The political situation, Colonel, at the present moment is most grave; the Assembly shows itself more and more openly hostile to the President, and before very long the conspiracy which is on foot, and of which the proposition of the Questors was only a first move, will burst forth. The intentions of the conspirators are no longer a secret from anyone.   To imprison the President in

Vincennes and get possession of the government is their aim. We are consequently menaced by civil war, the demoralization of the army, which will be dragged this way and that by persons who, on the morrow of their victory, will quarrel among themselves, and we shall be subjected in the end to a state of socialism worse than the Reign of Terror, in 1793, the ruin and shame of our country.

"'The President is anxious to prevent a recurrence of such disasters, and in order to do so has determined to dissolve the Assembly, arrest the principal agitators, and then appeal to the nation to support his action. I have counted upon you and your well-known energy to carry out the measures which this salutary *coup d'état* necessitates. Am I mistaken?'

"I replied that the President could rely upon me. I was then given a pass which procured me access to every corner of the National Assembly House. Without losing time I used my right of entry, and examined the position I was to carry; then, having spied out the weak points and made my dispositions, I returned to the Minister's house and guaranteed the successful accomplishment of the enterprise whenever he gave me the order to act.

This order was not long in coming. On the night of the first of December I was aroused by three commissaries of police, each bearing a letter, which, on opening, proved to be the mandates for the Questors' arrest; other instructions empowered me to take possession and command of the Palais Législatif, and, lastly, I was told to hand to President Dupin a letter from the Prince. The three commissaries appeared rather startled at first at the gravity of their duty, but a few firm words from me gave them confidence, which was further confirmed by my perfectly determined expression of countenance. From that moment I knew that I could rely upon them.

" About half-past two my regiment left the Military School. Two hundred men surrounded the Palais Législatif, with the order to let no one escape, and I presented myself with a strong force at the little door leading to the President's private entrance, asking to see first of all the officer of the guard, and then the commandant of the battalion in charge of the Palace. Without more ado the two officers, who were greatly astonished to see me there at such an hour, were forcibly arrested and placed in a room under a military guard. Thus being master of the Palace, I could proceed without molestation to secure the persons of the three Questors—Messieurs Baze and de Panat, and General Leflô. Monsieur Baze tried, without success, the effect of his eloquence on my men, who only laughed at him. General Leflô, in full uniform, wished to harangue the troops, and protest against the violation of the privileges of members, but I declined to allow him to speak, and, with all possible respect, informed him that I had a military duty to perform, and could not allow him, in defiance of my orders, to address the soldiers under my charge. On a sign from me he was then removed under guard.

"Having settled the Questors I presented myself

before Mons. Dupin, and gave him the Prince's letter, which assured him of the necessity of the course that was being taken and guaranteed him his liberty, but at the same time advised his remaining for the moment quietly within the precincts of the Palace. President Dupin assented, and said he should prefer to do so. Everything went smoothly, and day began to break. I then assembled, along with the troops under my command, who until then were entirely ignorant of the purpose of their mission, those who had been in charge of the Palace, and addressing them all, said : 'Soldiers, a conspiracy has been formed by several members of the Assembly with the object of usurping the power and imprisoning in Vincennes the nephew of the Emperor Napoleon. It was on the point of breaking out, but we have nipped it in the bud. I put it to you, will you be commanded by a lot of blackguards or by the Emperor's nephew ? ' My appeal was answered by the unanimous cry of ' Long live Louis Napoleon ! '

"Everything went well, but as an insurrection might nevertheless take place in Paris, and the Palace be attacked, I neglected no precaution. In the out-buildings of the Palace a large number of attendants and their families were lodged, and my orders were to allow the nurses and servants liberty to go to and fro. Profiting by this facility about sixty Deputies got into the Chamber, and were proceeding to discuss the deposition of the President when I got wind of what was going on. I at once commanded the officer in charge of the gendarme battalion to clear the room. He was received with hooting and angry cries, and I thought

at one time he would be killed; at last he was obliged
to beat a retreat. I then entered the room at the head of
my grenadiers, and was received with loud execrations,
the Deputies even proceeding to blows with the soldiers.
Wishing, however, to avoid all scandal, I endeavoured
to obtain silence, and said :—' Gentlemen, let me appeal
to your own dignity, do not dispute orders which I am
bound to execute, and oblige me to have recourse to
force.' Cries, vociferations, and insults drowned my
words; some of the more desperate ones seized my
soldiers by their coats. I could not allow such a scene
to proceed, and, in tones that dominated the noise and
tumult, ordered the gendarmes to carry them out.
The order was executed, but not without difficulty, for
some of the Deputies had literally to be transported
like so many bales. The more violent among them
stuck to their seats and would not move, and one, more
uncontrollable than the others, demanded to be struck,
and with so much insistance that a gendarme, at last
losing all patience, said, 'Is that your last word?' and
receiving a reply in the affirmative gave him a cuff
that knocked him down, and he was carried off crowned
in the full attainment of his prayers.

" The Palace being cleared, I proceeded to give my
military orders, thinking that I should now be free to
do so, when I received information that the Deputies,
on their expulsion from the Chamber, had roused the
populace and forced the guard in front of the door
leading to the Rue de Bourgogne. I hastened there
at once with one company, and succeeded in dividing
in two the invading crowd. After driving back into

the street that portion that menaced the guard I
addressed the Deputies, whom I had made prisoners at
their head, in these terms : —' In my eyes you are no
longer Deputies, but merely insurgents who are stirring
up the people to revolt and force the guard.   On any
repetition of violence on your part I will have you
instantly shot.'   My determined attitude cowed them,
and they did not utter another word, and were put in
a room in the Palace under view of a guard.   After a
time they adopted a gentler attitude and asked for
their liberty, whichI at once accorded."

I said to him :—" Colonel l'Espinasse, do you really
mean to say you would have carried into effect your
threat to shoot them if they had persisted in disregarding your order ? "   "Most certainly," he replied.   "My
head was at stake, and I was not going to lose it
through weak play."

The number of killed on the side of the insurgents,
including those afterwards captured and shot, is over
two thousand.   The suppression of the insurrection
has been terribly severe.   God grant that it may not
have to be repeated, although I hardly dare to express
such a hope.   Paris is like some wanton woman who
requires to be gratified with the lust of blood every
two or three years.   Such a spectacle is to her what a
bull-fight is to the Spaniards.

Lord Palmerston has fallen from the pedestal of
power, and his Machiavelian arts are defeated amidst
the plaudits of all Europe. Lord Granville is entrusted
with the seals of office.   Decidedly demagogism is
being vanquished on all sides.   Now the political

refugees will be watched, even if they are not expelled, and Italy will breathe again. Lord Palmerston has done incalculable injury to Europe, if not, indeed, to his own country. He was an evil genius who would willingly have set fire to the world in order to warm his feet with the flames.

The President is elected by 7,400,000 votes. His strength is enormous. We will see what use he makes of it.

He was at the opera yesterday, and received an enthusiastic welcome, at which he was deeply moved.

CHAPTER V.

1852.

January 1st.—The President, Ministers, functionaries, army, and National Guard have just returned from the celebration of the "Te Deum" at Notre Dame, where the crowd that had gathered received the Prince most enthusiastically.

At this moment the galleries of the Louvre are filled with officers of the army who are about to defile before the Chief of the State. A company of old soldiers of the Empire have also donned their uniforms in honour of the occasion. The weather is foggy, cold, and frosty, just such a day the " veterans " say as when the Emperor Napoleon was crowned. Marshal Jérôme Bonaparte was present at the function in full uniform, the colour of which it was impossible to distinguish for the lace. He was the only Marshal thus dressed.

The influence of favouritism is beginning to assert itself as under former *régimes*. Morny, who, by the wish of the President, retains his office as Minister of the Interior, is looking out for a place for his friend Montguyon. A year ago the latter was on the point of being made Director of Fine Arts. Now they are endeavouring to find something that will suit him in one of the Ministries. What has Montguyon done? An old opera beau, costumier of the green-room, and libertine on the unattached list, he has passed his life with this or that dancer, disputing with his comrades the affections of some creature or other, and spending his money in similar pursuits. Now, forsooth, he must have some indemnity, and the State is charged to find it for him. Before another two years are over he will probably be made an officer of the Legion of Honour, and we shall be told that merit is the sure road to fortune.

What oblations of devotion are offered up to-day! What a crowd of true believers! The same which collected under the balcony of Louis XVIII., crying out : "Long live the King and the Bourbons for ever," which called Charles X. " The Cavalier King; " Louis-Philippe " The Citizen King," and which in 1848 shouted for the Republic. Go, my noble friends of the new order, and ask for a bone to pick. There have been a number of promotions in the army. Captains of the Staff and the President's Orderly Officers are made Commanders of squadrons, but my friend Captain Saint-Martin, who has held the same grade for fourteen years, seven of which have been spent amid a thousand dangers in preparing a map of Tunis, has not been promoted.

January 4th.—England is beginning to feel the inconveniences resulting from the inconceivable latitude she has given to the fomenters of anarchy, and the freedom vouchsafed them for circulating their insensate doctrines. An association of working men, called the " Trades Union," are raising the flag of Socialism, and presuming even to dictate terms to the manufacturers themselves. The association has its own paper, *The Co-operative.* It asks for equality in wages, and, as a means of gaining its end, supports the different strikes out of a common fund consisting of 625,000 francs.

Social war has been proclaimed in England. Where will it stop? That country is now gathering the fruit of Lord Palmerston's policy. A State cannot with impunity shelter the enemies of society and civilization in the hope of injuring its neighbours. The

Kossuths, Mazzinis, Louis Blancs, and Ledru Rollins, *fêted* and sheltered by the English nation, have profited by the folly of their hosts by corrupting the residuum of their population. The Anglican, and especially the Scottish, clergy—subscribers to the Mazzini fund, which has been started with the object of upsetting the Papacy—have furnished the Socialists with the means of propagating their doctrines in the United Kingdom itself. The evil is gaining ground, and is preparing its code of rules and system of organization; it has its leaders, army, and newspaper organs, already adopts a dictatorial tone, and is ripe for mischief.

When I was in London in 1848 I witnessed the beginning of this business. English vanity affected to despise Continental agitators, who were permitted to enter Great Britain at will, and plumed itself on the excellence and invulnerability of the British constitution. The Socialist Clubs of Wardour and Princes Streets only provoked a smile, as much as to say to us foreigners: Your wild beasts directly they are landed on our shores become domesticated animals, who are rather entertaining than otherwise.

Between 1848 and 1852, however, the wild beasts have gone ahead, for England is, of all places in the world, the spot where eccentricity and vanity of opinion find the largest number of recruits and partisans. Magnetism, phrenology, quack medicines, and the most extravagant religious sects there find numberless disciples and the most credulous followers. At Brighton during the winter of 1848-9, I heard it

seriously stated that, in order to avoid all the maladies
to which flesh is heir, it was only necessary to extract
as children the three upper front teeth, and I actually
saw the wife of a colonel, a friend of mine, take her
eldest son, twelve years of age, to a dentist's for that
purpose.

January 11*th.*—Yesterday a decree was issued from
the Tuileries, signed "Louis Napoleon," expelling from
French territory sixty-six representatives of the Democratic party, with the threat of transportation if they
returned to it. Among these the most notable in the list
are : Victor Hugo, Charles Lagrange, and Colonel
Charras. A second decree is directed against
dangerous Parliamentarians; about eighteen of them
are temporarily expelled—Duvergier de Hauranne,
Creton, General Lamoricière, General Changarnier,
Baze, General Leflô, General Bedeau, Thiers, Cham-
bolle, De Rémusat, Jules de Lasteyrie, Emile de
Girardin, General Laidet, Pascal Duprat, Edgard
Quinet, Antony Thouret, Victor Chauffour, and Ver-
signy. The *Moniteur* also announces the transportation
to Guiana of Messieurs Marc Dufraisse, Greppo, Miot,
Mathé, and Richardet. Cavaignac's name is not
mentioned in any list. The Government, it is said,
have received his promise that he will not interfere in
any fresh political movement.

The journalists are terribly dejected ; the profession
is not quite so good as it was. Soon only the principal ones will be left, and the scribblers, who excite
the public mind morning and night with their pens,
will disappear. That cloud of grasshoppers, the

scourge of modern times, will go back to the holes
they came from, and which they ought never to have
left.

We are to be permitted to be governed in peace, and
to live in peace at last. As far as my memory carries
me back, I can recollect nothing but troubles, revolutions, and calamities, which have left an indelible impression upon my mind. At Versailles, where my
father lived, my young days were spent in the midst
of those who had escaped from the cut-throats of '93,
and who fostered to the day of their death the remem-
brance of the monstrous scenes of which they had been
witness.

I have still before my eyes the picture of that com-
munity so jealously and punctiliously retaining the
traditions of the 18th century; full of sad regrets,
religiously Royalist, and weeping in their hearts for
relations, friends, and institutions dead or destroyed.
Those unhappy gentlefolk furnished their apartments
with the insignia of the last royal race, and their walls
were hung with portraits in profile of the members of Louis XVI.'s family, with the outlines of a
weeping-willow allegorically guarding a tomb. All
wore the costume of the 18th century and retained
the language, predilections, and antipathies of that
time.

My father lodged at Number 7 in the Rue de
l'Orangerie, a few steps from the Orangerie railings,
and it was in front of this house that the Orleans
prisoners were massacred. A gentleman living in the
same house, the Marquis de Valfons, had witnessed

the tragedy from his window, and was never tired of re-
counting its horrors, the sight of which had frightened
poor Madame de Valfons into her grave.

Mons. de Valfons was a very kind-hearted man, who
came, I think, from the neighbourhood of Nîmes. My
brothers and I visited him nearly every day, and he
always received us with inexhaustible good-nature, in
spite of our turbulent youth. He was subject to
moments of great depression when his mind reverted
to those he had loved and lost; then he would draw
us to him, and, taking us to the window, would describe the massacre of the Orleans prisoners, amongst
whom were numbered many of his own friends.

Mons. de Valfons was, therefore, the mentor of my
youth, and from him I learned by heart the names of
the murdered and the murderers.

In his moments of quiet mirth he would go into
his kitchen and stamp upon some piece of pastry
about to be consigned to the oven the impression
of a *fleur-de-lys.* Delighted with this mute protest
against the Empire, he would come back to his
room and tell us long stories of Louis XVI., of the
Queen, for whom he cherished the tenderest affection, and of the tortures inflicted upon the young
Dauphin at the instance of that infamous Simon. I
also knew at that time—about 1807 or 1808—an old
Madame d'Angevilliers, who lived at Versailles in the
Rue de la Surintendance. She had her *salon,* or rather
literary *levée,* for she always received in bed after the
manner of her day. She wore a dress of pannier
fashion, which extended in ample flounces over her

bed, and her hair, which was crimped and powdered, towered above her head in the style of 1780.

Amongst those of distinguished birth or attainments who assembled at Madame d'Angevilliers' were Mons. de Feletz, of the *Debats*, and two abbés, Messieurs d'Andrezel and Saint Gérac, who, in those days, had very little of the abbé about them, but were, on the contrary, both excellent men of the world.

Who else shall I mention of all this Versailles world which had effected its escape from the Palace into the town after the destruction of Royalty and the pillage of the residence of kings? Madame des Escotais, the Duchess of Villeroy, an aristocratic and highly respected old lady, and the demoiselles de Chateaugirou, who lived in the Rue Satory, at the pavilion Le Tellier, where private theatricals often took place, for old tears, old regrets, and old people's griefs do not prevent young people from amusing themselves.

I became acquainted with the great Revolution through the sorrows of those whose relations had been its victims; of the Empire I learned through the agency of another sorrow, deep and poignant, although skilfully disguised. My father was chamberlain to the Empress Josephine; he had been her lover before she married Napoleon, and their intimacy was resumed after her divorce. The Empress always retained a sincere affection for the Emperor, and his fall was a mortal blow to her. After the Russian campaign, child as I was, my mind became saddened at the sight of the sorrow which overwhelmed the Court at Malmaison, where I spent most of my time.

The Empire had fallen. I saw it revive and fall again amid the blood and carnage of Waterloo.

January 21st.—The Ministry is unsettled, and begins to feel the effect of Persigny's baleful influence. Morny wishes to retire into private life; he is averse to the sequestration of the Orleans property, which Persigny is determined to bring about. The latter is the President's evil genius. He has great influence over him, although he is a mere vulgar intriguer, tortuous in his methods, and without the courage to oppose either men or measures frankly and in open day. A sort of insignificant cadet, of mushroom growth, the mere sight of him is sufficient to destroy any confidence one might have been disposed to place in him. An abject object in appearance, there is neither truth in his look nor conviction in his words; he is as pompous as a *laquais* and as spiteful as a beadle. Without seeming to notice an affront he will never forgive it. He is, above all, the counsellor of violent measures and crooked means. Such is Persigny.

January 23rd.—The property which Louis-Philippe abstracted from the State on ascending the throne, by a decree dated August 7th, 1830, has been confiscated, and is to be applied to the public service. The Orleans Princes are also required to sell their property within twelve months.

The President surrenders all title to the possessions taken from his family in 1814 and 1815.

Morny leaves the Ministry, and is succeeded by Persigny. Fould is replaced by Bineau, &c., &c.

January 24th.—Princess Mathilde is furious at the President's decrees, she has written to him begging him not to sign them, and even went so far as to say to me : " If Louis-Philippe had ever been jealous of Louis Napoleon he would to-day, had he been alive, have felt fully avenged."

Morny has had a quarrel with the President. His mistress, Madame Lehon, is the cause of it. She is an Orleanist, and has been trying to influence Morny to support measures favourable to that party. He had begged the President to write to the King of the Belgians, asking that Monsieur Lehon might be sent as ambassador to Paris.

We live in an age when adultery is publicly rewarded. Young Lehon, although still a minor and a Belgian subject, after acting for six weeks as principal secretary in Morny's department, has been promoted to the auditorship, and has received the cross of the Legion of Honour.

Walewski, an old *roué* without ability, but the illegitimate son of the Emperor Napoleon, is ambassador in London.

Cotterau, Queen Hortense's paramour in her latter days, is Inspector-General of Fine Arts, and Morny himself, the son of this same Queen by Count de Flahaut, was for a time Minister of the Interior.

The Orleans Princes excite a great deal of sympathy, and there is excellent reason too why certain people should commiserate with them. It is all very well to tell these persons " that the property of kings is the appanage of the State." They will not listen to you.

These poor people will only have a hundred millions to divide amongst each other, and tender hearts weep at the spectacle presented by that dear old king and his family who hadn't the courage to defend throne and country against a hideous insurrection which has since cost us all so dear.

They fled in all directions, each one anxious to save his own skin, abandoning women and children, honour and future fame. God punishes the assassin of Louis XVI. through his sons and grandchildren. He punishes, equally, the King without conscience, the bad parent and usurper. Justice does exist!

The aristocratic quarter of St. Germain is exercising its turn for humour in the same frivolous spirit that it showed under Louis-Philippe's reign. Here is a sample of it, intended for private circulation —" Anarchy is happily delivered of despotism; both mother and child are doing well."

January 30th.—Véron's brother has been appointed controller of the Government tobacco factories, which post is worth 9,000 francs a year.

Patronage is in strange hands, and appointments and promotions of the most startling kind are being made. Prince Murat is made a senator, because he is the legitimate son of his father; Walewski and Morny are placed in high offices because they are not the legitimate sons of theirs. Clavel is appointed near to the person of Persigny, because he was the dependent lover of the late Queen of Naples, Madame Murat.

We are not apparently reforming our era; on the contrary, we are acting the part of a bad Louis XIV.

and a detestable Louis XV. In the lower ranks of society we still hear voices exclaiming —" Sir, I am the bastard son of your apothecary."

February 11*th.*—I went to the Vaudeville Theatre yesterday to see one of Alexandre Dumas the younger's pieces. The theatres, be it remarked in parenthesis, are subject to a censor, appointed for the purpose of protecting public morality and public decency. The " Dame aux Camélias " of Mons. Dumas is simply an insult to the interests the censor is supposed to protect; a shame to the age in which we live, to the Government which permits it to be played, and to the public who go nightly to applaud it. The Vaudeville is crowded every evening, the Place de la Bourse is blocked with carriages, and women of good family are not ashamed to show themselves at the theatre. The whole thing is a gross public scandal.

During five whole acts the " Dame aux Camélias," or, in other words, the kept mistress, displays to a civilized public the hateful details of a life of shame. Nothing is wanting in the picture—neither the procuress, the gambler, the cynical expression, nor the scene borrowed from the lowest dens of vice. The whole play reeks with lewdness and debauchery, and the very actors chosen by the author to give it popularity are themselves ignoble in their parts. The " Dame aux Camélias " is supposed to represent true love ; true love, indeed ! . . . alternating between the caresses first of one lover and then of another, taking money from the rich man, who is not loved, to be spent in the entertainment of one who is. Then the scene with the father, who comes to reclaim his son, and tries to cure him of his affection by arranging with his mistress to resume her old and nameless occupation. Then the girl of pleasure, dying rehabilitated in the arms of her paramour, surrounded by his friends, and voluntarily pronouncing a eulogy on religion; finally the funeral oration spoken over her remains : " Much will be pardoned her inasmuch as she has truly loved."

It is impossible to analyse such transcendent vileness; it is coarse beyond expression, but the spectacle presented by the house itself is even worse.

February 22nd.—The Orleanists are on the war path. They wish to persuade the country that it regrets their absence, and that they only fell in 1848 through accidentally slipping on the political ice. The country is being inundated with pamphlets and protests, distributed with the object of provoking a revolution, in order that, when the storm has passed over, their restoration may appear on the political horizon like a rainbow.

But the country wants repose, and takes no heed of their machinations; the middle classes alone—the lice of the body corporate—are disposed to favour them. These bewail the lot of the poor Orleanists, whose goods the State has had the infamy to confiscate. The Orleanists are an accursed race, who have caused every insurrection that has taken place during the last sixty years. They are punished at last, and richly deserve it.

Bocher, their factor, an ex-Préfet and Deputy, has

been arrested on the charge of distributing their pamphlets, a large depôt of which was discovered at Madame d'Haussonville's. This lady's domicile was searched by the police, and large packets were found in her apartments, even secreted in her carriage. Mons. d'Haussonville, her son, who married Mdlle. de Broglie, has been expelled from Belgium for publishing a paper full of lies concerning French affairs. It was called *Les Bulletins Français.*

March 4th.—The journals say that Count d'Orsay has received the commission for a marble statue of Prince Jérôme to be placed at Versailles. So much the worse for Versailles.

The Count is an old "lion," whom nobody now knows or receives. He has lived with his mother-in-law, Lady Blessington, and everyone but his wife, Lady Henrietta d'Orsay, who was the mistress of the Duke d'Orleans, of Antonin de Noailles, and a host of lesser stars.

Count d'Orsay for twenty years lived on the aristocracy and the tradespeople of London. Steeped in debt, he has now turned artist, backed by a following of nonentities, who laud him as if he were a second Michael Angelo, and supported by journalists of Lord Wigmore's stamp, who perfume him with their literary incense. Every year he disfigures some contemporaneous celebrity either in marble or plaster; last time it was Lamartine.

D'Orsay has still great pretensions to elegance, and dresses like no one else, with a display of embroidered linen, satin, gold chains, and hair all disordered.

March 11*th*.—Here are three letters which will give an excellent idea of feminine relations, and the fortuitous jumble of society at the present time.

The first is from a Countess de Solms, *née* Wyse, whose mother was the daughter of the late Prince de Canino. She is young and pretty, and captured Pommereux from the Countess de Schulimburg, an old idiot who has never been even passably good-looking, but who has made herself extremely notorious and shown a ferocious jealousy with regard to this said Pommereux.

The letter is addressed : "To the Countess de Schulimburg, who has thought proper, during a fit of mental aberration and a fearful rainstorm, to wait five hours outside my door for the advent of I know not whom or what, sending every five minutes to make inquiry, and finally honouring me herself with an unexpected visit.

"*Monday Evening.*—You have thought proper to take a step to-day, madame, which it is impossible for me to pass over in silence. Such conduct is so utterly opposed to the usages and customs of good society, so foreign even to the practices of women of no pretensions to breeding whatever, that I am obliged to make a vigorous protest against my house and person being made the object of your ridiculous and extravagant behaviour. I have to beg, therefore, madame, that you will spare me a repetition of the open-air comedy you have been pleased to give to the great amusement of the Parisian public. In spite of a conscientious and most willing desire to do so, I am totally unable to

discover any reasonable solution for the strange pre-
occupation I have caused you for some time past, or
for the whimsical manner in which you have endeavoured to arrest my attention ; for, unless my memory
is greatly at fault, my acquaintance with you has been
limited to the honour of receiving you once or twice
on occasions when my rooms were thrown open to all
comers. Nor can I fail to acknowledge that I
have specially intended to cut short an intimacy
which the very difference in our ages rendered undesirable, and which was the more out of place, seeing
that my position as a widow of more modest pretensions obliged me in a measure to restrict my circle
to a few chosen friends and family dependents. It is
singular and superfluous, to say the least, that your
interest should have been excited in a woman who
knows so little of you, and who would ere now have
entirely forgotten your existence but for the trouble
you have taken to remind her of it. I cannot conceive,
madame, what my good friend the Count de Pommereux's relations with you may be, but whatever
they are I am not in the least concerned, and so
would wish entirely to ignore them; but as you
think proper to bring them to my notice, I can
only echo, without dwelling on the matter, what
everybody says, namely, that his family and those
who have regard for him have often deplored the
injury and ridicule to which he has subjected himself
for the past twenty years by so absurd a connection.
But everyone is free to do as he likes in this world ;
and if he has been pleased, either from weakness,

kind heart, or habit, to act for a time the more or less interesting part of one of Mons. de Balzac's heroes, his friends can only pity, not blame him. According as they are played, some comic scenes excite tears, some tragedies laughter.

" Enough, however, madame. I write this letter for no other reason than to tell you that you do not interest me in the least, and that I shall be infinitely obliged by your not sending your messengers to my house. I should be constrained to have them ejected, and, to speak frankly, my servants have no wish to disturb the even tenour of their ways by interfering in the extravagant caprices or nervous excitements of a fantastical invalid woman. You will allow, madame, that if all my friends' mistresses in the past, present, or future treated me so my house would become a perfect hell, and I should have to engage the fish market for their accommodation. All these childlike ways, madame, which you will readily understand are delightful at eighteen, when a woman wears the diadem of youth and freshness, become ridiculous, you will equally allow, when her brow is crowned with half a century —in ruins.

" There is a time in her life when she must learn to surrender with grace muslin dresses, attacks of nervousness, scenes of jealousy and plaintive romances, otherwise she makes a man, who is feeble or silly enough to tolerate such conduct, cut a sorry figure; his best friends are bored, and the woman herself is neither younger, more graceful, nor more amusing in consequence.

" To become fat is to grow old, said our witty friend

Becquet. Is it not equally true that to grow old to
some people is the same as to die? Good taste in
that case prescribes that the moribund body should be
made as attractive as possible by the assumption of all
those qualities and graces which are the outcome of
common sense and a benevolent mind. Let me offer
this 'friendly' advice, madame. Among the subjects
to which I have given my serious attention is that
of the science of medicine, and I know that there
is a critical period in the life of women when they
are the victims of a kind of fever which Lafon-
taine has so delightfully described in his charming
fable. This critical period renders some women uncontrollable, and they only find relief in the last
extremity. Others, again, more reasonably constituted, or of better judgment, become resigned, cir-
cumspect, even sometimes pious, forgetting the smell
of the rose, and learning to renounce the world before
it in turn renounces them. I am wrong, I know, and
give way to too much good feeling in pointing out what
your conduct should be; but in any case it is already
rather late. The fever is at its height, and your precautions should have been taken earlier; but really I
pity you, and have sufficient friendship for Mons. D—,
and compassion for Mons. de P—, to try—having
already coerced myself into writing to you at all—to
prevent your going to Charenton. The place is un-
comfortable, and, I assure you, most unhealthy, for
the dresses that are worn there are of very villainous
style—black and tight fitting—and one's wrinkles and
crow's-feet are shown up by a frightful white fall; in

addition to which the cooking is bad, it is a long way off, the roads are wretched, and I should have some difficulty in obtaining news of you through some kind friend—Mons. de Pommereux, for example—for, believe me, madame, I am extremely anxious about your health. I wish, upon my honour, that for your sake I could find some of that famous elixir of youth, the loss of which you experience so keenly ; but here a matter of grave doubt occurs to me, and I beg of your good nature to put an end to it. That wonderful fountain was supposed to restore beauty to those who had lost it. Were you ever pretty in your life, madame ? But this prattle must cease. I have endeavoured to disguise, under a jesting form, a lesson you have richly merited, and which you will do well to take to heart.

"In which hope receive the assurance of my distinguished sentiments.

" COUNTESS DE SOLMS,
" née BONAPARTE-WYSE."

The two other letters formed a little correspondence which passed between two *actrices* of the Comédie Française, Mdlle. Rachel and Mdlle. Nathalie. The latter had sent a picture by Diaz of somewhat suggestive meaning to Mdlle. Rachel after carrying off her lover, Emile Augier :—

" MY DEAR COMRADE,—

"Your Diaz is scarcely veiled enough to ornament my little house. Although I sometimes like the reserve unclothed of a charming mind, I cannot stand that kind of nudity which Molière's Arsinoë was so fond of. Do not think me too prudish, but why deprive yourself of a picture which I myself should be obliged to hide away? A thousand thanks all the same, and believe me ever your devoted comrade,

" RACHEL."

" DEAR AND GREAT COMRADE,—

"I must have been mad, almost impious, to have thought that my little picture was worthy to be placed upon your altar, but my foolish error has, at least, procured for me the most valuable information as to the limits of your innocence. Permit me, however, to differ in my reading of the comedy which you invoke, as it appears to me in an entirely wrong sense, for it was precisely in pictures that Arsinoë did not care for nudity.

> In pictures she hides the bare form with a screen,
> 'Tis in life that she loves to have nudity seen.

"I take back, therefore, my little Diaz, who is a little confused with his rash excursion. His blushes shall be hidden in my alcove, where only Mons. Augier can see them.

"Your devoted servant,
" NATHALIE."

These three letters speak volumes for the age in which we live.

March 27th.—I dined a few days ago with Rachel at her charming little mansion in the Rue Trudon. Morny, Rouher, late Minister of Justice; Fould, late Minister of Finance; Caumont, the Senator; Manuel, the stockbroker; Roqueplan, manager of the opera;

Arsène, manager of the Théâtre Français, and her two sisters were among the guests.

The mansion is furnished luxuriously, but with good taste, and the dinner was perfect. In the evening more people came, and we had some music and a little dance, followed by an excellent supper. It is impossible to meet with a more charming hostess or a better bred woman than the mistress of this house. Her lover, young Lehon, was at the dinner and the dance, but no one could have guessed from his manner the position he occupies in the establishment. The house is gilded like a court dress of the 18th century. It is filled with pictures, sculptures, and bronzes; the silver is magnificent, and the servants are numerous and well trained. Rachel fully understands the charms of good manners and choice conversation, but it is said that there are times when she easily dispenses with either.

In spite of everything said or done to the contrary, the Empire is in course of preparation. The Senate and Corps Législatif will propose it, and it will be proclaimed by the army at a grand review. The President, who is disposed to take nothing but receive everything, will consult the nation. His family and the persons surrounding him are more impatient for the Empire than he is himself. The former aspire to the title "Imperial Highness," and the latter, as in the case of Edgard Ney, and Fleury, want to be appointed Masters of Hounds or Principal Equerries. The French nation is ever the same with its Marquis's habit and Spanish tambourine. Whoever

wears the one and shakes the other proclaims to the
world at large that they are the happiest people on the
face of the earth.

March 28*th.*—I dined at Princess Mathilde's yesterday, and was there informed of the almost total destruction of the Austrian Fleet during a storm. Twenty-five
ships and every soul on board of them lost. It is horrible
to think of; but the Emperor would put out to sea in
spite of his officers' advice. He himself owes his
safety entirely to the presence of mind of one of the
sailors, who took command of the ship and ran her
ashore.

April 11*th.*—While dining at the Princess's yesterday with Marshal Exelmans and General Rebillot,
the conversation turned for some time upon Marshal
Marmont, and I am pleased to relate that both of those
old officers did him full justice. In Exelmans' opinion
Marmont in no sense betrayed the Emperor; he is the
victim of a thoughtless remark on the part of the
Emperor in 1815, and of an historical lie. Although
wounded, Marmont fought to the last against superior
numbers, but his division had been corrupted in his
absence by General Souesme, who, along with the
Duke d'Albuféra and the Duke de Reggio, was for
some time in treaty with the enemy. Marmont was put
in the pillory of history, and the two Marshals got off
almost scot free. Reggio even tried in 1815 to induce
General Exelmans to abandon all thoughts of defence,
and was sharply taken to task by Madame Exelmans
when he appealed to her for support. Justice has at
last been done to Marmont in the presence of the

Emperor's niece by one whose opinion is not without weight. The Princess, for the sake of keeping up the argument, referred to the surrender of Paris in 1814. I quoted the order of King Joseph, upon which she said : " Mons. de Viel Castel, you are aware that I do not care to hear my relations accused." With all possible respect I rejoined : " I am ; but it is not fair to excuse their weakness at the expense of an innocent general." Upon which she repeated twice : " I never had any prejudice against the Marshal, nor have I believed in his great culpability."

It appears that the news of the loss of the Austrian Fleet was an entire fabrication.

In order to get rid of the President the Orleanists rely upon an affection of the spinal marrow, from which he is supposed to suffer, but one of their agents did not scruple quite recently to remark : " If the malady is not sufficiently expeditious we have some devoted men who will not hesitate to give him the pistol illness."

CHAPTER VI.

1852 (*continued*).

July 23rd.—The President's journey to Strasburg
was a veritable triumph. He was received with
ovations everywhere. It is rumoured that he is to be
married to one of his nieces, a daughter of Princess
Wasa. Prince Wasa is a member of the Sweedish
royal family, which was ousted by Bernadotte.

The day before yesterday Marshal Exelmans was
proceeding to the Pavilion de Breteuil, St. Cloud, to

call on Princess Mathilde.   When at a place called
Point du Jour, in front of an inn kept by a man
named Malfilâtre, his horse took fright and he was
thrown violently to the ground.   His head came against
a stone, and he was killed on the spot, in the same
way as the Duke of Orleans.   In spite of his 77 years
the Marshal had the vanity to wish to appear young,
and generally went about on horseback.

The President loses a sincere and independent friend,
who was not for ever boring him with useful truths.
He had a true and loyal heart, and was of incorruptible
honesty.   His death will be regretted by everybody,
except Marshal Jérôme, who was terribly afraid of the
old soldier's jokes.

The Prince of Moskowa has been appointed to a
colonelcy in Africa.   His daughter, Madame de Persigny, refused to call up his mistress, Madame Murat.
A quarrel between father and daughter thereupon
ensued; the son-in-law interfered in his character of
minister, and the father-in-law has been exiled under
pretence of joining his regiment.

Count d'Orsay is dead, and all the papers are
mourning his loss.   He leaves behind him, they say,
many *chefs d'œuvres*, and on his death-bed requested
Clésinger to finish his bust of Prince Jérôme.

D'Orsay had no talent; his statuettes are detestable
and his busts very bad; but a certain set cried him up
for their own purposes, and called him a great man.
One newspaper goes so far as to affirm that on hearing
of his death the President said: "I have lost my best
friend," a statement which I know to be perfectly
false.

D'Orsay's friends were the President's enemies—
the Jérôme Bonapartes, Emile de Girardin, Lamartine,
&c. He never pardoned the Prince for not appointing
him ambassador to the Court of St. James's, forgetting,
or purposely ignoring, the fact that such a thing was
impossible. No Government would have received him.
His debts are fabulous. For a long time he was the
leader of fashion in London and Paris, and tailors, per-
fumers, carriage builders, &c., supplied him without
payment for the sake of his custom. The papers inform us that he has been buried at Chambourcy (on
the property of his sister, the Duchess de Grammont)
in the same grave as his mother-in-law, Lady Blessington. The incident is sublime; to make it complete, perhaps they will engrave on his tombstone:
"That his inconsolable and heart-broken widow,"
&c., &c., &c.

He died ten years too late, for he became at last
merely a ridiculous old doll. The President does not
lose his best friend; on the contrary, he is well rid of
a compromising schemer. If he could but lose twenty
more such friends Louis Napoleon might sing a Te
Deum.

August 12th.—The Bonapartes are feathering their
nests. Jérôme has received two millions, Murat one
million, and Madame Camerata one million. The latter
thinks proper to attack Princess Mathilde—who, by
the way, receives nothing—because she has had to pay
one of her father's debts.

August 18th.—Here are two curious unpublished
letters of the Emperor Napoleon. I insert them at

this point as being more interesting than an account of the Paris *fêtes* of the 15th instant, the balls at St. Cloud and the Central Market, or the strained relations between the President and his mistress, Miss Howard, on account of his approaching marriage.

"Paris, Thermidor 30th.

"I congratulate you on having rejoined the army, where, being of use, you will have the tender satisfaction of knowing that you are promoting your country's welfare. Fortune changes, and men's favour and esteem are in perpetual oscillation, but the pardonable pride of having been useful, and having merited the recognition of the few who can appreciate genius and art, is as unchangeable and ingrained in you as is the harmony and delicacy of a sentiment so natural in itself. Influence has been brought to bear to induce me to serve in the Vendée army as a General in command. I have not accepted the post, as many officers are better fitted than myself to lead a brigade, having been more successful in the command of artillery. . . . I take a back place, conscious that the injustice which has been done to one's services is not ignored by those who are in a position to judge of their value.

"You are, my friend, in a delicate position; if a man of practical genius, of consummate experience, were . . . at the head of the army, and your tyrants, who are served by incapable agents and environed by quacks, were a versatile Government . . . instead of perverted rascals, let us add, he could not make or merit a reputation . . . but, my friend, in this best of all possible worlds, to do the best one can, and feel recompensed by the consciousness of it, that is the great secret which saves one from ever being either impostor or flatterer, sour, importunate, vindictive, or criminal.

" There is nothing new here. Hope is not yet altogether lost to the man of sense, that is to say, in the enfeebled condition in which this Empire happens to be.

" Friendship, constancy, gaiety, and never discouragement if you find men ungrateful and wicked. Remember the great, if somewhat droll, maxim of Flavius : ' Let us be thankful to them for the crimes they have not committed.'

" B.

" To Citizen Sucy, Commissioner of Ordnance, Army of Italy, Nice."

Second Letter.

" In circumstances of difficulty, the post of honour for a good Corsican is to remain in his country, and in that conviction my relatives insist upon my being amongst them. Nevertheless, as I do not know how to compound with my duty, I purposed sending in my resignation. The principal officer in command of the district, however, offered me a ' mezzo termine,' which reconciled everything. He offers me the post of adjutant-major in the volunteer battalion.

" This commission will postpone the renewal of our acquaintance, but I shall look forward to it very soon if things improve.

" You, sir, have entirely neglected me, for I have not heard from you for an age.

" Things are going better here, and I hope that by the time this reaches you political apprehensions will have ceased, at least for this campaign.

" Our enemies would be very foolish to hasten on hostilities ; they know very well that the defensive state is as ruinous to us as actual war. If you can spare the time to think of an old friend, you might give me some information as to your position at the present moment. If your nation loses courage she is lost for ever. If you have kept up your relations with St. Etienne, I would beg of you to have made for me a pair of double-barrel pistols, seven or eight inches long, and 22 or 24 bore, as nearly as possible. As to the price, I will forward seven or eight louis in paper money.*

" If you can undertake the commission, the pistols can be sent through Marseilles, to the care of Mons. Henri Gastard, merchant, Rue de Paradis.

" I am, Sir, and dear Sucy, your servant,

" BONAPARTE.

" Corte, February 27th."

The letter is addressed to Monsieur Sucy, Commissary, Valence, Department of the Drôme. It is sealed with red wax and stamped with the letters B and P, interlaced.

These letters must have been written in the year

* Worth then from 227 to 259 francs ; 74 francs in cash=100 francs paper money.

1792, for in 1791 there was no question of Volunteers, and in 1793 Bonaparte was already in command of one of their battalions.

August 20th.—I dined with Véron at Auteuil yesterday, and sat between Sainte Beuve and Musset.

In the middle of dinner Véron told us the following anecdote :—

"On his return from visiting the French seaports, Prince Jérôme went to report to the President the ovations he had received, and handed him the statement of his expenses. This the President declined to pay, telling his uncle that he had already given him more than two million francs, with a pension of three hundred thousand francs a year besides, and that it was impossible for him to do more. An altercation ensued. Jérôme lost all control over himself, and ended by saying, 'You have nothing of the Emperor about you.' 'You make a mistake,' replied the President, with perfect composure, 'I have his family about me.'"

August 21st.—In the course of a walk which Princess Mathilde and I took together at Versailles on Sunday last, our conversation turned upon the more than free and easy manner assumed by young ladies of good family nowadays, and she told me a story on that subject which I will repeat.

"Fleury, the Prince President's aide-de-camp, about a year or so ago was very much smitten by a certain Mdlle. de S—, who afterwards married a man in very high position. The Princess was commissioned by Fleury to ask for the young lady's hand in marriage, and while negotiations were proceeding with her family, in order to give the two interested persons an opportunity of meeting, she arranged a dinner for them at her house in the Rue de Courcelles, and Fleury and Mdlle. de S— were placed next each other at table. During dessert the young lady turned to the aide-de-camp and said to him in an under-tone : 'If we were in a room alone together, what would you do ?' Fleury, taken aback, scarcely knew how to reply, and when dinner was over went to the Princess and informed her of the circumstance, beg-ging she would no longer trouble herself about the marriage."

On Sunday evening I dined at Breteuil with General Daumas, who often saw and had frequent oppor-tunities of conversing with Abd-el-Kader. He looks upon this Arab Chief as an extraordinary man, and one whose name will occupy an important place in history. He says that political necessity may perhaps require that he should be detained a prisoner, but that plighted faith has been violated in consequence.

When Abd-el-Kader arrived in France Daumas was sent to receive him at Fort Lamarque, and proposed that if he would make complete submission to the Government, and consent to live in France, a royal residence should be placed at his disposal, together with a mosque and a pension of three hundred thousand francs. Abd-el-Kader listened to this pro-position with a scornful smile, and replied : " I am a prisoner, in spite of the plighted word of France. I reject your offer, and will never abandon my people."

He then took off his burnouse in the keen sea breeze, and, rolling it up, continued : " Place in this all the riches of France and I would treat your offer thus," and he threw his burnouse into the sea.

September 10*th.*—I met Mons. de Cavour at Morny's yesterday morning, and we stayed for two hours talking over the events of December 2nd, or rather in listening to Morny. He told us several things which I think worth while noting. During the time of the Constituent Assembly the question of a *coup d'état* had been already under consideration, and Morny, Thiers, and Changarnier had had many interviews on the subject. Thiers and Changarnier were equally of opinion that the Assembly should be dissolved, but the former, in making out the list of indispensable arrests, would not include that of Cavaignac or Lamoricière, which, he said, would be a dangerous step, on account of their popularity. Changarnier, on the contrary, declared that it was necessary, and said : " I don't care a rap. I feel that my position is sufficiently assured to arrest both of them."

Every one desired the *coup d'état* for his own advantage, Changarnier no less than the rest.

Some hours before the *coup d'état* was put into execution Morny was at the Opera Comique, and sat by the side of Cavaignac. During the play Madame Liadières signed to him to come to her box, where he met several Orleanist Deputies, who said to him : " Well, a few days more and we shall have you imprisoned in Vincennes."

Maupas, the Préfet of Police, was very wanting in

firmness and strength of character during the troubles,
and, although his prefecture was guarded by a battalion
of a thousand men, when it was attacked by a few hundred insurgents he sent to ask for reinforcements.
Morny replied chaffingly, begging him to defend himself. Maupas also sent the most incredible reports, such
as : " The Duke of Bordeaux is approaching with the
6th Dragoons," &c.

All the correspondence of the revolutionists, arrested
at the lines, contained the same instructions to their
provincial allies : " Push on the movement decreed
for 1852, obtain as much influence as you can, and
seize all Bonapartists and Royalists." No single
General was in the secret, and Morny was very uneasy
for a time at seeing Canrobert and Leflô talking in
low tones with the Questor for more than an hour. In
spite of his connections, however, Canrobert went
straight.

When Morny reached the Ministry of the Interior
at five o'clock in the morning he would not allow his
men to disturb the Minister, who only awoke at eight
to learn that the *coup d'état* had taken place, and that
he had lost his office.

October 12*th.*—The President's journey through the
Southern Provinces of France, where he has been
everywhere received with the greatest enthusiasm, is
nearly at an end. People are anxiously expecting the
Empire; even those who until lately have shown the
greatest hostility cry out for Napoleon III. The
papers give but a faint idea of the general excitement;
at Marseilles, Toulon, and Bordeaux the same unani-

mity, the same desire shows itself. At Bordeaux the Prince made an admirable speech, firm, clear, and to the point, which is approved by all men of good feeling or impartial minds. " While France is at peace Europe is tranquil." " The Empire means peace," &c., &c.

On Saturday the Prince returns to Paris, where a magnificent reception is being prepared for him. He will go straight to the Tuileries, where the members of his family will be waiting to receive him. The Council of State are drawing up a *senatus-consultum*, declaring the Empire. This decree is to be adopted by the Senate, and then presented to Louis Napoleon, who will elect to resort to universal suffrage. The Empire is an accomplished fact. The more extreme sections of Orleanists and Legitimists are furious, and evince their anger in the choicest invectives.

The Prince will have a great many things and a great many men to reform, and he will do well to begin with his own *entourage*. The officers of his household form a sort of Regency ; they take women to Fontainbleau when they go there to hunt, and their orgies are the talk of the town. The Imperial hunts have been· organized, and thirty persons selected to " receive the button," that is to say, who are authorized to wear the Prince's hunting livery and colours.

October 16th.—The weather is magnificent, the National Guard and troops are under arms, and the Boulevards are crowded with people who have come to see the Prince and his retinue pass. Workmen's societies and associations, with their banners and mottoes, are interspersed with the troops, and triumphal arches have been erected. At two o'clock the Prince is to arrive amid salvoes of artillery and peals of bells. Never will a sovereign have received a more splendid reception. I heartily wish, however, that the day was over. I have always a sort of dread of these popular assemblages in Paris.

The arches are covered with the inscription "To Louis Napoleon, Emperor," and last evening medals, inscribed "Napoleon III., Emperor," were being sold in the streets. The number of strangers at present in Paris is enormous.

Three o'clock.—I have just returned from the Railway Station, where the Prince was received by the Senators, Deputies, Councillors of State, members of the diplomatic body, and representatives of the Courts of Justice amid cries of "Long live the Emperor!" He is now proceeding along the Boulevards to the Tuileries, and cannon are being discharged every minute.

October 23rd.—Yesterday evening Prince Louis Napoleon was present at a grand representation of "Cinna" at the Théâtre Français. His arrival was announced by shouts of "Long live the Emperor!" from the crowds in the Rue St. Honoré and Rue de Richelieu, and on coming into the theatre similar cheering took place, everyone uncovering and standing up. The ladies were in full evening dress, and the sight was magnificent. The Prince warmly applauded the passages where Augustus displays his clemency. Cinna's part was played by Beauvalet. Rachel's

Emilie was a marvellous piece of acting. After the tragedy was over, Rachel recited an ode which had been specially written by Houssaye in honour of the Prince.

October 30th.—There was a State performance at the Opera the day before yesterday, at which the President was as well received as at the Théâtre Français. Abd-el-Kader was present, and the object of general curiosity. Gudin, the marine painter, always desirous of making an exhibition of himself, went to the ex-Emir's box and embraced him publicly. Better disposed persons were shocked to see the President's mistress, Mrs. Howard, covered with diamonds, in one of the principal boxes; it had a very bad effect. Prince Jérôme also had his mistress with him. This placarding of mistresses is a great deal too common now; it is a fashion which belonged to an entirely different age.

October 31st.—Everybody is discussing the reported disaffection in the army, and the gossips say there was a plot among the regiments garrisoned at Fontainbleau to carry off the President and proclaim the House of Orleans. The real facts, I believe, are that a conspiracy had been got up by some non-commissioned officers and soldiers of the 43rd regiment to fire on the President on his arrival in Paris. The affair got wind and was nipped in the bud; the plotters are probably at this moment on their way to Cayenne.

November 5th.—The Senate met yesterday, and the Prince's message was very cordially received, but nine out of the ten bureaux would not agree to the succession of the Jérôme family in the Imperial line in case of future eventualities. Public opinion supports the action of the nine bureaux. Jérôme and his son are generally despised; both have helped to ruin a magnificent position by their misconduct and secret intrigues.

I was talking yesterday with a statesman of Louis Philippe's time, and he told me the following story :—

While Dupin was in the Cabinet, in the days of July, 1830, Louis-Philippe received a letter from Charles X., in which that unhappy monarch requested him to accept the Lieutenant-Generalship of the kingdom under the Duke of Bordeaux. Louis-Philippe showed the letter to Dupin, expressing his sympathy with the fugitive, and the obligation he was under to him, and appeared on the whole disposed to accept the proposal. Dupin, whose official conscience, personal feelings, and middle class prejudices revolted at the idea, exclaimed, " Prince, it is too late to accept the King's abdication in the Duke of Bordeaux's favour; the country will not tolerate the elder branch." " But," urged Louis-Philippe, " I cannot betray the interest of my relative and profit by his misfortunes." Dupin hereupon commenced an argument under three heads in support of his view of the position, and all the prejudice and vanity of his class disclosed themselves in his words. Louis-Philippe gave in, but his heart was so full that he begged Dupin to write the answer, for which Charles the Tenth's aide-de-camp was waiting. When it was finished Louis Philippe said, " I am a family man, my dear Dupin, and have a habit of doing nothing without my wife's advice. I will go and show her your letter." He then took the letter away, and on his return, twenty minutes later, put it in an envelope and sealed it up. " My wife's feelings," he said, " were for some time opposed to the sending of this letter, but the reasons you had placed before me, dear friend, overcame her scruples at last, and the refusal shall be sent off." Tears were in the Duke of Orleans's eyes when he handed the letter to the aide-de-camp, and for some time afterwards he remained silent and depressed.

The next day, however, Charles X. announced the appointment of the Duke of Orleans to the Lieutenant-Generalship.

A year afterwards Berryer gave Dupin the key of the enigma. Louis-Philippe had acted a little comedy. Dupin's letter had not been sent, but in its place a respectful acceptance of the proferred position.

November 19th.—Jérôme has resigned the presidency of the Senate, after attacking the President in a most violent manner, and saying that he does not share his nephew's political views. He is opposed to any reconciliation with the upper classes, and predicts Louis Napoleon's fall from a position he is not qualified to fill. In face of the Senate's hostility to him he pretended that he would resign all his offices, and carry his griefs to the Emperor's tomb.

The *Constitutionnel* and *Pays* newspapers have been bought by a syndicate, of which Mirès is the head. It was impossible for Véron to stand against the determined resolution of the Ministry to carry their point. The Government are desirous of getting the press into their hands, but I cannot understand why they rely upon Mirès for that purpose.   He is a schemer with a doubtful reputation, who has made six million francs since last year by speculations on the Bourse.

Guéronnière takes the management of the *Constitutionnel,* and Granier de Cassagnac that of the *Pays.*

November 25th.—The majority of votes for the Empire is already enormous.   The Empire is, therefore, a settled thing, and the campaign for places at Court has begun.

On Tuesday last Princess Mathilde gave a grand reception to celebrate the opening of her new house (formerly the Queen of Spain's) in the Rue de Courcelles.   Prince Louis Napoleon was there.   He was in excellent spirits, and extremely gracious to everybody.   During the evening he thanked me for my design for his new menu cards.   After dinner he set the example, and we all smoked in a large marble court, which had been arranged like a winter garden. Mdlle. de Montijo, a young Spanish lady, of fair complexion and aristocratic birth, has been the object of the Prince's attention ever since his journey to Fontainbleau.   I wonder what my brother Louis, who has been for years on the most intimate terms with her mother, will say ?   The young lady is very prepossessing in manner, and of ready and remarkably agreeable wit, with too much strength of mind ever to allow her heart or feelings to get the mastery of her.

Billaut told Princess Mathilde in confidence that by a decree of the Senate she was about to receive the title of Her Imperial Highness Mathilde Bonaparte and a pension of 500,000 francs. It is also said that Napoleon, Jérôme's son, is to be made Heir Apparent.

December 2nd.—The guns are firing, and Louis Napoleon re-enters Paris as Emperor, having been elected by 7,824,189 ayes to 253,145 noes. The Tuileries Palace is to be prepared for his reception.

December 3rd.—Yesterday evening there was a grand dinner and reception at the Palace. The Emperor said to Princess Mathilde: " My dear Mathilde, until there is an Empress you will always take the first position here, and sit on my right hand."

Is there then to be an Empress ?

Miss Harriet Howard boasts that she can prevent the Emperor marrying.

Jérôme said to Baroness de Talleyrand, who is strongly in favour of the Emperor's early marriage in order to ensure the perpetuation of his dynasty: "But, my dear Baroness, such a marriage would interfere with my son's rights." I had this from Baroness de Talleyrand herself, with whom I spent the evening yesterday.

December 7th.—Being in a gossiping mood, I may as well relate the following story :—

Romieu, speaking to me about Deutz, the betrayer of the Duchess de Berry, told me that he was himself informed by Mons. de Montalivet that when that Jew came to him the first time to open negotiations he said to the Minister: " You are anxious, sir, to discover the whereabouts of the Duchess de Berry, and I am the only person who can deliver her into your hands. I am, doubtless, in your eyes a vile spy, and you look upon me with contempt; but, nevertheless, I have only decided upon taking this course out of love for my country, in order to spare her the anguish of a long civil war and the horrors that would follow. I am well aware that my name will be execrated, that I shall be placed in the category of the most shameless criminals, and that when dead even my grave will be defiled; that from this day forth I am a pariah, a leper in the eyes of all men. I shall only be able to exist by the magical effect of money. If I ask for 'five hundred thousand francs,' therefore, it is not as the price of treachery, but in order to fly from the country I am saving." The price was agreed upon, and after the Duchess's capture Deutz received from Monsieur de Montalivet's own hand five hundred notes of one thousand francs each.

Marshal Bugeaud confided to Romieu that from her manner and what escaped the Duchess de Berry he was convinced that Deutz was the father of the child she carried. Monsieur de Mesnard was also of the same opinion. The Duchess, on learning by whom she was betrayed, exclaimed, and kept repeating, " What, him ! betrayed by him ! by Deutz !" Marshal Bugeaud had no manner of doubt that the tender relations which had existed between them were the cause of the Duchess's condition.

December 23rd.—To-day's *Moniteur* publishes the decree fixing the order of succession. Jérôme and his heirs male are designated heirs to the throne in case the Emperor should die without issue or formal act of adoption.

The Court is still at Compiègne—dancing, hunting, and making merry.

The Emperor is over head and ears in love with Mdlle. de Montijo, the lovely and elegant young Spanish lady whose sister is married to the Duke d'Alba. She is invited to every entertainment, and is received with marked favour, but I doubt if she has become subject to the law of the conqueror. Her mother, who was formerly called Countess de Teba, had a very flighty reputation, and was on extremely intimate terms with my brother about 1825.

CHAPTER VII.

1853.

THE EMPEROR'S HOUSEHOLD—BALL AT PRINCESS MATHILDE'S
—MDLLE. DE MONTIJO—THE CREDIT FONCIER—MATRI-
MONIAL SCANDALS—PRINCESS MATHILDE THE CHAMPION
OF JUSTICE—THE DUCHESS OF VALENTINOIS AND THE
ITALIAN REFUGEE—MINGLING THE REMAINS OF ROBES-
PIERRE AND LOUIS XVI.—RUMOURS OF THE EMPEROR'S
APPROACHING MARRIAGE—HE SILENCES DISCUSSION ON THE
SUBJECT OF MDLLE. DE MONTIJO—OPINIONS ON THE SUBJECT
—OFFICIAL DECLARATION—MDLLE. DE MONTIJO'S DIPLO-
MACY—DUPIN'S OPINION—THE MARRIAGE CELEBRATED—
THE EMPEROR REPROACHES SAINT-ARNAUD—LEGITIMIST
PLOTS—THE EMPRESS AND MARIE ANTOINETTE—SUICIDE
OF COUNT CAMERATA—LIST OF NEW SENATORS—CHAR-
ACTER OF THE OFFICERS OF THE HOUSEHOLD—THE EMPEROR
PROMISES THE AUTHOR THE LEGION OF HONOUR—THE
ENGLISH ALLIANCE—CLOUDS IN THE EAST.

January 3rd.—The principal offices at Court have
been filled up, and Marshals Magnan, Vaillant, Saint-
Arnaud, and the Dukes of Cambacères and Bassano
have been appointed to them.

On the 1st January I was at the evening reception

at the Tuileries, and yesterday I dined with Her Imperial Highness Princess Mathilde, who had sent me in the morning a very pretty tea-service in Sèvres porcelain for a New Year's gift.

The Emperor's household is being formed, and everybody wants some position in it. What the Court most requires at present are men of probity, for the Emperor is being robbed in a disgraceful manner by the people in his confidence, who make him pay for everything a third more than the proper price and put their hands upon whatever they can pillage. Of this I have proof. The furnishers, for fear of losing the Emperor's custom, are obliged to give receipts for a third more than the value of the goods supplied, and the difference goes into the pockets of the officers of the household. Eight days ago the purchase of a pair of phaeton horses fell through because the seller would not consent to give a receipt in excess of the money paid him. When these transactions do come to the Emperor's knowledge a good many people will be included in the clearance. Standish tells me that during the last trip to Compiègne Persigny took his father-in-law, the Duke de Mouchy, aside, and said to him, pointing to Bacciochi and the ordinary suite: "You have frequent opportunities of talking with the Emperor. Just advise him to turn all those blackguards out of doors."

It is again reported that Jérôme's son has been made a General of Division, and that he is to have the command in Algeria. This appointment is extremely distasteful to me. Prince Napoleon is ambitious, cunning, and unscrupulous, but time will prove if I am wrong or not in my estimate of him.

January 6th.—Walsh, brother of the late director of the *Mode*, always called the Stammerer because of his queer way of speaking, has been appointed Chamberlain. Four months ago he said to Nicolaï, who himself told me the circumstance, " Who will have the kindness to rid us of that gentleman by putting a bullet through him ? " That gentleman is at the present moment the Emperor, and the Stammerer is his Chamberlain.

January 7th.—I was dining with la Guéronnière last night. He told me to read the article in to-day's *Pays*, which has been written under dictation from high quarters. He had seen the Emperor in the morning, as he frequently does, on matters connected with his paper. The article in question is a sort of cunningly devised sop for the Parliamentarians.

The recognition of the Empire by the principal Northern powers has been received, and the silly stories invented by the Legitimists and Democrats will fall to the ground ; these gentlemen will have to cudgel their brains for some new mare's nests. The aristocrats of the St. Germain quarter are again exercising their wit—and in their habitually useful manner—by christening Fould the Duke of Vilegew.

January 10th.—There was a ball at Princess Mathilde's yesterday. About three o'clock in the morning thirty of us, who had stayed late, made up a merry supper party. Morny was at the ball, as well as the Countess de Teba and her daughter, Mdlle. de

Montijo. The Emperor is still very much engrossed with this handsome young person, and she is certainly most elegant, amiable, and intelligent. For more than an hour they were engaged in private conversation, which no one had the temerity to interrupt. The Emperor seemed to enjoy himself very much, and did not leave until two o'clock in the morning. Mdlle. de Montijo wears her favours with gentleness and good grace; she and her mother are hoping that a marriage may take place, and all their diplomacy is being exerted in that direction. Mdlle. de Montijo is much sought after and courted, and her influence with the Emperor is already invoked. The Ministers pet her, and she is at every *fête;* it is the old story of the rising sun over again.

Fould, the foxy Jew, has been making himself very important, and trying to walk over everybody's head. In order to obtain (in his brother's name) the charter for the Crédit Foncier Bank he has never ceased saying to the Emperor: "Your Majesty must absolutely enfranchise yourself from the tutelage of the Rothschilds, who are governing France in spite of you."

The Emperor did not like the word tutelage, and was only too anxious to find the means of escaping from it. Fould allowed him to seek, and one day proposed the establishment of the Crédit Foncier, this was agreed to, and he secured ten millions as his share of the transaction.

January 11th.—I dined at the Princess Mathilde's yesterday with Chaix d'Estange and His de Butenval, who has just been appointed to Brussels as *chargé d'affaires* in place of Bassano, who becomes Grand-Chamberlain. The dinner was very informal and pleasant, and we discussed a thousand different scandals. Chaix d'Estange told us about the Chaponays' case, in which he is engaged on Friday next. A year ago the Marquis de Chaponays married a Mademoiselle de Courval, grand-niece on her father's side of the famous Cardinal Dubois, and granddaughter on her mother's of General Moreau. Mademoiselle de Courval, besides being very pretty and agreeable, is well educated and clever; but she was brought up by a mother whose mode of life excited a good deal of comment. After a year's marriage, and as the result of a very dangerous confinement, the young couple ceased to cohabit, but as many stories got into circulation, to the discredit of Mons. de Chaponays, concerning the reason of the separation, he applied to the Court for redress and restitution. Madame de Chaponays defends herself on the ground of her husband's brutal exactions, and the case comes on on Friday, when lovers of scandal will doubtless crowd the Court to listen to a disgraceful violation of the secrets of married life.

Another case, that of Madame de Montesquieu, daughter of the Countess de Charette, is of a graver nature. In this instance the husband is charged with cruelty of the grossest description, the effects of which are observable in his unfortunate wife's ruined health. By an order of the Court the care of the daughter born of the union has been confided to the mother; but

Mons. de Montesquieu is a relative of General Goyon, the Emperor's aide-de-camp, who has written to De Maupas and exerted his influence to arrest the course of justice, to such purpose indeed that the poor lady cannot find a magisterial officer, gendarme, or police agent ready or willing to execute the judgment of the Court.

Princess Mathilde, when she heard Chaix d'Estange's narration, was overcome with indignation, and said : "It is not possible that the Emperor can be aware of such an atrocious interference with justice." "Certainly not, Princess," replied Chaix d'Estange; "but the Emperor is surrounded by people who abuse their position and influence; others are afraid to gainsay them, and the result is that he is visited with their iniquities; the truth is hidden from him, and there is no one to open his eyes." Upon which the Princess, whose generous anger is always roused at the bare mention of a mean action, exclaimed : "Give me Madame de Montesquieu's petition; I will take it myself to the Emperor and tell him what use is made of his name. You shall see, Mons. Chaix, if an order of the Court shall be obeyed or not, and if Mons. de Goyon has the power to suppress truth and justice."

After dinner, in a corner of the drawing-room, the Princess told me the following anecdote :—The young Duchess de Valentinois went to her some months ago to beg she would procure her the post of lady-of-honour, near the person of the Empress, in the event of the Emperor marrying. The request seemed natural and proper, and the Princess promised she

would speak to the Emperor and use all her influence
with him in the matter. A few days afterwards, however, Duke Proto, a Neapolitan refugee, who is rather
a chatterbox, came to her and said: " Your Highness
is good enough to receive some singular noble dames."
" What do you mean, and to whom do you refer ? " said
the Princess. Proto replied : " Yesterday I happened
to be at the Café Cardinal, at the corner of the Rue de
Richelieu, in the company of some refugees, like myself, when one of them, who is known to be a man of
bad character, said that he had met the Duchess de
Valentinois at Baden, and had made her his mistress,
and that she now often came to see him at his rooms.
I would not believe a word of the story," said Proto,
" but my countryman told me that if I went to the
house where he lived on the following day I could see
her arrive. I did so," he continued, " and saw the
Duchess go to his apartment."

The story created some stir, and came to the ears
of the Duchess de Valentinois herself, who wrote to
Proto to go and see her. He went, and she asked him
what opinion he had of the Neapolitan refugee. He
replied : " This man, Duchess, is a swindler of the
very worst description; you had better be careful of
him, for he is equal to any rascality." The Duchess
listened attentively to what Proto said, and then
begged him to be the bearer of a letter to the Minister
of Police, requesting the man's removal from Paris on
the ground of his being a dangerous character. After
taking the letter, Proto returned to the Duchess's to
inform her of the result of his mission, when, on going

into her room, to his great surprise he beheld the
rascal himself seated there. An explanation, it appeared, had already taken place, and a second letter
had been sent to the Minister begging him to consider
the first as not having been written. I asked the
Princess if she believed the story, and she said: "Yes,
every word of it. I made particular inquiry, as I
was bound to do at the time, and it is true in every
detail."

Surely Brantôme and Tallemant des Reaux have
calumniated no one, and invented and exaggerated
nothing. Their world was depraved as is our own,
because of the influence of the upper circles, because
family life was unknown, and because everybody lived
for gallantry and amusement. Our children, profiting
by the example of their parents, will carry corruption
to yet greater limits.

January 17th.—Herbette, the ex-Deputy, has just
left my office. He and I have been discussing a
multitude of topics, and last but not least that of the
Great Revolution. He tells me that he has seen in
Mons. de Saint-Albin's possession the original
Memoirs of Barras. Saint-Albin is an old *sans-culotte,*
whose real name is Bousselin, but who found it
desirable when the restoration took place to destroy
the identity of the companion of Robespierre, Marat,
&c. With this object, and for a certain money consideration, he prevailed upon an old Marquis de
Saint-Albin, who was without a sou or a rag to his
back, to adopt him as his son. He took his adoptive
father's name, dropped his own, and then, the better

to hide all traces of Bousselin, published an obituary pamphlet containing an account of that worthy's last moments.

So much for Saint-Albin; let us return to the Memoirs of Barras. The old director herein mentions that he assisted after Robespierre's death in opening the ditch where Louis XVI. was buried, and that he had a lot of quicklime thrown upon the bones of the unhappy king, and then, in expiatory spirit (singular mode of expiation !), he disentombed from the gaping foss the body of Robespierre, in order, he says, to place the executioner beneath the victim.

Barras made this incredible statement at the time that what were believed to be Louis XVI.'s remains were being removed to the memorial tomb in the Rue d'Anjou, and he mentioned, in proof of his assertion, that they ought to come across silver shoe buckles and gold breeches buckles, as Robespierre always wore on his nether garments and shoes buckles of different metal. This turned out to be true, but he was begged not to mention the matter any further, and Robespierre reposes to this day beneath the marble monument of Louis XVI. Towards the end of his memoirs Barras (fallen greatness) bitterly bewails the baseness of the great ones, dead and living, who formerly, while he took his bath, waited in his antechamber patiently for whole hours at a stretch until he was at leisure to receive them, and pressed forward to kiss Josephine's (the Empress's) hand as she passed from his room.

These memoirs furthermore contain many details concerning Bonaparte and letters of the future Emperor, full of complaints of Josephine's infidelities.

The chances of Mdlle. de Montijo becoming Empress of the French are at the present moment the topic of conversation. Why not? We are living in an extraordinary century, and nothing would surprise me. The most important thing for France is to see the succession to the throne well assured. Complete, sire, your history as fairy stories end! " They lived happily ever after, and had a large family." Such is my prayer.

January 18*th.*—I have this moment been told by Crozatier, the metal-founder, who has charge of the Tuileries bronzes, that he has received an order to have the " Empress's " apartments in readiness by the 6th of February. The matter is so pressing, that, to save time, only indispensable arrangements are to be made. We are to have an Empress, then, by February 6th. Is it to be Mdlle. de Montijo ? . . .

January 19*th.*—It is apparently decided that Mdlle. de Montijo is to be Empress. There were a number of people at Princess Mathilde's last night, and the news was being whispered about. I played whist with the Minister of Marine, but he and the rest of the Ministers were impenetrable on the subject. As to the simple mortals outside the Ministry, some blame, others approve, the Emperor's choice; but a great many ladies were in anything but good humour at the prospect of having to call Mdlle. de Montijo for the future " Your Majesty." The far-sighted ones predict difficulties as to the manner in which the marriage will be received, both by the nation and by foreign Courts, and scandalizers rake up stories about the *fiancée's* maternal ancestry, saying that her mother, Madame de Montijo, is the daughter of an English merchant, named Fitzpatrick, who was British Consul in Spain, and died a bankrupt.

It is also stated that when the Emperor acquainted his Ministers with the approaching marriage he would listen to no objections on their part, and said : " There can be no observations or discussion on the subject, gentlemen.   I am resolved upon it, and the marriage has been fixed."

The Emperor brings to bear in everything he does or says an iron will ; he takes no one's advice, and carries out his purpose regardless of obstacles.   His *amour-propre* was piqued by the difficulties placed in the way of his marriage.   Mdlle. de Montijo pleased him, and he would not consent to be dictated to by Europe.

The Emperor, it must be admitted, is perfectly right in saying, " The State is myself," for, good or bad, everything proceeds from him ; he knows mankind, and generally despises them.   A good hand at dissembling, he acquaints no one with his projects, thinking that the great art in politics, as in war, is to hide your intentions from the enemy.   When once his mind is made up nothing stops him, obstacles are brushed aside and emotions do not count.   His quiet and meaning smile, vague, veiled look, and slowness of speech and action, point to the man who consults

with himself more than those about him, and who
listens to the promptings of his own thoughts rather
than to the voice of would-be counsellors.

He owes his future to no one, and no one has the
right to dictate how he shall use it. In his case
there was a double reason why he should marry, and
marry quickly :

Firstly : To destroy the hope of the Jérômes, and
reassure the country as to the possibility of their ever
reigning.

Secondly : To deprive the princely houses of Europe
of the pleasure of putting him under matrimonial
quarantine.

Europe having declined to give him a consort of
royal blood, he takes a young girl by the hand, places
the purple mantle on her shoulders, and makes her his
Empress. Call out against it as much as you like,
you Russians of quality, but tell us, in the first place,
where your great Catherine sprang from ?*   Swedes,
whence came your Bernadotte? As to the country,
to France herself, what does it matter to her where
her Empress comes from, so long as she has one who
shall bear as many children as the Queen of England?

Many of the more ambitious ladies are distracted
between a desire to have some place at Court and the
disgust they experience at having to call their companion of yesterday " Your Majesty." The Legitimists, like the intelligent and humorous party they

---

* Mons. de Viel Castel here confounds the wife of Peter I., an
innkeeper's servant, with Catherine (the Great) the wife of Peter
III., a princess of the house of Anhalt-Zerbst.

are, will devote themselves to endless pleasantries on
the subject.   For my part, I am in considerable doubt
as to what the Emperor will do with his Court—nearly
all the principal officers of which lead such equivocal
lives—when he places an Empress at its head.   Mdlle.
de Montijo will, perhaps, be one day allegorically
represented as a Hercules cleansing the Augean
stable.   God grant that it may be so.

January 20th.—The marriage is making the devil's
own noise, and the funds dropped two francs yesterday.   The old Royalists are waking up, and crying
out scandal, the national honour is compromised, &c.,
and starting all sorts of calumnious rumours about
Mdlle. de Montijo.   The St. Germain quarter in this
leads the way, but the Emperor quietly pursues his
object without a word.   Thiers remarks to anybody
who will listen to him, "That there is nothing to be
feared from people who are slightly intoxicated, but
you must beware of them when they are quite drunk."

January 21st.—The marriage of the Emperor is to
take place on Monday week, and the new Empress's
household is already formed.   The Duchess de Vicence
is mistress of the robes, and the Duchess de Lesparre
and Countess de Montebello are ladies in waiting.   The
religious ceremony is to take place at Notre Dame
with great pomp.

Madlle. de Montijo, with whom the Emperor has
been deeply in love for two years past, has guided her
bark with the greatest address and skill.   She induced
the Emperor to mention the marriage first, and then
said to him : " You must yourself write to my mother,

who, out of affection for both of us, and fully appreciating the distance which divides us, may be inclined to refuse her consent."

The Emperor wrote, and the letter will remain among the Montijo family archives to prove that the first advances were made by the Emperor, and that he had been obliged to overcome the mother's scruples. Well played, indeed !

On hearing of the marriage Dupin said : " People take little notice of what I say or think, and maybe they are right, but the Emperor does better in espousing a lady who pleases him than in allowing himself to be bargained for by some scrofulous German Princess with feet as big as my own. When the Emperor kisses his wife it will, at least, be for pleasure and not from duty."

Pending the marriage the new Empress is to reside at the Elysée.

January 22nd.—Smart things are being said on all sides. Here is one attributed to Thiers : " The Emperor has always seemed to me to be a man of wit, but now he shows himself to be a man of forethought, for he makes certain for the future of a Spanish grandeeship." Poor French nation ! She lives on smart sayings and revolutions.

January 23rd.—The ball at the Tuileries yesterday was very brilliant, and the Emperor was in great spirits. That old fool of a Duke of Brunswick was there in a hussar's uniform, pomaded, painted, and decked out like a marionette. He made me admire his diamonds and decorations.

January 31*st.*—The marriage *fêtes* are over, and the Court is at St. Cloud. I will not refer to the ceremony, which was very beautiful, as all the newspapers describe it in detail. The Imperial procession was favoured with magnificent weather; the whole population was on foot, and the Emperor and Empress were received with enthusiastic loyalty. The Court will remain at St. Cloud for some time.

February 6*th.*—Many rumours regarding Ministerial changes are afloat, but that which is most probably true is Saint-Arnaud's retirement. After a recent Cabinet Council the Emperor detained him, and said : " Saint-Arnaud, I am very much annoyed with you. I do not like my Ministers to gamble on the Bourse and make large losses. I hear that you have been gambling and lost heavily." Saint-Arnaud tried to excuse himself, and said that his losses had been greatly exaggerated, and then asked : " Who has mentioned the matter to your Majesty ? " The Emperor replied that it was Fould, the Minister of State. " Fould ! " cried Saint-Arnaud, " why, sire, he has been speculating for a fall and I for a rise. The only difference between us is that I believed your Majesty's Government would inspire a feeling of confidence, and I lose, your Minister of State has calculated on a panic, and he wins."

This is how the Emperor is served.

February 9*th.*—Some of the Legitimist party have been arrested on account of their dissemination of pamphlets and correspondence inimical to the Empire. My cousin, Viscount Edward de Mirabeau, was apprehended by mistake on Sunday morning instead of his brother, the Marquis de Mirabeau, but I procured his release later on, and he was able to come to Princess Mathilde's ball. I met the Minister of Police, Mons. de Maupas, at the ball, and complimented him upon the perspicacity of his agents in arresting a Mirabeau friendly to the Government instead of a Mirabeau hostile. The Minister seemed rather embarrassed.

These arrests have been brought about in consequence of some feeling of rivalry between the Ministers of the Interior and Police. They detest and wish to do each other all the harm they can, and this accounts for the clumsy zeal in their respective departments.

News of a serious nature is current this morning. Lombardy, it seems, is again in insurrection against Austria. This is the work of secret societies, and it may possibly stir up the embers of revolution in France. Details are wanting, and the extent and importance of the insurrection are not yet known.

As long as revolutionists find assistance in any country whatever, Europe will never know repose. France, Switzerland, Piedmont, and England above all, merit grave reproach on this score. Not only are revolutionists received in these countries when they have been hunted from their own, but they are placed in possession of funds, either by an allowance from the State or by means of public subscription. In England these matters have a deeper significance; there revolutionists are permitted to hold meetings and invite subscriptions, which are intended to excite all Europe against royalty. England would be only too pleased to see the whole of Europe ablaze for its own profit. That nation represents to my mind a big pirate vessel, hidden within some archipelago, sallying out and plundering all ships that come within her reach. The war being waged by Turkey against the Monte-negrins engages public attention on account of the complications which Russian and Austrian diplomacy may bring about. Directly the great Powers begin to feel easier on the score of internal troubles they revert to the narrow jealousies and blunders of their old policy.

February 11th.—The Emperor and Empress visited the Sovereigns' Gallery at the Louvre yesterday and complimented Nieuwerkerke and myself on its arrange-ment. The Empress wished to have read to her Marie Antoinette's beautiful testamentary letter to Madame Elizabeth. While it was being read the Emperor was in deep thought, and seemed profoundly moved. Souvenirs of Louis XVI. and Marie Antoinette always have a great effect upon him. There was something sad and soul-thrilling in listening to this letter in the presence of a young and beautiful Empress at the beginning of her reign, and in the first intoxication of an almost undreamt-of happiness. The Queen's farewell message seemed to borrow addi-tional solemnity from its distinguished listeners; it was like a communication of misfortune, a sob from the past, impossible to describe in a simple narration.

The Empress listened in silence, and with tears in her eyes, to the last words of the Queen about to be led to the scaffold, of the mother who, even in that supreme moment, was not allowed to embrace the children she left in her executioners' hands.

The effect produced upon the Empress by this letter will be repeated; all mothers who come to the museum will respond from the bottom of their hearts to Marie Antoinette's appeal, when before her judges, and beneath the weight of the most monstrous accusations, she arose proud and dignified and bequeathed to posterity those simple words: "I appeal to all mothers."

February 25th.—Father Lacordaire has been exiled from France in consequence of a sermon in which he grossly insulted Napoleon I. and the present Emperor. This Lacordaire is an ambitious man, who began life with Lamenais and Montalembert, and has always been consumed with a desire for popularity. Madame de Solms, daughter of Madame Wyse, and one of the Lucien Bonapartes, is also expelled.

It appears from what I hear this morning that the Emperor of Austria's assassin came from London. He went first of all to Milan, where he received the instructions of which we know the result. London is the asylum for all these scoundrels. The English Government aids and abets in the concoction of conspiracies directed against the rest of the world, and then when the plots are ripe those who are commissioned to execute them receive English passports under borrowed names. The policy of England is something infamous.

February 28th.—Things are going badly in Constantinople. Russia and Austria are in arms, and the three Northern Powers are much incensed against England. What will be the upshot of it all?

March 5th.—Count Camerata, the son of Princess Bacciochi, blew his brains out yesterday morning. The papers which announce the fatality attribute it to brain fever. The real reason is that the Count has lost 200,000 francs on the Bourse, and neither his mother nor King Jérôme, to whom he applied for assistance, would help him. Seeing nothing before him, therefore, but bankruptcy he resolved to commit suicide. He explains the whole matter in a letter he has left behind him, in which he mentions Jérôme's refusal, and the fact that Jérôme owed him 400,000 francs. This last brother of the first Emperor is an infamous rascal, and the Camerata affair was not wanted to prove it. At the same time he enjoys an income of a million francs, and the Palais Royal is being furnished for him.

March 7th.—The *Moniteur* contains a new list of Senators. The wonder is where the Government finds all these conscript fathers. Amongst others the name of the Marquis de Boissy is mentioned. He is the husband of Guicioli, Lord Byron's mistress, and was the most irritating, disagreeable, and troublesome member of Louis-Philippe's peerage. When our legion repaired to the Tuileries on February 24th, 1848, he accompanied the rear of my battalion, and kept inciting the National Guards to cry out, " Let us have reforms."

General Magnan, General Saint-Arnaud, and Colonel

Fleury are also in the list. These gentlemen are improving their reputations and becoming very moral now. This ought not to be a difficult matter.

Magnan receives as General-in-Chief of

the army of Paris	80,000 francs
As Marshal of France	40,000 ,,
As Master of the Horse	40,000 ,,
As Senator	30,000 ,,
As Grand Cross of the Legion of Honour	6,000 ,,

Making a total of 196,000 francs. And the rest are equally well treated. The inferior officers of the Imperial household are also, many of them, nothing but low fortune-hunters, and it is with such materials that the moral tone of the young Empress's court is to be maintained. Moreover the officers of the household are to be looked upon with respect, and the members of the Senate are to be taken seriously. What rubbish !

March 15th.—The Emperor and Empress visited the Louvre yesterday, and the former said he would give me the Cross of the Legion of Honour on the 15th August next. The Empress added : "I will not let him forget his promise, for the Viel Castels are friends of my own." She then asked for news of my brothers, and was extremely affable and gracious.

March 19th.—A piece of news which was received yesterday has put the Bourse in a tremor. The English fleet, it is said, has left Malta and forced the Dardanelles. The evening journals give a qualified denial to the rumour. The facts are these : On the arrival in Constantinople of the Russian envoy, and in view of the Russian demands, Turkey, believing her independence to be menaced, had recourse to England. Colonel Rose thereupon, it is said, sent off a despatch boat to Malta, with an order to the English fleet to repair to him immediately. The fleet at once left for Constantinople, but it is not yet known if it will force the Straits, which it can hardly yet have done.

The event is full of gravity. Russia cannot recede, and in that state of things a general conflagration may be brought about. The relations between England and the Northern Powers were already very strained, and the Eastern question may involve us all in consequences the end of which it is impossible to forsee.

As to France, the more prudent ones say neutrality is forced upon her, but a neutrality on the watch. If the Ottoman Empire disappears from the European map, and France allows Russia to take Constantinople, she ought to take Egypt, and for that reason Russia and England should not be allowed to settle the division, for whoever holds Egypt will be mistress of the commerce of the world, and hold the key to the Indies. Egypt would complete our Mediterranean possessions and influence. Already we possess the important ports of Toulon and Marseilles, the island of Corsica, and the 250 leagues of Algerian seaboard. Egypt in addition would make us all-powerful. Our alliances are in the south. Spain, Portugal, Italy, and Sardinia ought to be attached to us by indissoluble ties. The frontier of the Rhine would not be of the least utility, whereas possessions in the Mediterranean would double our power, and guarantee the security of our fleet and our commerce.

Puritan England will ally herself with the Turks against the Russians, and let loose the Rünges, Mazzinis, and Kossuths against Germany, Italy, and Hungary, to upset them and make a diversion. There would be employment for these refugees. It would be good policy for us to ally ourselves with England against Russia.

March 20th.—The French fleet has left Toulon for the Grecian Archipelago, and three maritime powers will find themselves face to face—England, France, and Russia. People are uneasy as to the complication that may arise in consequence. Russia has shown herself too impatient in her desire to suppress the Turkish Empire, and her ambassador's manner to the Ottoman Ministry has been most insolent.

CHAPTER VIII.

1853 (*continued*).

March 30th.—An Imperial decree, issued by Mons.
Fould in the Emperor's name, distinctly settles that
only the Grand-Marshal of the Palace shall be allowed
to use the Imperial livery. This was inserted in the
Moniteur of March 17th, and is called by the public
the "Rachel decree." The reason is as follows:
Prince de Canino having thought it in good taste to
send a carriage and four horses with the Imperial
livery to drive the great actress to Longchamp, the
public, mistaking the occupant of the carriage, have

saluted her for the Empress, and the same error has permitted Rachel to use the Empress's private passage through the Arc-de-Triomphe.

As he is not to be trusted, Prince de Canino has been deprived of the right of using the Imperial livery. Rachel remarked that "it was extremely disagreeable to be mistaken for the Empress."

April 2nd.—The day before yesterday there was a grand ball at the Princess Mathilde's. The Emperor and Empress were there, and stayed until one o'clock. During the evening the Emperor came and spoke to me very kindly for a few minutes, and the Empress a little later on also did me the honour to converse with me for some time. She spoke to me about my brother Louis, whose estrangement she regretted, and begged I would remember her to him very cordially.

Pastoret was at the ball, and gave me the following account of the admission of the Duke de Chartres (eldest son of Louis-Philippe) to the Order of the Holy Spirit:—

The ceremony took place at St. Cloud, in Charles X.'s private room, in the presence of the officers of the Order, of Louis-Philippe, Marie Amélie, Madame Adélaïde, and the Messieurs de Pastoret. The Duke de Chartres knelt in front of Charles X., who, before investing the new knight with the collar of the Order, said: "My dear nephew, this Order was instituted in a time of great trouble and perturbation for the purpose of uniting the nobility, royalty, and princes together. Those unhappy times may return; have ever before your mind, therefore, the fresh obligations which your position as a Knight of the Order impose upon you, and never forget the double title which attaches you to royalty as a Prince and a Knight of the Order." Louis Philippe, who could not restrain his tears, then knelt behind his son, and putting his hands, together with the Duke de Chartres', into the old King's, said, in a voice full of tenderness and emotion : " Permit me, sire, to renew my vow as a Knight of the Holy Spirit, and to identify myself more closely with the meaning of this royal ceremony. I am nothing except by your goodness; I owe you all. You have accepted my repentance with generosity, and have extended to me your entire forgiveness. May it please your Majesty to receive the assurance of a devotion which I offer you here in the presence of my wife, my sister, and the officers of the highest Order attached to the Crown of France. Yes, sire, father and son are entirely devoted to you and your royal dynasty."

Charles X., surprised at this act of homage, thanked the Duke of Orleans with effusion. This ceremony took place in 1828 or 1829. In 1830 Louis-Philippe was King of France, and the Order of the Holy Spirit was abolished.

June 16th.—Table-turning has been completely outdone, for we have now tables that talk. Yesterday at Princess Mathilde's, in the presence of Saulcy, a member of the Institute, Abbé Coquereau, Almoner of the Fleet; the Princess, Nieuwerkerke, and others, a table was put to the test. Piétri, the Préfet of Police, came in, and was highly amused at the expense of the spirit-rappers. He was invited to ask a question, and he inquired his age. Forty-seven knocks came from the table, which Piétri had to acknowledge was correct. Then, in order to put the spirits to more severe proof, he asked: "How many men were implicated in the secret society which I arrested yesterday?" Eighteen knocks came from the table. "How many among them," he then asked, "had resolved to assassinate the Emperor?" Three knocks came. Piétri was obliged to admit the correctness of the answers. I only state a fact, explain it who can!

On leaving the Rue de Courcelles in the evening Piétri told Nieuwerkerke that people ought to beware of their cab-drivers when engaged on any delicate mission. A lady of note had taken a cab to call on a gentleman at Passy. The driver, suspecting the motive of the visit, found means to enter the room where the gentleman was closeted with his visitor, and convinced himself of their tender relations. Two hours afterwards the lady returned to Paris in the same cab, the driver of which declined to accept twenty francs as his fare, saying that he wanted ten thousand francs, not as fare, but as hush-money. The lady re-entered the cab, and told the man to drive her to the Prefecture of Police. On being shown into the Préfet's room she said to him: "I believe you to be a man of honour, sir, and the repository of many secrets. I am Madam X—, and have been to visit a gentleman at Passy. The cabman who took me there has discovered my secret, and demands ten thousand francs as the price of his silence. He is in your courtyard." The Préfet rang his bell, ordered the man to prison for five days, and told him that if he allowed his tongue to wag he should be turned out of Paris.

June 17th.—When visiting the exhibition yesterday the Empress was shown the statue of a young girl representing innocence. She criticized the extreme narrowness of the shoulders and body generally, but Nieuwerkerke pointed out to her that a young girl's figure should show less development than that of a woman of riper years, and that the slenderness of the figure accorded in fact with the idea of chastity. The Empress replied, without thinking of the exact meaning of her words, and with that vivacity of speech which is so natural to her : " One may be very chaste without being so narrow. I don't see the necessity for it." No one laughed, although many of us had a mind to.

July 2nd.—We are nearer to war than ever, for Russia seems resolved upon resorting to the ordeal of battle. England and France are arming their fleets and preparing for any emergency. The Emperor Nicholas is carried away by the enthusiasm and sentiment of old Russia, which he has himself evoked.

Vice-Admiral La Susse, chief of our Dardanelles squadron, has been recalled and placed on the reserve list. The cause of his dismissal is recent, although it had been decided for some time to remove him at the end of his two years' service. La Susse is rather a drawing-room sailor than a real salt-water one, and is, moreover, very unpopular with his men and officers, who resent his arrogance and harsh manners. He is also accused of immoral conduct. His squadron was at Salamis when he received the order to leave at once for Besika Bay at the entrance of the Dardanelles, where he ought to have arrived three days before the English, who were at anchor in the Malta roads. Mons. la Susse kept the order in his pocket for four days, and when he arrived found the English had been there two days before him.

The Emperor was furious, and without further delay deprived the Vice-Admiral of his command.

There was a grand dinner-party at St. Cloud yesterday; the evening was a pleasant one, and all the guests enjoyed themselves immensely. The Emperor opened a box of presents sent him by the Iroquois Indians, which contained, amongst other things, bonbons made of maple sugar.

The news that the cholera is at Copenhagen reached us yesterday. To be visited by that scourge would complete the disasters of the season, which will probably include a famine after the rain and frosts.

This year is one of the worst we have had. After revolutions come epidemics and ruin.

July 4th.—I went to spend Sunday with Princess Mathilde at the Pavilion de Breteuil, where the room I had last year is still kept for me. At four o'clock I accompanied the Princess and Madame de Serlay on a visit to Prince Murat at his new château near St. Germain.

Murat was at dinner when we arrived. He left the table and came to receive us, and took us to the dining-room, where we found about twenty guests. Canino was among them, but neither the Princess nor I took any notice of the loathsome wretch. I was made to drink two glasses of chambertin, two of claret, and two of champagne.

Marshal Saint-Arnaud and his wife came to see us in the morning at Breteuil. The Marshal complains bitterly of the vulgarity and rudeness of his colleague, Marshal Magnan, towards the officers of the camp at Satory. He has been nicknamed the "peasant."

About one o'clock the Princess went to St. Cloud to pay the Empress a visit. Nothing can be more monotonous than Her Majesty's life. She rarely goes out, never occupies herself with any needlework, and reads very little. Her Court is a strange medley. The jester is no other than the first Chamberlain himself, Count de Tascher. In the middle of a conversation between the Empress and the Princess the Chamberlain was heard acting the buffoon in the waiting-room adjoining, and he was requested to come and amuse the Princess.

When he came the Empress said to him : "Imitate a turkey," and he at once proceeded to do so, clucking and strutting and looking more like a turkey than the real bird.

"Imitate the sun," said the Empress, and the Chamberlain, with all sorts of stupid grimaces, did the sun.

"Imitate the moon." He assumed an idiotic air, and giving his already ugly features a still uglier look, said, "That is the moon."

Then he imitated a storm, and committed every farce, in fact, that his position required.

It was ignoble to the last degree to see a man of forty-eight giving himself up to such antics in order to make himself laughed at.

July 7th.—The Emperor and Empress went to the re-opening of the Opera Comique yesterday. I was dining at the Café de Paris, and saw the Imperial carriages driving through the throng of people that lined the boulevard, and heard many cries of "Long live the Emperor!" About ten o'clock I was going towards the Opera Comique, through the Rue de Richelieu, at the very moment the police were arresting in the theatre itself several members of a secret society who were taken with arms in their hands. These men defended themselves with energy, and one of them wishing to get rid of his pistol tried to throw it through a window. The window, however, happened to be protected with wire-work, and the pistol falling back among the police was seized, and on examination was found to be charged with ball. It appears that the plan of the conspirators was to surround the Emperor's carriage as he got into it to return, and to fire together from all sides. The police got wind of the plot and were enabled to frustrate it in time.

I know some foolish Legitimists who rejoice at all this; they are only concerned about the future of their Pretender, and treat aught else with contempt.

Russia, on entering the Principalities, has published a Manifesto, and sent Mons. d'Ozeroff to resume negotiations at Constantinople, but she does not appear to have modified her demands. It is clear that she only wishes to gain time, concentrate her troops, and exhaust her adversary's resources.   The present inactivity of France and England she takes for weakness; their fleets are at the entrance to the Dardanelles, but she does not believe they will dare to take them into the Bosphorus.   The old Russian party are urging the Emperor to undertake a crusade against the Turks, possess himself of St. Sophia, and take the whole of the Greek Empire with Constantinople as the capital. They dream of universal dominion and the resurrection of the old Roman Empire; in order to ruin England they prey upon her commerce in the East, and undermine her relations with Persia and Turkey.   As regards us Frenchmen, the Czar has more friends here than he is aware of.   The bourgeois class assert with an air of profound knowledge: "Let him take Constantinople, England may have Egypt, and we will take the Rhine frontier."

These stupid middle class politicians are still bent on the Rhine frontier; it is impossible to make them understand that we have no interests in the North, and that the day Russia and England divide the Mediterranean among themselves France ceases to be a great power.   An accession of territory, simply, would not increase our power an inch; what we do require is a position on the Mediterranean which would mean the prow of our vessels turned towards the East and the development of our maritime resources.

July 11*th.*—Yesterday, Sunday, Nieuwerkerke, Saint Marsaut, Préfect of Versailles, and his wife, Baroness de Serlay, a few other people, and I went to dine at the Little Trianon, in the house belonging to the Lord of the Manor, which is situated in the middle of the park, on the borders of the lake, and towards evening, favoured with delicious weather, we went over the chateaux and parks.

It is always a melancholy visit; the memory of Marie Antoinette, of her Court and the *fêtes* she organized are everywhere present. Now all is silent, sad, and abandoned, the royal dwellings are unpeopled, and the parks bereft of their guests; the spectacle fills you with emotion, and impresses you with an inexplicable feeling of sadness. The deserted palaces bear witness to the passage of the Revolution, gaiety is out of the question.

In the evening I slept at the Pavilion de Breteuil.

There is still no news, either from Constantinople or Russia. The Emperor Nicholas does not draw back, and is bent on trying the fortune of war.

France and England are only injuring their position by hoping that anything will come of diplomacy; weakness or indecision at this juncture would be fatal. Austria is anything but frank in this matter, nor does Russia express herself very clearly. Russia is not a power to threaten merely; she will only give way to active measures. Our delay may cost us dear.

July 18*th*.—I have just come from Breteuil, where I spent the day yesterday. I found the Princess in trouble over this Russo-Turkish question. "The Russian Emperor," she said, " has no political ambition in this matter, and the intentions of Russia are not aggressive. That power cannot reach Constantinople, and does not desire to take it in any sort of way." I replied, with some warmth, that I regretted the prejudices which prevented her from seeing the question in its right light; that Russian policy never varied or shifted its course, and in that consisted its strength. From the time of Peter the Great Russia has worked her way towards Constantinople, and religious matters are pushed to the front merely to hide her real object. In truth, it ill becomes the persecutor of Catholics in Poland and Mussulmans in Northern Russia, to assume the position of avenger, which should only belong by right to a power united by ties of common faith to the people oppressed.

At a time when Holland is persecuting its own Catholic subjects, it is strange to hear Europe protesting against the intolerance of the Turks.

All these diplomatic delays, despatches, ultimatums, &c., make me uneasy. Russia wishes to gain time, ruin the Porte, cause friction between France and England, and fortify her position in the Principalities.

Princess Mathilde thinks it is perfectly natural for Russia to champion the great cause of the Greek Church by possessing itself of the Holy Places, but she blames France for pretending to the same privilege. " Why mix herself up in such matters ? " she says.

The Princess is very little interested in religious subjects, and has no sympathy with the clergy. I have frequently been distressed to hear her speak as she does before her servants of the Pope, the College of Cardinals, and priests generally.

July 19th.—Marco de Saint-Hilaire, whose mother

was tire-woman to the Empress Joséphine, showed me yesterday the following account for the year 1806 from L. H. Leroy, Court draper to Her Majesty. I have copied it in order to show how profuse Her Majesty's expenses were in matters of dress and odds and ends.

Particulars of account due from Her Majesty the Empress and Queen for dresses and fashions, supplied by L. H. Leroy, as under:—

Account previously rendered	48,000 francs
Interest	15,000 ,,
Month of January 12,264 ⎫ These three months hav- ,, ,, February 12,347 ⎬ ing been paid are only ,, ,, March 11,206 ⎭ mentioned to show the account	
February, for Mdlle. Tascher	1,425 ,,
,, for H.M. the Queen of Bavaria	575 ,,
April	34,590 ,,
May	10,209·50 ,,
June	16,843 ,,
July ... ... 13,881·75 ⎫ In addition for black heron's plumes 10,000 ⎬	23,881·75 ,,
August	7,370·75 ,,
September	9,665·50 ,,
October	10,275·10 ,,
	177,837·60 francs
Received October 14th...	2,000 ,,
Balance due on October 30th, 1806	175,837·60 francs

August 10*th*.—When I was dining with Prince Murat at Businval a short time since we talked about Fould, the principal Minister of State, for whom he entertains a royal dislike. He told me that on the occasion of the Emperor's marriage Fould walked into the room where the Imperial family, high dignitaries, and Ministers were awaiting the arrival of the Emperor and Empress with the airs of a little sovereign. He went about shaking hands with the members of the Imperial family with an assumption of extreme importance. When he got to Prince Murat he held out his hand in his patronizing way, but the Prince shrugged his shoulders, and told him to pass on, adding : "I decline to give my hand to such a man as you." Fould, taken aback, tried to insist, and asked the reason. The Prince replied : "Deuce take it, sir ; pass on, and at once, or must I repeat my words?" Fould went off but he complained to the Emperor, who wrote to Prince Murat "that he could not permit one of his Ministers to be abused in that fashion at the Tuileries." To which the Prince replied that he fully allowed that the Emperor was master in his own house, and, as he could not obey him, he should abstain from coming to the palace. The Emperor specially invited him, and showed him marked attention, but was not able to reconcile him with Fould; indeed, Murat said to him : "I will never shake hands with a man I despise."

The result of Prince Murat's conduct was that a crowd of marshals and general officers wrote their names in his visitors' book. Fould is very properly despised and condemned by everybody. He and Persigny are on excellent terms. Prince Murat says that it is because they have learned to know and to respect each other's little infamies. "If I told all I knew about Persigny," said the Prince, "it would be sufficient to send him to the galleys."

What unfortunate men for the Emperor to have about him! At this very moment Princess Mathilde is taken in with Fould's cajoleries, just as she is by de Laborde's and the pleasant manners of her reader, Madame Desprès, who is merely placed as a spy about her. This lady even had the audacity to say on Sunday last : " All the Princess says is repeated at St. Cloud." The Courts of Louis XVIII. and Charles X. never had a more miserable and despicable set about them than has Louis Napoleon's.

The old nobility do not go to the Tuileries Court, and are not therefore responsible for the fulsome conduct of those who do.

August 14*th.*—Three days ago the Empress said to the Emperor after breakfast : " Louis, you promised Mons. de Viel Castel the cross ; try not to forget it." " We shall see," replied the Emperor. But the Empress, not satisfied with the answer, rejoined, " No, it is not we shall see, but we must. You made the promise and ought to keep it."

In my turn I say : " To-morrow we shall see." In the *Moniteur* of this morning there are four nominations of officers and knights of the Order. The officers are : Mocquard, the Emperor's secretary ; and Conneau, principal physician. The knights : Ch. Thélin, treasurer of the purse ; and Acar, principal chemist and druggist. Conneau is a devoted friend, and Thélin, I believe, a foster brother, against whom no objections can be raised; but as to Acar, the druggist, and Mocquard, the Emperor's white eunuch about the person of Madame Howard—poor Legion of Honour!

All that has transpired with regard to the note which Russia has accepted leads me to fear that, in spite of a good deal of noise and movement of the fleets, we shall in the end submit to the Czar's dictation. It presages a snub to the powers and an increase to the prestige of Russia, to whom will be conceded the protectorate, and Austrian mediation will be accepted, because Nicholas will not recognize the right of France and England to intervene in Turkish affairs. Russia pushes her condescension to the extent of not requiring Turkey to pay the expenses of the war, in recognition of which proceeding the collective note says nothing about the evacuation of the provinces, the good faith of the Emperor Nicholas being considered a sufficient guarantee. The pleasantry is excellent, but I don't think it is altogether to John Bull's taste. Russia wished to see how far she could go, and she now knows. She is the only great power left, England and France not knowing how to support her feeble allies.

The diplomacy of France and England has been so admirably conducted that Turkey comes out of the conflict completely crushed. She is nothing more than a Russian subject, and is fully aware now to what extent she can for the future rely upon her great friends, France and England. Russia reigns alone; it is sad to reflect upon, but so it is; we have lost our second battle of Waterloo.

Mons. Drouin de Lhuys has received the grand cordon of the Legion of Honour; it is really prodigious. If I were the Russian Emperor I would make him a Prince. Under Louis XV. Poland was allowed to fall; in 1853 Turkey is placed under the vassalage of Russia.

Napoleon I. said that before fifty years were over Europe would be either Republican or Cossack.

August 16*th.*—I am fifty-one to-day. Yesterday the Emperor was to have given me the cross, as he had himself promised, but he has not kept his word. Fould opposed it. The Emperor told Nieuwerkerke yesterday: " I could not nominate Mons. de Castel, as Fould's list was full; but it is only deferred."

August 17*th.*—Reiset, our second Secretary of Legation at St. Petersburg, has arrived. I dined with him on Sunday at my brother's at Enghien. He thinks that the Emperor Nicholas will resume his pretensions as regards Turkey in a few years, and considers the indecision of England in not consenting to force the Dardanelles when Russia entered the Principalities as a grave error. The Emperor Nicholas has felt his way, and now knows positively what he always suspected, that England is satisfied with a little diplomatic palaver. He does not like the Emperor Napoleon, but he respects him, and re-marked sententiously : " He is my friend, for friends can choose each other, whereas brothers are forced upon each other by nature."

August 19*th.*—Count de Tascher, the Grand Chamberlain, has just left me. He tells me that yesterday, at St. Cloud, the Empress did not go to bed until past midnight, as he and she had an animated discussion on the subject of the Duke de Reichstadt's death. She maintained that he was poisoned by the Austrians, and Tascher defended the good faith of the Austrians against such a charge.

The Emperor in private life amuses himself like a child; he has organized the game of football, and devotes himself to the exercise with perfect enthusiasm. The Empress passes her time in breaking in ponies and hanging new pictures about her rooms.

August 23rd.—I have just had an interview with Mrs. Beecher-Stowe, the authoress of " Uncle Tom's Cabin." Hers is another phase of modern charlatanism. She came to the Louvre with Belloc and his wife to see Gabie's Diana; the rest of the museum of antiquities did not seem worthy of her attention. She was shown a cast of the Venus of Milo, but did not care to see it in marble, and she turned away from the Achilles statue for reasons of modesty.

Mrs. Stowe is a short, thin woman, rather elegant, but with no actual pretensions to beauty. I should judge her to be about thirty. She cannot speak a word of French. Her reputation, which she is just now stalking round Europe, has turned her head somewhat, but I don't think she is very much flattered by her cool reception in Paris. No little ovation, no attention, no public reception; and she walks through the streets without exciting the least notice. Society does not throw itself at her feet, there is no Duchess of Sutherland to do lady of honour, nor aristocracy to act the sycophant to this apostle of negro democracy. What a misfortune that Schoelcher is in exile! She is not applauded on entering the theatre, there is no wreath, in fact, for this muse, this Republican blue-stocking. We shall be well reviewed, I expect, in the book she will doubtless publish on her European travels. Belloc introduced her to Béranger, and the old revolutionary poet paid the most outrageous compliments to the friend of the blacks.

" Uncle Tom " is the book of Protestant hypocrisy, the Bible of philanthropic societies. You may thrash, if you like, in the interest of discipline, soldiers and sailors; torture by solitary confinement white prisoners, but to touch a negro, or attack his dignity, is revolting to the sense of Protestant humanity.

Leave us, Mrs. Stowe, and rejoin the children who are awaiting you in Philadelphia. While you are making the tour of Europe cease to drag your poor supernumerary husband behind your chariot, and get someone to translate for you the epitaph of the Roman matron : " *Domum Mansit, Lanam fecit.*"

CHAPTER IX.

1854.

War—Views of the Ministry—Recall of the Russian Ambassadors from Paris and London — Reported illness of the Czar—Passage of English troops through Paris—Mdlle. Denain—The Empress consults the spirits—Conversation with the Empress—The author and Count de Laborde—Secret attempt to get possession of Madagascar—Condition of the fleet—Fresh plot to assassinate the Emperor—Prince Napoleon—Revolution in Spain: Espartero, Christina, Isabella—Baroche asks to be made a Senator—Germans in Paris—Death of Marshal Saint-Arnaud—An infernal machine—General Canrobert and Lord Raglan — Algeria a bad school for French soldiers—Barbarous conduct of the Russians—Cowardice of Prince Napoleon.

January 4th.—War is decided upon; a manifesto will appear in the *Moniteur* to-morrow or the day after. Thirty thousand French and twenty thousand English troops are to embark for Constantinople.

January 8th.—Preparations for war continue, the funds are falling, and men's minds are full of the crisis.

I dined with Princess Mathilde yesterday, and dine

with her again to-day. Everybody talked about the
Russo-Turkish question, and seemed to have lost his
head, La Rochejaquelein especially. He wanted to be
sent as ambassador to St. Petersburg, and, although he
did not precisely say so, led one to understand that
he believed he could have arranged matters more
satisfactorily.

Mons. de Las Cases and I talked for some' time
about Napoleon. He told me that at St. Helena
Napoleon sometimes spoke about his weakness in
matters of the heart. He did not look upon Count
Leon as his son, but thought that Murat was the
father.

January 13*th.*—The war is still the only topic of
conversation. The fleets have received orders to enter
the Black Sea, and new vessels are in commission.
Turkey accepts the note of the four Powers, but
Russia does not.

January 23*rd.*—People are beginning to doubt the
neutrality of Austria, and the Oriental question is becoming more and more serious. General Bosquet had
an interview with the Emperor a day or two ago, and
begged to be permitted to serve with the expeditionary
forces. The Emperor replied that he could only
authorize him to serve with the Turkish contingent,
which the General declined. The Emperor then expressed his doubts as to the neutrality of Austria, upon
which General Bosquet said, "You have an expeditionary corps in Rome, sire. Anticipate Austria
by reinforcing it, and then take possession of Trieste
and Venice."

January 25th.—Nothing definite has yet been decided with regard to the Eastern dispute, and some people still cherish the hope of peace.

In the Cabinet there are three different views. Persigny is of opinion that Prussia and Austria ought to be coerced into joining France and England, or else treated as enemies of the public weal. Drouin de Lhuys hopes that the presence of our fleets in the Black Sea may act as an example to Prussia and Austria, and that these two Powers may be induced to overcome Russian obstinacy with their armies, as they will be the principal sufferers from Muscovite ascendency. This means letting things take their course.

The third opinion is the only right one, namely, to succour Turkey by sending her 50,000 French and 20,000 English troops, in view of which contingency the Russians are already hastening to cross the Danube. Russian diplomacy is to keep negotiations going on while her troops are being pushed forward. Turkey, having spent six hundred million francs since the commencement of the war, is exhausted, and without help will have to surrender at the Caudine Forks. If such a thing were allowed to happen France and England would cut a very sorry figure, and the two Cabinets would find it difficult to defend themselves before public opinion.

The Czar's reply to the collective note is said to be evasive as usual. Are we going to allow ourselves to be deceived once more ?

February 4th.—The Russian ambassador left Paris this morning, and Brunow has also left London.

February 12*th.*—Count Orloff, who was sent to Vienna by the Czar, has not succeeded in his mission. Austria informed him that the passage of the Danube, or a prolonged occupation of the Principalities, would be regarded as a declaration of war. Our fleet is at Brest, *en route* for Toulon, where troops are to be embarked.

A letter from Count de Reiset announces that the Czar has—an unusual circumstance—kept his room for two days. The doctors say that he is suffering from a first attack of gout, but he will not listen to them. Some rumours were current that the doctors have recognized the premonitory symptoms of the same illness that Alexander died from.

February 15*th.*—Yesterday the *Moniteur* published an admirable letter which the Emperor has addressed to the Czar. It is dated the 29th ultimo, and is in the form of an ultimatum. The reply to it is known in anticipation to be a refusal.

England is embarking her soldiers, and we are about to do the same.

Princess Mathilde has just told me that Pietri, the Préfet of Police, has been to beg her not to dine with Haussman, the Préfet of the Seine; he says he is a thief, and that proofs of his robberies have been placed in the hands of a Paris solicitor of his acquaintance. They are at last becoming aware of the Préfet's villainies even in the Municipal Council itself.

February 19*th.*—The *Moniteur* of this morning announces the Czar's refusal of the Emperor's propositions. I always thought that this refusal would be made known after the Court Costume Ball, which took place yesterday. We are launched into war, therefore.

At yesterday's ball the Emperor wore the dress of his new body guard, a regiment of heavy cavalry whose uniform is of white and gold.

February 24*th*.—Yesterday some English troops, bound for the seat of war, passed through the Rue Neuve de Rivoli.

Marshal Saint-Arnaud will command the Army of the East, and among the generals under him are Bosquet, Pélissier, Espinasse, Canrobert, Bonat, and, some say, Prince Napoleon.

February 27*th*.—Fould has thought proper to deprive Mdlle. Denain of her part in the " Verre d'Eau," and to give it instead to Mdlle. Brohan. Mdlle. Denain, in consequence, asked for an audience of the Minister, and protested against her removal. Fould, in answering her, said : " I am the interpreter of public opinion, which has adjudged your acting of the part not only indifferent, but bad."

Mdlle. Denain : " I must confess, your Excellency, that I was not prepared for such a compliment ; moreover, the course you have taken is contrary to custom, and an infringement of my privileges."

The Minister : " Your privileges—custom. Really, mademoiselle, you must learn to know that my will is law. The members of the Théâtre Français are paid public servants who must obey instructions."

Mdlle. Denain : " Then, sir, you will force me to defend my rights before the Tribunals."

The Minister (laughing) : " Bring your case before

the Courts and win it. My wishes will be carried out nevertheless ! ! ! "

What a proud thing to be French when one's Minister of Fine Arts is a bankrupt Jew !

March 3rd.—Simon, the doctor attached to the Museum, has been to see me. He tells me a funny story about table-turning. He is attending the Marquis de Galvo, brother of the Duke d'Alba, who recently broke his arm at the Tuileries, and he sees the Emperor and Empress very often in the sick man's room. A little while ago the Empress was interrogating a table in Galvo's room on the subject of the East, and she asked if the Czar would be long before he replied to the Emperor's letter. The table indicated by taps that the reply would arrive within twenty-four hours. In point of fact, it arrived on the following day. She then asked if many Russian vessels would be burned, at which moment the Emperor entered the room. " Come here, Louis," she said ; " I am talking politics with my table." The table then proceeded to answer, in its ordinary way, that no Russian vessels would be burned, that there would be no battle, and that the war would only be a pen and ink one. " That's very satisfactory," said the Emperor, smiling. " If rivers of ink are used, there will be no rivers of blood spilt." The table went on to assign a duration of seven months to the war. " That is better than a seven years' war," said the Emperor. Then he took the Empress aside and said something to her in an undertone, and the Empress made some inquiry of the table, the answer to which Simon did not hear. The Emperor then turned to Simon, and said to him : " What do you think of table-turning, doctor ? "   Simon replied : " I do not know what to think, your Majesty ; but it all seems to me very strange."   " It is, indeed, very strange," said the Emperor ; " and not to know what to think is the most rational view to take."

On the following day the Empress brought with her the Bishop of Nancy, who, after some resistance, was induced to ask this question of the table : " What becomes of the soul after death ? "   But the table was silent, and no answer could be got from it in the Bishop's presence.   Why do we laugh at the sorcerers of the middle ages or the credulity of our forefathers ?

March 14*th.*—The policy of Prussia and Austria is still dark.   Our army is being embarked, and Marshal Saint-Arnaud takes command.   Marshal Vaillant replaces him as War Minister.

May 6*th.*—Odessa has been bombarded, the batteries destroyed, powder magazines blown-up, thirteen war vessels burned, and about the same number of transports with munitions of war taken.   The French ships detained in port have also been freed.

May 19*th.*—The Emperor sent his principal chamberlain to me two days ago to invite me to dinner to-day. The Emperor and Empress received me most graciously. The latter sent to ask me to come and talk with her. After twenty minutes' conversation, seeing the Brazilian Minister approach, I moved away ; but she despatched Count Tascher de la Pagerie, her chamberlain, after me to beg me to return and renew our conversation, which lasted this time for nearly an hour.

The Empress thanked me for the ring I gave her
which had belonged to Louis XVI., and I took the
opportunity of adding the pocket-knife which had
been seized by the keepers at the Temple with the
King's effects. The Empress attaches the greatest
interest to all that belonged to that unhappy monarch,
and especially to any souvenir of his Queen. I
promised her I would search for the least relic of
Marie Antoinette. "What I should like to find,"
she said, "is the portrait that was done of her at
the Conciergerie."

I sent the Empress, through Tascher, the invitation
card designed by Guervelot for the ball given at
Versailles on the occasion of the marriage of Louis
XVI. and Marie Antoinette.

After my two conversations with the Empress I was
a man of mark, and people came and spoke to me who
had hardly noticed me before. Rothschild came up to
me twice and did the amiable, but the *servum pecus*
was as *servum* as possible, and will always remain so.

The Empress told me that she relied a good deal
upon her mother to bring about a reconciliation with
my brother.

May 26th.—I have always forgotten to copy into my
book the only correspondence which ever took place
between Count de Laborde and myself, and which is
the cause, they say, of the hatred he bears me.

The Count was in London as French Commissioner in
connection with the Universal Exhibition, and he
wrote to thank me for a very handsome fancy dress I
had lent him for the ball given by Queen Victoria.

Instead of giving me some interesting account of
the Exhibition, this gentleman thought proper to
write me a letter full of twaddle and frivolity, as if
he were addressing some boulevard coxcomb. The
following is his letter, which is stamped at the head
with the English Arms:—

" *Great Exhibition of Works of Industry of all Nations,*
1851.
" *President :*
" His Royal Highness Prince Albert, Etc.
" *Office of the Executive Committee :*
" Exhibition Road, Kensington Road, London.
" 14th July, 19, Bury Street.

"I trust, my dear Castel, you are not wanting
the costume you were so good as to lend me, but if
you are I will return it at once. I shall be back in
Paris again early in August, when I will deliver it
personally with renewed expressions of gratitude for
your kindness. London life, which you know well, is
not more jovial than it used to be. Always the same
flood of invitations to lunches, dinners, and at-homes ;
always the same weary round of pleasure and
colossal expenditure which rank and fortune impose.
Of amusement very little, gallantry none, and morality
enough to make you sick. Are you not of the same
opinion as the Englishman who said that the morality
of the women in London corresponded with the archi-
tecture ? You can see from the street into the rooms
on the ground floor, and if you pull the blinds down
the whole neighbourhood is scandalized. On the first

floors the doors open out upon you, and the very carpets are in league with the husbands. In no country, not even Germany, have I ever met women so easy to win as here; they have absolutely no defence. It is not so much their temperament as a proneness to swoon, which takes complete possession of them."

The rest of the letter, comprised in a few lines, contained expressions of regret at having abandoned his work at the Louvre.

This was my reply :—

" MY DEAR FAUBLAS,—I disengage myself with difficulty from the arms of the little President to send a few words of reply to your charming and amiable letter. Do not thank me for the sacrifice, for I begin to have quite enough of Robin's wife. Her husband does not conspire with the noiseless carpets, but on the contrary leaves his tender half full and entire liberty. Let me chide you a little, my dear Faublas, or, at least, let me express my astonishment at finding you so changed, so different from what I once knew you. What you, the hero of twenty encounters, you, the organizer of charades, the conqueror of Madame B—, you dread the silent carpet or consider the husband! But where would be the pleasure in vanquishing the wife if husbands were blind or carpets muffled their footsteps? Be yourself; shake off the English fog that cools your ardour—in a word, be Faublas. I can imagine all your successes; the *veni, vidi, vici* astonishes me not in your mouth.

" That you tire of the English women as you tired

of the Germans nothing could be better ! . . You think that the women of perfidious Albion depend solely on architectural accident. I acknowledge the archæological simile, as our Academy professors say. But, my dear Faublas, you walk in the public gardens and follow the beaten track . . . out upon you ! that smacks of the pleb with a vengeance. Leave such ladies and their tarred petticoats and attack bravely and resolutely one of those good little Quakeresses, one of those fair, soft creatures in floods of brown and cambric, with features hidden beneath a penthouse, which they call a bonnet. Faublas, my dear Faublas, succeed in compromising a Quakeress and I abdicate in your favour. That would be really grand, prodigious, inconceivable."

May 24*th.*—The following prophecy was found in a book, entitled "Quarenii Euclid terræ Santæ, Antuerp," 1639. T. I., f. 265 :—" *Hoc regnum (Turcicum) et secta penitus destructa et abolita erunt anno Domini,* 1854 *vel* 1856."

June 4*th.*—The Emperor a few days ago received the Chancellor of the French Academy (Salvandy), who introduced the two most recently elected immortals, the Bishop of Orleans and Mons. de Sacy. The Emperor received them admirably, and with ceremonious dignity. He expressed to Salvandy the pleasure he felt in seeing him at the Tuileries, and Salvandy replied that political differences did not interfere with literary duties. The Emperor also congratulated the Academy upon having chosen a man from the ranks of the clergy, who merited the distinction on account of his talents and enlightenment, and he was equally complimentary to Mons. de Sacy, whose polemics in the columns of the *Debats* have always been characterized by their attic tone. He likewise laid stress upon the marked position he occupied in the Academy as a writer of classical French.

"I read you assiduously," he said; "and am charmed to find you maintaining the reputation of our best prose writers."

Towards all three academicians the Emperor showed the greatest courtesy.

About the beginning of August the Emperor is going to take command of the camp of 100,000 men which is being formed in the north.

June 5th.—There is in course of preparation—very secretly, but with the full approval of the Government—an expedition, the object of which is to dethrone the Queen of Madagascar, and set up her son, Tamatave, in her place. Sarda Garriga, the old Governor of Bourbon, is at the head of the enterprise, the details of which have in a great measure been planned by Mons. Rantonei, a very rich banker, who has large interests in Bourbon and Madagascar. A few retired officers, amongst others Messieurs de Montferrier and du Planty, and a dozen non-commissioned officers of the Spahis, compose the *personnel* of the expedition. Prince Tamatave has a great part of the population on his side, and his men are armed with rifles, but they have no cannon. Some guns, therefore, and a quantity of powder are being taken out to him. Sarda Garriga leaves on Saturday to complete his arrangements with Tamatave and sign the necessary stipulations. The Imam of Mascat will supply provisions. Sarda takes to Tamatave the portrait of a young lady of good family whom it is proposed the young Prince should marry. The project, which was conceived and is to be carried out by a hardy band of adventurers, was communicated to me this morning.

The idea is to make Madagascar a sort of French colony, administered by French agents, nominally under Tamatave, who will be the shadow of a king, a mere gilded puppet in our hands. It is a magnificent dream. Will it be realized?

June 18*th.*—To-day is the 39th anniversary of the battle of Waterloo, and we are again at war, but this time on the side of the English and against Russia.

I saw a Frenchman, who has just arrived from St. Petersburg, yesterday, and he tells me that the Emperor has in a few months aged by several years. The Russians are discontented, overwhelmed with taxes, and expecting to be beaten. In Russia trade is dead, and the money of the country is being poured like water through the Danaides' sieve, the effects of war are on every side visible, and the resources of the nation are filtering away.

July 15*th.*—Admiral Napier has written to the Admiralty to say that it is impossible to take Cronstadt in the present condition of our fleet. On reading his dispatch the Minister of Marine said : " In the next campaign I will send the Admiral such a fleet of gunboats that nothing shall be impregnable."

The cholera has broken out amongst our sailors.

One vessel has lost eleven from it in five hours, and another forty from small-pox.

A plot against the Emperor's life has just been discovered. Forty persons have been arrested, and their papers and correspondence seized.

A very singular circumstance, which I ought to mention, occurred a day or two ago. Prince Jérôme received a letter from his son, Prince Napoleon, just as hostilities on a large scale were about to commence in the East, in which that future hero begged that his father would have a steamer placed at his disposal. " If the Emperor were assassinated," he said, " it would be of the utmost importance that I should return with all speed."

The Emperor remarked when he heard this : " If he returns to Paris without my leave I will abandon him and never see him again."

The Prince is on the worst possible terms with Marshal Saint-Arnaud, who complains bitterly of his conduct. He is a bad man, cunning, cowardly, and without gratitude or generosity. He has intelligence, but of a low order, he is in relations with extreme men, and his principal counsellor is Girardin. His dissolute life makes him look years older than he is.

If ever he should come to the throne, which God forbid, France will have a bad time of it. In appearance he is like Napoleon I., without his expression ; all that was grand in the uncle's nature is mere astuteness and vulgar instinct in the nephew's. The bitter enemy of Napoleon III., no acts of kindness can reconcile him, any favour conferred on him he attributes to the fear he inspires. If he were brave one would pray that a bullet might carry him off, but there is no such hope. The Empress ought to bring into the world a son thirty years of age!

July 21st.—The Emperor and Empress have gone to Biarritz. The last words the latter said to Nieuwerkerke, before getting into the train, were: " Give my best thanks to Viel Castel; he has given me an immense pleasure." I sent her eight days ago the portrait of Marie Antoinette, done from nature in 1791, by Dumon, her miniature painter. The Queen is represented seated at the foot of the little temple in the Trianon garden, holding a vase on which is a medallion of Louis XVI.

Spain is in open revolt, and has declared against the Queen mother and her Ministers. Espartero is at the head of the whole movement, which has been brought about by Christina's rapacity and Isabella's immorality.

August 9th.—The news from Spain is still very bad. The Generals are making themselves Marshals and proscribing their adversaries; already, too, they are quarrelling amongst themselves, and the men of the barricades are gaining power. These latter gentlemen are composed of some seven or eight thousand demagogues of French, Polish, and Italian nationality.

It is said that the people will not let Queen Christina leave her palace without paying a heavy ransom.

Queen Christina, on reading her daughter's proclamation to the Spaniards, boxed her ears before the Council, exclaiming: " You are degrading royalty."

Too long, unhappily, both mother and daughter have themselves and in their own persons brought disgrace upon royalty ; the Neapolitan branch of the Bourbons has done nothing but supply European thrones with wantons.

It is said that Prince Napoleon is coming back from the East. Whether he has been recalled or not I cannot say, but what I do know is the universal dislike he inspires. In the East he collected about his General's quarters all the refugees and bad characters he could get together, so much so that the Duke of Cambridge refused to see him.

Ministers and dignitaries of State are preparing for any future emergency, and try to keep on sufficiently good terms with Prince Napoleon. That is the reason too that they tolerate *La Presse* and its hostile articles.

Drouin de Lhuys caresses the editors of the *Siècle*, and would betray the Emperor the first time he could make a franc by doing so. Billaut, Minister of the Interior, would return to his eloquent demagogism of happy '48. Fortoul would sell himself to the highest bidder ; luxury is necessary to him, and there is nothing he dreads so much as relinquishing his present high position. Before he became Minister he was a sort of Government spy in the Chamber.

Baroche is a scoundrel. His Excellency has a salary of 120,000 francs as President of the Council, and an income of 80,000 francs besides, but the ambitious bourgeois is not satisfied.

Having discovered, after profound reflection on the uncertainty of human fortunes and the insecurity of

Empires, especially in France, that the most solid
position for the last fifty years has been that of senator
or peer, whose incomes have invariably been paid, he
had the audacity of a porter asking for a Christmas-box
to go to the Emperor and say to him : " Your Majesty,
I have an overpowering desire to become a member of
the Senate." The Emperor replied : " It is not possible,
my dear Baroche, except you resign the presidency of
the Council of State." Baroche, pale with fright,.
hastened to say that such a sacrifice was far from his
thoughts. " Then you cannot be a Senator," repeated
the Emperor; " the functions of Councillor of State
and Senator are incompatible. The one makes laws,
and the other criticizes and adopts them." Baroche
twisted his hat in his hands, having held it out without shame, and, with the voice of a blind beggar and
the attitude of a person offering holy water, tremu-
lously said : " If I felt the desire to be a Senator, your
Majesty, it was not for the distinction it would confer
upon me; did your Majesty know me better you
would admit how little given I am to the vanities of
the world, but I have children who are not good-
looking, and who are too conscious of their dignity to
be discriminatory, and a wife who is difficult to manage.
To maintain my family, rank, and name, therefore, is
a hard matter, and the 30,000 francs as Senator
would have been very useful. Pity me, therefore,
sire."

The Emperor looked at Baroche in his expression-
less way, and dropped the Senator's office into his
hat.

Persigny has been called to Biarritz. It is asserted that this one is honest; perhaps they will find out to-morrow that he isn't.

Pietri, the Préfet of Police, is, I believe, in the absence of proof to the contrary, a man on whom the Emperor may rely, but he is not always fortunate in his agents. There is, moreover, a matter to which he does not pay the attention it merits, and that is the invasion of certain parts of Paris by Germans from the Rhine. The Marsh and the St. Antoine suburbs are full of these savages, who are ready for any mischief and stick at nothing.

They were German workmen known to Crozatier, the metal founder, who, in 1830 and 1848, were the first to enter the palaces and destroy the beautiful furniture and vases in order to secure the bronzes. For the last two months the Marsh and St. Antoine quarters have been deluged with these objectionable men—half Germans, half Jews—who monopolize the more expensive kind of cabinet making. To these may be added the working tailors and shoemakers, nearly all Germans and of the worst description. It is high time that this population received the attention of the authorities.

August 15th.—To-morrow is my birthday, and my fifty-second year will have revolved. Fould wrote to me yesterday to say that by a decree of the 5th of this month the Emperor has made me a Knight of the Legion of Honour.

Princess Mathilde, in placing the ribbon in my button-hole, said, " Give me a kiss, then." It appears that I did so in a very clumsy and embarrassed manner, like a schoolboy.

October 11th.—Marshal Saint-Arnaud has died from the effects of an internal complaint from which he has been suffering for some time past. To sufferings which his strength of mind alone enabled him to battle against, was added some short time since an attack of cholera. At the battle of the Alma he was for twelve hours on horseback, and, during constantly recurring attacks of pain, had to be supported in his saddle by two officers.

The Marshal's end was a manly one; he died like a Christian soldier, in a spirit of resignation, within sight of Sebastopol, and at the head of a victorious army. He was comparatively young, only fifty-three. He had led a restless and rather adventurous life, but was a man of action, good feeling, and intelligence. His last years more than compensated for the wildness of his youth, and he dies universally regretted. General Canrobert succeeds him in command.

I have learned several details with regard to the infernal machine that was placed in the Boulogne tunnel with the object of wrecking the Emperor's carriage on his return from the camp. The machine was buried in a place hollowed out of the masonry inside the tunnel, and was attached by a wire to an electric battery placed some distance away. The vibration as the Emperor's train passed was relied upon to start the apparatus and cause it to explode. One of the railway servants, during a tour of inspection, noticed a place newly cemented in the wall, and on examining it discovered the machine.

It is said that twelve persons have been arrested, but the affair is kept quite secret.

October 19th.—There is no news from the Crimea, but the bombardment of Sebastopol has, we know, begun.

By an order, recently issued, women of light fame are excluded from the principal places at the Opera, where up to now they have been permitted to flaunt themselves and their diamonds. Some people, however, are opposed to the measure on the grounds of free trade even in vice.

October 27th.—Princess Mathilde tells me that after the battle of the Alma General Canrobert wished to follow the retreating Russians at once into Sebastopol; according to his opinion, the demoralization of the Russian army at the time would have enabled us to take the place with comparative ease. Lord Raglan, however, was opposed to the French General's view, and to this opposition we owe the present siege and its wearying delays.

The cholera has made frightful ravages in our army; an officer in the Crimea, whose letter I have seen, says that he has lost fifteen friends who went out with him in the same ship.

November 22nd.—The guns at the Hôtel des Invalides are firing in commemoration of the victory of the allied armies at Inkerman on the 5th inst. It is also reported that another battle took place on the 13th. General de Lourmel, an officer of great distinction, has been killed, and the Duke of Cambridge and General Canrobert are slightly wounded.

Prince Napoleon says he is not well and has gone to Constantinople. A nephew of Princess Mathilde's writes from the seat of war to say that the Prince's retreat has had a most deplorable effect on the army; in France it is equally condemned.

The war is becoming very severe, and is assuming colossal proportions; every day new reinforcements leave for the Crimea. The loss of so many relatives has had both in France and England a depressing effect upon society, and mourning is general. It is very sad, but I doubt if the grandeur of the campaign has not elevated the moral tone in both countries.

The Zouaves are behaving like heroes. The whole of our army, in fact, is magnificent on the battle-field. The veterans (old leathern breeches) of the first Empire are altogether in the wrong, and will have to withdraw their favourite saying, that Algeria does not make either good officers or soldiers, and that in the event of a great war all these African heroes would make pitiable figures before Russian or German troops.

The Empire will suffer in public opinion from the fact that no Prince of the Bonaparte family is with the army. Pierre Bonaparte very nearly got the reputation for cowardice in Africa, at the siege of Zatcha. Prince Napoleon leaves the army at an important moment. Young Murat, who is a soldier by profession, does not volunteer for the Crimea, and the other Bonapartes are satisfied to draw their senatorial salaries in obscurity. Madame Patterson's grandson bears the honour singly.

November 26th.—On Monday week the Emperor will review his body guard at the Champs Elysées and at the Tuileries. Lord Palmerston is to be present. This statesman, they say, has come to Paris to confer with the Emperor about a loan that is to be raised on joint English and French security; also to arrange about the subsidy that the English Government is to pay the French for sending larger reinforcements to the East.

The war will be conducted with bitterness on both sides. The Russians are behaving like savages, and their officers even order the wounded on the battlefield to be killed. One Russian major, who is strongly suspected of having given such orders, has been made prisoner, and will be tried by court-martial. Generals Canrobert and Raglan are about to demand from Mentchikoff explanations on the subject of these atrocities.

November 28th.—It appears that Prince Napoleon, in spite of the order he received, did not lead his division to the assistance of the English at the battle of Inkerman. He allowed the English troops to be decimated without giving the aid they had a right to expect from him. After this unjustifiable conduct General Canrobert said to him : " One thing only can excuse your behaviour, Prince. You were unwell. Go and restore your health at Constantinople."

This wretch may be a Prince, but he certainly isn't a Frenchman.

CHAPTER X.

1855.

January 3rd.—The Empress has sent me a very
beautiful watch as a New Year's gift. The case is of
polished red jasper, with my monogram and crown in
raised gold. To this is attached a chain with key in
gold and jasper, and a locket made from two cameos,
encircled with rubies and diamonds.

The Emperor has the gout, and could not preside at

the family dinner party on New Year's Day. His place was taken by Prince Jérôme, who received the Emperor's guests, and profited by the occasion to become reconciled with his daughter, to whom, by the way, he made the first advances. On Tuesday he paid Princess Mathilde a visit, and brought her some very beautiful presents, saying as he offered them : " You have made me pass a better night than I have had for a very long time."

There is no very startling news from the Crimea. The Duke of Cambridge's illness has been greatly exaggerated. He never lost his reason, but here the most extraordinary stories are in circulation.

January 10*th*.—Yesterday the Emperor reviewed the Guards, who are leaving for the Crimea. After the review the Empress took the Emperor's arm, and they passed through the ranks together amidst the enthusiastic cheers of the soldiers. The Empress, deeply moved at the sight of so many brave men about to shed their blood for France, could not restrain her tears, on perceiving which the enthusiasm of officers and men knew no bounds.

February 17*th*.—I met Princess Mathilde at Madame Lehon's last evening, and had a long talk with her about the Emperor's proposed visit to the Crimea. She told me that all the arguments against his doing so were futile. She had spoken to him on the subject yesterday, and he had told her that the capture of Sebastopol would bring about peace, and that Sebastopol must, therefore, be taken. The Empress urges the Emperor to join the army, and proposes to accompany him part of the way.

February 18*th*.—It seems almost decided that the Emperor will leave on Thursday. Admiral Hamelin says he can take him to Sebastopol in eight days.

The Council of Regency, in his absence, will be composed of Prince Jérôme, as President, of Troplong, and De Morny. Morny will be the principal man in the Council; he is furnished with sealed letters, which, in case of emergency, will give him full powers.

I begin to think that the Emperor's visit to the Crimea is necessary; there is a kind of dissension among our generals there owing to feelings of rivalry. This morning I saw a letter addressed by Canrobert to General Forey, asking him to withdraw the resignation which the latter had sent in in consequence of having been put aside when promotions to commands of large divisions had been made. General Forey is accused of being the cause of General Lourmel's check and death, as he did not support the attack with his division. Had it not been for his selfishness and jealousy the fort would have been taken, and Lourmel would still have been at the head of his troops.

The engineers and artillery are also disagreeing; everyone, in fact, is looking out for himself without caring about public interests. Always the same miserable jealousies, this one pleased because that one has met with a reverse, which he would not help to bring about, but which neither would he try to prevent. Denunciations are becoming frequent, the most obscure ensign ventures to write to the papers criticizing the operations of some General-in-Chief; then colonels in the army, jealous of the Guards, communicate their feelings to their subordinate officers, who in turn influence the privates.

Our generals, again, are a little too inflated with their own importance, they all dream of the marshal's baton, and what I fear is that they dream of it merely as a stepping-stone to further power. If the greater part of these "captains" were deprived of their sword and epaulettes, what moral obliquity would be disclosed !

February 21st.—I stayed until two o'clock at Madame Lehon's fancy ball, which was very bright and merry ; the costumes were charming, and there were a few dominos. Madame Lehon's second son and E. Delessert as clowns, with their faces covered with flour, were marvellous. Giraud, the painter in chalks, was taken for a real Turk, for Vély Pacha in fact. The clowns predominated, as was only right they should ; they thought themselves in fancy dress, the blades. Not a bit of it, good sirs, you would be equally at home in the real character !

Madame E. Lehon, Mdlle. Lehon, Mdlle. de Reiset, and Madame Manara carried off the palm for beauty.

The Marquis de La Valette did not leave Princess Mathilde's side. This diplomatist, who has been shelved to the Senate, was once a well-known opera green-room dandy ; he is now as fat as a little quail, drags his jealous cannon-ball of a wife behind him, and tries his last seductive powers upon the heart of an Imperial Princess, who amuses herself at his expense.

In spite of the excitement of the ball it was evident that a good many people were preoccupied with the thought of the Emperor's departure. Many will not yet believe it, and hence the conflicting rumours : He is going ! . . . He is not going ! Statesmen envelop themselves in imposing silence, but the officers of the household are waiting for orders from day to day and dare make no engagement for the morrow.

Princess Mathilde, who is very vexed at his departure, does not mention the subject to outsiders, but she had a long conversation about it with Persigny, and later on with Colonel Fleury, who, in his double capacity of first equerry and Colonel of the Guides, ought to be well informed. All the big-wigs who are connected with the Court have sold their stocks and shares, as they rely upon a fall in prices the day the Emperor leaves, and then they will buy back again.

Mazzini's party is very active, not only in Italy but throughout Europe generally. Marquis Visconti informed me of a letter he received yesterday from an Italian refugee in London telling him to warn the French Government that emissaries charged by Mazzini to assassinate the Emperor were leaving for France and the Crimea. Mazzini only sees in the Emperor an obstacle to his anarchical projects—another old man of the mountain—and has decreed his death in consequence.

February 23rd.—Princess Mathilde has received a charming letter from the Czar, in which he says : " In truth I do not know why France is waging war against me." The old Czar is the same as ever, and thinks he is going to hoodwink the whole world with his artifice. The Princess is delighted with the letter, and is more Russian than ever. We are living veritably in funny times when the Emperor's own cousin corresponds with a monarch with whom we are at war, and her brother, Napoleon, who has been nicknamed since the Crimean business "Craint-plomb," instead of Plon-plon, as formerly, only associates with democrats and conspires against the Constitution.

"Craint-plomb" is the author of an anti-French pamphlet published in Brussels, which takes the form of a report to the French Government on the military situation in the Crimea, and is signed, " A General Officer." The French Government are taking steps in Brussels against the publisher and still "unknown" author of the pamphlet, and Prince Napoleon has been threatened with arrest, but he swears " on his honour " that he has had nothing to do with the publication.

February 26th.—Yesterday evening at Princess Mathilde's I had a long conversation with La Guéronnière on the state of affairs. He is the author of the article which appeared two or three days ago in the *Moniteur*. The Emperor asked him to go and see him at the Tuileries, and said, " Write an article in such and such a sense and you will do me a service." Fould thought that the publication of such an article would be impolitic, but the Emperor wished it to appear. During the interview, as may be imagined, the question of the Emperor's departure for the

Crimea was a good deal discussed. The Emperor has decided to go, the dissensions among the generals, their jealousies, and the absence of any high authority require him to be there ; the soldiers themselves want to be reminded by his presence that the army is his one and constant thought. " I wish it to be known," said the Emperor, " that I am going to Sebastopol in the interests of peace, which can only be secured at the scene of action. The incidents of the campaign will bring this about more than any diplomatic conferences, and, moreover, the Emperor Nicholas will also probably come to the Crimea! . . ."

La Guéronnière, in fact, thinks that the Emperor is decided upon going, for he said to him, " If Sebastopol is to be taken I must assist at its capture."

Marquis Visconti, who dined with the Emperor on Saturday, and had a long conversation with him about the doings of the Italian refugees, told me the same thing, but with less detail. The offensive alliance with Austria will only be an accomplished fact the day Sebastopol is in our power. The Emperor places no reliance on that power, and said to Visconti, " I shall believe in the good faith of Austria when I hear her guns fire."

Lamartine, in private conversation among his intimate friends, approves of the resolution. He thinks it grand and noble. He says, however, that the Emperor must take Prince Napoleon with him, or put him under a guard of honour in Vincennes during his absence. Berryer also praises it, and says that it is an idea worthy of a French prince.

March 3rd.—At seven o'clock yesterday the news arrived that the Emperor Nicholas had died of paralysis of the lungs. At once Senators, dignitaries, &c., rushed off to the little Bourse in the passage de l'Opera to make capital out of the information, and stocks went up two francs fifty centimes.

April 1st.—The Emperor and Empress will leave for England on the 16th. They will only be absent a few days. The Emperor did not give his family dinner on Easter Sunday. Princess Mathilde dined with him and the Empress alone, at which the Jérômes and the other Bonapartes are very jealous.

April 17th.—The Emperor and Empress are at Windsor. The Emperor has been received in London as the protector of Old England. The people and aristocracy lean upon him, and he is to be made a Knight of the Garter. His reception, in fact, has been unexampled. It is a beautiful revenge for his uncle's death. England for fifteen years made war upon Napoleon I.; chained him until he died to a rock in the middle of the ocean, and now it is Napoleon III. who protects this same England with his arms and his alliance. The reception given to the Empress is also a remarkable circumstance. The English Court hesitated for a long time, but the Emperor has grown so powerful during the last twelve months that everything yields to him.

April 25th.—I was interrupted just as I was about to mention an anecdote about the famous Count d'Orsay. About 1846 Louis de Noailles, who was then very Legitimist in his sentiments, was one evening at Lady Blessington's, at Gore House. In the drawing-room, besides himself and Lady Blessington, were Count Alfred d'Orsay and Prince Louis Napoleon. Louis de Noailles on the occasion allowed his tongue to wag rather indiscreetly about Louis-Philippe and his family. A few days afterwards he received from Pinet, principal secretary at the Prefecture of Police and a kind of connection of his, a friendly letter coun-selling him to observe the greatest prudence in his conduct. The whole of his conversation had been transmitted to the French police. It cannot be sup-posed that Louis Napoleon was the author of the report. It therefore lay between that infamous couple, Lady Blessington and Count d'Orsay.

April 27th.—The Emperor is not going to the Crimea; a counter order has been given. He stays in France. Prince Jérôme wanted full powers in the Emperor's absence, and the Ministry threatened to resign if he received them. Under the circumstances, and to settle the matter, the Emperor has decided not to leave. I think he is right.

The Universal Exhibition will open in a day or two, and the English papers say that the Queen of England will arrive here on the 4th May.

April 29th.—It seems that the Emperor's life was attempted yesterday afternoon at five o'clock. The particulars were given me by Flamarens, who had them himself direct from the Emperor. The Emperor, accompanied by Edgard Ney and Valabrègue, was on horseback in the Champs Elysées on his way to the Bois de Boulogne. The Empress had preceded him in her carriage about a quarter of an hour. Suddenly a fairly well dressed man came into the roadway, and placed himself in front of the Emperor, who thought that he had some petition to present. Instead of a petition the man presented a pistol, which he fired almost point blank at the Emperor, but Providence seemed to interpose, for the ball did not take effect. Edgard Ney then threw himself between the Emperor and the would-be assassin, but not before the latter discharged the pistol a second time, happily again without result. The assassin is one of Mazzini's Italians, just arrived from England. He had on English-made clothes, and carried nothing but English money in his pockets.

The Emperor continued his ride to the Bois, where he joined the Empress, and they immediately returned to Paris together. All the people on foot, both men and women, to the number of several hundreds, acted as his escort, and he was greeted with constant and enthusiastic cheers. The crowd understood that at that moment the destinies of the world were in one man's keeping, and they were grateful that he had been spared. The Empress, pale and trembling, put her handkerchief frequently to her eyes. At the Tuileries the Princes, Princesses, Ministers, and a few other people who had been informed of the attempted assassination, were waiting to receive their Majesties, and the Emperor said, in answer to their cordial greetings: "You see that it is not so easy."

At nine o'clock the same evening I saw the Imperial carriages arrive at the Opera Comique, and if I had not been present should certainly have taken the accounts in the papers for adulation and courtly flattery. The cheers and cries of " Long live the Emperor ! " were like discharges of artillery, and were taken up and echoed far and wide. The emotion was universal. I saw people cry—not one person, but twenty, thirty. Old Colonel Porcher, who commanded a regiment of Cuirassiers before 1848, and has always remained an ardent Orleanist, actually shed tears. He was by my side, and not far from Victor Grouchy (gazetted the day before yesterday to the command of the Strasbourg division); overcome with emotion, and, turning to me with the tears running down his cheeks, he said, wiping his eyes, " I can't help it." At the theatre the Empress was pale and anxious in spite of her attempt to appear calm, and the Emperor himself was thoughtful. On their return their Majesties were greeted with the same ovations as on going, and the houses were resplendent with illuminations.

April 30th.—The man who shot at the Emperor is called Liberani, he is a Roman subject, and one of Garibaldi's band. At Princess Mathilde's yesterday evening it was stated that he refused for a long time to answer Pietri's questions, but, after repeated and energetic endeavours, and Pietri's pretending that he would have him shot instantly in his prison, he revealed everything.

The Emperor in his reply to the Senate's address yesterday, said : " I have no fear of assassins so long as my mission remains unaccomplished."

May 1st.—The assassin had assumed a false name

in the Sardinian passport which he carried. His real
name is Giovanni Pianori, he was born at Faenza, and
is a boot maker by trade. His trial will take place at
the next Assizes.

May 7th.—The French ambassador at Madrid has
just told me some curious details concerning the Court
of Spain.

The King, it seems, was the instigator of the
Queen's assassination, and he it was who placed the
knife in the assassin's hand. This attempt on her
life, which nearly succeeded, as the Queen it must be
remembered was wounded, is not the only one of which
the King has been guilty. One day, at Aranjuez, two
men rushed upon the Queen, but they were killed on
the spot by the officers on guard, and buried in the
garden. The affair was then hushed up.

The relations between the King and Queen are
limited to official appearances, otherwise they do
not even see each other. Isabella knows her spouse,
and all he is 'capable of. She fears, therefore, to
become his victim, watches all night long, and only
goes to bed when morning comes.

The *Debats* describes the whole scene that took
place between the Queen, Espartero, and O'Donnel
when her signature was requested to the new law
passed by the Cortes, the object of which is the sale of
Ecclesiastical property. The Queen only gave in at
last on being threatened by the two generals that if
she did not sign they would proclaim a Republic,
expel her, and retain her daughter as hostage.

May 12th.—Letters from Spain give the most

ignoble details of the violence practised upon the
Queen by O'Donnel and Espartero. O'Donnel seized
her by the head, and menaced and shook her roughly.
Narvaez will one day bring these gentlemen to book.
Isabella may have grave faults to reproach herself
with, but on the other hand how has she been brought
up ? What sort of husband was she married to ?
With what kind of relations is she surrounded ?
Her mother had but one object in life, namely, to
pillage Spain for the advantage of the children by her
second husband. Her aunt, her husband's mother, and
her father, Don Francis de Paul, have been and are still
her bitter enemies. They are all a bad race, without
shame, conscience, or intelligence.

May 17th.—The Universal Exhibition was opened
yesterday. I was present in uniform with the rest of
the household, at the foot of the throne, as near as I
could get to His Majesty. I could hear nothing, however, either of the address read by Prince Napoleon, or
the Emperor's reply. There was a deafening noise
throughout the vast edifice, and ill-bred people kept
crying out to people to sit down. The ceremony was
imposing, but very short.

May 29th.—On Saturday last I went to an at-home
at Prince Napoleon's ; there were a number of people
present, but very mixed. La Guéronnière tells me that
when he was dining with Prince Jérôme, at Vilgenis,
a few days ago, he saw Prince Napoleon arrive about
the middle of dinner. During the evening the Prince
took him into an unoccupied room, apart from the
rest, and engaged him in a confidential conversation.

La Guéronnière said to Prince Napoleon: "Since your Imperial Highness speaks to me as you do, I owe you perfect candour in return. France looks unfavourably upon the line of conduct you have adopted, and if the chances of life should ever place you upon the throne you will find many more enemies than partisans." Prince Napoleon, who likes paradoxes, and rather cultivates them, said, in answer to La Guéronnière's remarks, "The advantage of my position, Mons. de la Guéronnière, consists in my bad reputation; it would be almost a misfortune for the heir to a throne not to have a bad reputation. In that case all kind of evil things are expected of him, and the least act of virtue is consequently appreciated at a hundred times its real value. Do you suppose, moreover, that I should establish a bad Government with a light heart and reign in a manner to make myself detested? No; once upon the throne, I should be the Emperor! As to partisans, the *Moniteur* would find me plenty the day of my accession by the insertion of these very simple words: 'All public functionaries are retained in their offices.'"

Since the nomination of Pélissier to the post of Commander-in-Chief of the Army of the East matters have been vigorously pushed forward. We have carried a very important position under the walls of Sebastopol, and have occupied the line of Tchernaïa, and at Kertch and Yenikale, on the Sea of Azof, we have forced the Russians to retreat, after capturing thirty ships, loaded with provisions and war material, and three fifty-gun frigates. In their retreat the Russians burnt their stores, the rest of their fleet, and blew up their

batteries.   Pélissier's plan is being developed; he is
isolating Sebastopol little by little, cutting off provisions and reinforcements, and gradually getting
within range.

The War Minister, who pretended to direct the
military operations from the recesses of his closet, had
at one time recalled the expedition from Kertch and
enjoined upon Pélissier not to attempt taking it again,
saying that it would be better to keep his forces con-
centrated instead of dividing them in detached operations.   Pélissier replied : " Your orders, marshal, are
impossible to carry out.   I want space and forage, and
must go forward.   The possession of Kertch is also
necessary in order to prevent reinforcements reaching
the Russian army, and I have therefore ordered the
expedition to proceed."

June 8th.—Our squadrons are mistresses of the Sea
of Azof and the Black Sea, and are now advancing towards the Circassian coasts ; the bombardment of
Sebastopol is resumed and Cronstadt is being recon-
noitred.   Germany and Austria are distinctly neutral.

In the English Parliament during the last four days
political parties have been debating at length the question of peace and war.   These discussions show once
more how miserable the parliamentary system is when
matters of delicacy have to be dealt with.   Orators
only speak from their own selfish point of view, and
treat the graver interests of their country with scant
regard.   Then there are the " saints," who are indig-
nant at the help given to Turkey, and men of ambition
who would sacrifice England to Russia if they could

but regain power, and who dangle before the people's eyes the bribe of peace.

I met Alexandre Dumas, the elder, at dinner at Princess Mathilde's on Sunday last. I have already said how awkward I consider the presence of that man in the Princess's house, and I persist in my opinion. Dumas poses as a politician and an opponent of the present Government, says very compromising things, and puts himself on a par with the Emperor. "The Government has robbed me," he says; "the Government is ungrateful, and has refused me the management of the Odeon Theatre," &c., &c. He said to the Princess: "Call me simply Dumas; I have worked for that for twenty-five years." Then he remarked to us all: "In four years' time I shall go for an extended voyage, and shall leave behind me, as a farewell to my country, two unfinished novels with this inscription upon them: 'Frenchmen! you, who bear that splendid name, are a nation of thirty-five millions; there are five thousand writers among you. Well, I defy any of you to finish my two novels.'" From seven to eleven o'clock Dumas monopolized the conversation and spoke of no one but himself.

The manner of writers of our time is to praise themselves without reserve or shame. Dumas is like Georges Sand, who canonizes herself in the history of her life. She tells us now that she will not acquaint us with the inmost recesses of her heart, because she has no right to reveal secrets which do not belong to herself alone! When her mother was in question she was not restrained by any such scruples, and she thought it necessary to degrade the author of her being that she might the better raise herself. For example, she was not ashamed to put in print—" When my father resolved upon marrying my mother she was the mistress of General X—." In the last chapters published by the *Presse*, Georges Sand calls all those who have said that she has been eccentric in her vices " Cowardly liars."

I know that Madame d'Agout was deeply corrupted through her intimacy with Georges Sand, in speaking of whom, twenty-five years ago, Merimée said : " She is debauched to the core, but more from curiosity than from temperament." Her principal lovers were de Séze, Jules Sandeau, Merimée, Musset, Listz, Chopin, &c. I was dining eight days ago with Eugène Delacroix, the painter, and said to him, " Were you ever Madame Sand's lover ? " " Certainly," he replied, " as everybody else was ! "

June 12th.—Yesterday, on arriving on the ground where the manœuvres were to take place, the Emperor informed the cavalry officers, who were about to execute some important movements, of the good news which had reached him from the Crimea on Sunday evening last. Marshal Magnan said to the Emperor : " Would it be indiscreet to ask your Majesty at what hour the news reached you ? " " No," replied the Emperor ; " Fould sent me the news at ten o'clock." " That is very extraordinary," said Magnan ; " Fould had it sent to me before eight." The Emperor made no observation, but twisted and stroked his moustache as is his habit when put out.

CHAPTER XI.

1855 (*continued*).

RESTORING PICTURES AT THE LOUVRE—MARSHAL CASTELLANE'S STRANGE BLUNDER—MARRIAGE OF COLONEL FLEURY—THE MARCHIONESS DE CONTADES—AN ULTRAMONTANE BISHOP —THE DEPARTMENT OF THE DORDOGNE—A VILLAGE PRIEST —PRÉFETS AND CLERICAL INFLUENCE—THE QUEEN OF ENGLAND IN PARIS—ENTHUSIASTIC RECEPTION—PRINCE NAPOLEON AND THE ORDER OF THE BATH—KING JÉRÔME —PRINCE NAPOLEON AND ARAGO—SOCIALISTS—ALPHONSE DE ROTHSCHILD — CAPTURE OF SEBASTOPOL — PRINCE MURAT AND THE NEAPOLITANS—THE KING OF PIEDMONT —THE MARQUIS DE CASTELBAJAC—ANOTHER PLOT TO ASSASSINATE THE EMPEROR.

June 20th.—Since the last movement of the combined fleets in the Sea of Azof there is no information from the seat of war, but every day news of some decisive action having been fought is expected.

The artistic world and the public generally are very much exercised just now about the unfortunate restoration of the Louvre pictures, under the direction of Mons. Villot. I wished to ascertain for myself the

merits of Godefroy, the Conservator's favourite restorer, who in my hearing had threatened the Rubens
collection and the Medici gallery with indiscriminate
restoration, after mutilating in the most deplorable
manner Claude Lorraine's "Village Fête." I had
myself transported, therefore, to the studio of this
respected picture restorer, whom I found armed with
a heavily charged palette before Vandyke's equestrian
portrait of Francois de Moncade, which Mons. Villot
says in his catalogue, "is reported to be Vandyke's
finest equestrian picture."

That being so, let us see how Godefroy understands the work of restoration. I will repeat his
conversation : "You have some difficulty, Count, in
recognizing this portrait ! It is very changed since I
have taken the varnish off. . . . Painters who had
begun to copy it will have to begin over again."
(Here Godefroy laughed immoderately.) "The head
of Moncade shows up vigorously on a light sky,
but its clearness is actually lost on a florid background ! There was the trunk of a tree in the first
plan, now there is only a stone ! . . . The horse's
quarters are lost, the contour has gone, but if Mons.
Villot will bring me an old engraving of the picture
I will put in the hind quarters." (Here Godefroy
threw his head up proudly.) "I find the general
tone of this picture really very cold," I remarked.

Godefroy took a bottle, in which was some stagnant
kind of black mud, and said : "Here is my remedy.
With a little of this sauce I will revive the Vandyke.
When I take the varnish off a picture I keep the

old varnish dust, add some spirits of wine to it, and
there is my sauce for reviving old masters." After
this exquisite harangue, Godefroy took up his brushes
and began to repair the sky in some landscape, the
painter of which I have forgotten. *Ab uno disce omnes.*

June 25th.—A few days ago Marshal Castellane,
who commands at Lyons, received a letter from Paris,
announcing the death of someone of his acquaintance.
Either from inattention to the name, or some odd
hallucination, the Marshal thought he had been
furnished with news of the Emperor's death, and at
once despatched one of his aides-de-camp to summon
the official printer. The man had scarcely arrived
when the Marshal closed the door and said to him :
" The Emperor is dead; you must go at once and
print for me a proclamation, of which I will give you
the text, announcing to the population of Lyons the
accession of Henry V." It was in vain that the
printer, in a great fright, protested that he could not
mix himself up in such a grave matter, or incur so
heavy a responsibility, and that it was a serious thing
for the town of Lyons to take the initiative in a circumstance of so much importance. The Marshal
would not listen to him, and at last the printer was
obliged to write from the Marshal's dictation the
proclamation he was to print.

Immediately on the printer's departure the aide-de-
camp is called in and learns the news from the
Marshal's lips. The aide-de-camp at once expostulates
with the Marshal, and protests against the proposed
proclamation, asking how the fatal news has come to

hand. The Marshal shows him the Paris letter, the aide-de-camp reads it through, but can see nothing about the Emperor, only the announcement of the death of some stranger. With difficulty, however, he opens the Marshal's eyes and gets him at last to withdraw the proclamation.

A few days afterwards the incident was communicated to the Emperor, who merely remarked to his informant, stroking his moustache and looking perfectly unconcerned all the while : " I did not know that the Marshal was a man of initiative."

Fleury, the Colonel of the Guides, is to be married to Madame Calais St. Pol, a lady who has amassed a large fortune in business. The Emperor gives him four hundred thousand francs, against which nothing can be said. Fleury is a man who has been of great use, and is very devoted to the Emperor; for a long time, however, he has been on tender terms with the Marchioness de Contades, in fact, to speak plainly, he has kept her establishment going. La Contades is no longer beautiful, and has very little chance of finding a suitable successor to Fleury. She has, moreover, a son by the Marquis de Coislin, and, in addition, the inestimable privilege of possessing a brother, a cavalry officer, who has just been received back into the army from which he had been expelled, and of a father, Marshal Castellane, of whom I have just spoken. The Marchioness has prevailed upon the Empress to undertake the education of her boy, and the Emperor gives her a pension of twelve thousand francs as an indemnity for the loss and ex-propriation of Fleury.

Thus rehabilitated the Marchioness has, it is said, been taken back by her husband.

An attack against the Malakoff fort has failed through the fault of the English, who having neglected to furnish themselves with hurdles were unable to cross the ditch and co-operate with the French. Our losses are heavy.

July 14*th.*—I came back from Périgord yesterday and at once resumed my duties. The journey enabled me the better to appreciate the manner in which the clergy, or at least the more ambitious among them, profit by the protection they receive from the Imperial Government.

I found the department of Dordogne in a state of irritation and annoyance caused by the bishop's conduct. This dignitary is the most downright ultramontane I know. He launches his edicts against dancing and theatres, and refuses absolution to the members of his flock who indulge in the polka and redowa and go to the play. Instead of instituting a sisterhood to look after the poor, the want of which is very much felt in his diocese, he fosters the Capucine Order, and even goes so far as to apply the Romish " *Index expurgatorius* " to the Dordogne.

The population, although naturally religious, are exasperated by all these interferences, and to turn the tables on the bishop have got together in Perigueux itself a little troop of Protestants who are just in sufficient numbers to demand the building of a church.

The good people of Périgord, believing that it is easy to approach the Emperor, have asked me to lay their grievances before him ! The clergy of the Dordogne who do not enter into the views of their bishop are inhibited in large numbers, so that the rest are driven in zealous emulation to preach against dances and plays.

I have brought back with me the peroration of a sermon preached by the parish priest in the little commune of Gonterie, which is not altogether without originality, and ought to take an honourable place in the humorous history of the Church.

This is the translation of the provincial *patois :*—
" What I have been telling you is not to prevent you from dancing, for the Holy Virgin danced herself, but she danced decently, and this is how the Holy Virgin danced." And the good man danced in the pulpit, holding up the two sides of his surplice like a woman, and chanting a pious refrain the while.

The clergy think the middle ages have come back, and are trying to reimpose upon us their once sovereign authority, a pretension which may lead to deplorable consequences. In the greater part of the towns the préfets have neither sufficient authority nor intelligence to withstand the power of the bishops, in addition to which their position is not so settled, promotion, of course, being their constant aim and object.

The préfets have no firm root in their departments, being but the delegates of a central authority, which is always more or less in antagonism with the people, but the bishops have a real influence and hold upon the hearts and minds of their flocks. The confessional and the right of administering or refusing the sacrament gives them an enormous power. Whatever sovereign may govern the country, the bishops' receptions are always well attended, while those of the préfet are very often the reverse. The Government will be forced one of these days to take the growing pretensions of the clergy seriously in hand, to make them feel that a state within a state is not to be tolerated nor dictation allowed. The Emperor ought to have, like Charlemagne, his *missi dominici*, which gave him direct information. Official reports are never very trustworthy.

The Bishop of Angoulême, a crafty, cunning priest, slyer even than his brother of Périgord, has taken upon himself to deprive the clergy in his diocese of the pleasure of smoking. The whole Episcopate, in fact, avails itself of its power for purposes of tyranny. A single concession made to the clergy at once renders them unreasonable, and they begin to clamour for the position they occupied in the middle ages. With very little excuse they would, if they had the opportunity, put the whole country under an interdict and excommunicate the sovereign.

August 19th.—The Queen of England arrived yesterday, and went through Paris when it was almost dark. It was twenty minutes past seven when she reached the Boulevard de la Madelaine. The National Guard and the regulars lined the entire route from the Strasbourg Railway Station to St. Cloud, and the streets were crowded with people. The windows of the houses were arranged like boxes at the theatre, and the very roofs were filled with spectators. The trades guilds from the environs of Paris, with their leaders and the different mayors, turned out and mustered under their respective banners. Then there were mottoes and flags on which the people had inscribed in English their expressions of welcome to the Queen. Triumphal arches were erected along the Boulevards, the Strasbourg Railway Station was covered with flowers, and the second battalion of the National Guard had erected a monument representing France and England. The leading portion of the procession was composed of six carriages, each drawn by four horses. In the first, seated with their faces to the horses, were the Queen and her daughter, and opposite them were Prince Albert and the Emperor. The Queen looked about her with interest, and the Emperor seemed pleased to do the honours of his capital. The Marquis de Lowoëstine, General of Division, commanding the National Guard, presented Her Majesty with a beautiful bouquet in the name of his corps.

My almanack says that yesterday, the day of the Queen's arrival, was the festival of St. Helena. St. Helena! . . . What an occasion for the reconciliation of the two peoples! The Queen, led thither by the Emperor, ought to go and pray at the tomb of Napoleon I. Well might we adopt Racine's saying: " Never was an age more fertile in miracles." The good sense of the two nations repu-

diates their old hatreds, and the blood spilt is forgotten ; both behaved like foemen worthy of each
other's steel, and they can now shake hands with
mutual respect. This day will ever remain memor-
able in history. Our united armies are engaged in
destroying Sweaborg on the Baltic, while on the
borders of Tchernaya they are victoriously opposing
Liprandi and his sixty thousand Russians. These
engagements are like two bouquets sent by our brave
troops in honour of the Queen of England's arrival.
The whole week will be observed as a general holiday.

August 28th.—The Queen left yesterday. During
her stay the *fêtes* have been magnificent. Those at
the Hôtel de Ville and Versailles were beyond all
praise. The Queen, Prince Albert, the Prince of
Wales, and the Princess Royal, accompanied by the
Emperor and their attendants, visited the Louvre
yesterday. We received them in morning dress. The
Queen was most gracious, and had a kind word for
everybody. She was pleased to say that she had three
of my drawings in her album—which they were I forget. Her admiration for Paris and its monuments and
museums betrayed itself at every step. " I am jealous
of everything I see," she kept repeating ; "I have
nothing to equal it in England."

Prince Albert was very much struck with a painting
at the Exhibition, by Meissonnier, called " A dispute."
The Emperor bought it for twenty-five thousand
francs, and made him a present of it. The Emperor
seemed delighted with the Queen's visit, and was in

excellent spirits, and most affable; the Empress, on account of her condition, and the necessity for remaining quiet, showed herself very little in public.

Nothing, no description, can give an idea of the appearance of Paris during the past week; the streets and boulevards were literally waving with banners, and everywhere were to be seen triumphal arches and the escutcheons and monograms of the English and French Sovereigns. During the evening illuminations everywhere, and hundreds of thousands of people anxious for a sight of the Queen, whom they greeted with enthusiastic acclamations. At the Opera, where everybody was in evening dress, her reception was most cordial. At the end of the Opera, the principal artists, supported by the choruses, sang "God Save the Queen," the whole of the audience, without distinction of sex, rising; then, when the anthem was finished, the audience, still standing, turned towards the Queen and gave her the heartiest cheers, round upon round. The Queen, deeply moved, made her acknowledgments to the house, and as she prepared to leave on the Emperor's arm the spectators again sang the National Anthem and renewed their cheers.

The Queen, Prince Albert, and their children, in strictest incognito, drove all over Paris, and made purchases at several shops. The review of the troops was a splendid affair. Prince Napoleon received the Order of the Bath *for his eminent military services!* Censorious wits assert that this will not make him clean, and that the Queen would have done better had she simply sent him a good-sized cake of Windsor soap.

At Boulogne yesterday, before the embarkation of the Royal party, there was a review of forty thousand men. King Jérôme came all the way from Havre on Sunday last to pay his respects to the Queen of England, an act of homage which people say must have tried his Royal pride, and cost him a good deal of heartburning. I believe, for my part, that the cost must have fallen on the Emperor's purse, for the old wretch does nothing without a money bribe. Like a cabman he must be paid according to distance, and always reckons his fare as beyond the radius. When Rothschild wants him he sends for him, and King Jérôme never minds waiting in the ante-room. His Majesty knows how to conduct himself before a little Jew to whom he owes more than two millions of francs. The Emperor's connections are a bad lot, who occupy a low place in public opinion. Their ill-disguised anger at the Empress's condition is curious to witness.

September 3rd.—I dined with Princess Mathilde at St. Gratien yesterday, and met Prince Napoleon and Count Walewski. Arago, who was there, refused to go on the water because the motion of a boat always made him ill; but the Prince, who treats him like a buffoon, insisted on his doing so, in spite of his entreaties, in order to have the pleasure of seeing him sick.

Some Socialist workmen belonging to the State quarries at Angers, five or six days ago, marched upon the town, armed with rifles, pistols, hatchets, and scythes, for the purpose of sacking it. Having been hemmed in in the outskirts of the town of which they had taken possession during the night they were nearly all captured. They had with them a cart containing over four hundred pounds of powder and inflammable material with which to set fire to the town. In order to procure arms, the workmen had robbed little isolated detachments of the gendarmerie, and village firemen. A secret society, called the " Marianne," instigated the movement.

September 4th.—Yesterday Sefels, who is attached to the Turkish Embassy, gave us a dinner at the Trois Frères Provenceaux. The guests were the Pascha of Egypt's nephew and heir, Alphonse de Rothschild, Abbé Coquerean, Sefels, and myself. The dinner was superb. The Egyptian Prince speaks French like a Frenchman. We discussed at some length, but without heat, and from a historical point of view, the differences between the Christian, Mahommedan, and Jewish religions. Alphonse de Rothschild is a man of intelligence and trained capacity. The dinner was not over before ten o'clock.

September 10th.—On Saturday a young man from Rouen, twenty-two years of age, named Beltimore, who had been condemned at sixteen for swindling, and again in 1852 to two years' imprisonment in Belle Isle for a political offence, and who has only recently received his discharge, fired at the Emperor on his arrival at the Italian Theatre. The papers want to make out that he is mad, but he is nothing of the sort. He is under arrest.

September 17th.—Sebastopol has been taken at last. The assault has cost us six thousand men, killed and wounded, and five generals are among the slain. Details are awaited with anxiety. The English papers pretend that twelve hundred pieces of artillery have been taken. Te Deums have been performed in all the churches throughout France, and illuminations have been general.

The King of Naples, who has disgusted everybody by his tyrannical conduct, has at last quarrelled with France and England. A small detachment of the English fleet has been despatched to the Bay of Naples, and we are to increase our contingent in Rome by two regiments.

In their limited selection of capable men the Neapolitans have addressed themselves to fat Prince Murat, who, in a proclamation to the people of the two Sicilies, and unknown to the French Government, has declared his readiness to undertake the management of the Neapolitan State. Casa Bianca is the Prime Minister of this King in expectation, who does not perceive that, in order to give him a chance of restoration, a general war, the subordination of Austria, and a sweeping alteration in the map of Europe would be necessary.

October 19*th.*—The *soirées* at the Louvre begin again to-day. For a month I have added nothing to this book. I have been ill and staying at St. Germain for a little change and fresh air.

Sebastopol having been taken our armies are trying to turn the Russian flank, and before very long we shall have some news of importance.

The Duke and Duchess of Brabant came to visit the

Louvre yesterday. They are not very enamoured of the arts, and said to Nieuwerkerke : " It is very kind of you not to press us to see anything."

October 27th.—The French refugees in the island of Jersey and the political refugees generally have at last exasperated the English press and public. Their paper *Man* has been attacking not only foreign princes, but the Queen and English people as well, and has been advocating the principle of assassination. Victor Hugo has been mixing himself up in the matter. It is to be hoped that England will send this tribe of bandits off to America.

The Legitimists, with the intelligence and patriotism for which they are so distinguished, are more Russian than the Cossacks themselves. The Marquis of Mirabeau, who is as devoid of sense as he is of education, is prominent among the more violent spirits of the party.

December 6th.—The King of Piedmont, who passed through Paris a day or two ago, has returned from his official visit to the English Queen. He is to shoot to-morrow and the day after at Compiègne with the Emperor.

The King's tone and manners are those of a private soldier. He prefers the society of the commoner class of women, and is strongly disposed to treat the whole sex cavalierly. His conversation is loose, and his natural inclinations are not even disguised in the form of decent language ; in fact, he affects coarse expressions. He also talks without reserve of his successes, and does not hesitate to mention by name, and in the most casual manner, the Turin dames of high position who have fallen victims to his allurements. When a family belonging to the highest aristocracy was mentioned in his presence, he smiled and said aloud that he had been intimate with both mother and daughters.

The Marquis de Castelbajac, who represented France at the Court of St. Petersburg before the beginning of the war, is one of the heaviest Christians I know. The rupture with Russia and the audacity of that power in the East were probably owing to his want of ability. The Marquis became the courtier of Nicholas, and applauded him in everything. He praised every action of the Czar, and stood transfixed and charmed under the fascination of his royal favour. The unhappy mortal at last even went so far as to congratulate the Emperor Nicholas upon the result of the atrocious butcheries at Sinope. It was useless for the English envoy to protest, nothing would ever convince the Emperor—judging of France by her ambassador—that an alliance between that country and England was possible. He believed in the weakness of our country, and we know the consequences. The Marquis de Castelbajac submitted to the grossest affronts, as, for example, when the Russian Government refused him permission to order a mass in celebration of the Emperor Napoleon III.'s birthday.

December 28th.—The Imperial Guard, on their return from the Crimea, will make their public entry into Paris to-morrow. Preparations are being made for their triumphal reception. Arches are being erected, the

National Guard are ordered out, and the Bourse and public offices will be closed. Unfortunately the secret societies are alive and moving in their dens, and the Government are not without alarm. Some workmen have been asked to fire at the Emperor, and an attempt upon his life is feared. Princess Mathilde, who paints a good deal after Nature, is at the present moment using as her model a young girl in poor circumstances, to whom, as well as to her family, she has shown great kindness; in fact, the Princess has been a sort of Lady Bountiful to them. The day before yesterday the young model came to the Princess, and told her that her brother, who is a member of a secret society, had been asked by his old accomplices to shoot the Emperor, but the crime was repugnant to him after the Princess's goodness to them all, and he offered to reveal everything. The Princess has accepted his offer, and Collet Megret is to go to her house this morning to see the young man, who is to be brought there by his sister.

CHAPTER XII.

1856.

January 2nd.—The official visits are over, and everybody at Court is dissatisfied, as their long-drawn faces show. The Emperor and Empress have given presents to no one, neither to their household nor to the members of the Imperial family; and the Paris shop-keepers, where the Court have usually made their purchases of New Year's gifts, are irritated at the neglect. The Princes attribute this parsimony in the way of presents to the Empress, who is not so sparing with regard to her own family. The mansion in the Champs Elysées (the Hôtel Lauriston), which has been bought for the Countess de Montijo, has already cost three millions of francs, including the additional land and alterations.

The Emperor has given the Empress a breakfast and dinner service for her own room; it is in silver gilt, and has cost no less than sixty-five thousand francs. The *layette* of the long and impatiently-expected child has cost two hundred thousand francs. This year Murat's children, the youngest of whom is the Emperor's godchild, have not received invitations. What completes the dissatisfaction felt by the family is that the same economy is not practised with regard to the Queen of England and her family, and Lord and Lady Hamilton.

On the other hand, Prince Napoleon is doing Achilles for a quarter of an hour in his tent; the august chief-tain is in the sulks. He is furious at not having been placed at the head of the army on the day of the Guards' entry into Paris. He would simply have been hooted. This sulking on his part has led to the inser-tion of the notice which has appeared in the *Moni-teur* placing Canrobert, *by command*, at the head of the army.

January 8th.—People are talking about two promotions to the Order of the Legion of Honour, which have not, and for very excellent reasons, been gazetted in the *Moniteur.* Grand crosses have been given to the Duke d'Alba and the Duke of Hamilton. These two strange promotions have been made merely to annoy the Imperial Family, Prince Lucien and Prince Murat, for instance, who are only officers of the Order. The Duke of Hamilton is merely a blind to mask the distinction conferred upon the other.

The Empress will favour her family to such a point that she will rouse public criticism. The unhappy Queen, Marie Antoinette, owed all the calumnies of which she was the victim to her imprudent partialities, which, for every friend, made her a hundred thousand enemies.

The Imperial Family do not care for the Empress, who, for the matter of that, does not give herself very much trouble to propitiate them. The whole family, which ought to be united and homogeneous, disregarding the necessities of their position, do nothing but work for their own individual interests, and speak ill-naturedly of each other. Then there are always the inevitable drawbacks to every Court—the schemers, sycophants, and flatterers.

January 14th.—I lunched with Morny yesterday; there was only Count Lehon present besides myself. We conversed principally about the *coup d'état* of the 2nd December. "What made me believe," said Morny, "that the Emperor would not be badly received by the people was a conversation that took place in my hearing, after a shooting party in the neighbourhood of Senlis. We had just left the dinner table, and were a pretty numerous party, consisting of some Parisians and people belonging to Senlis, amongst whom was a druggist, an old leader of the local Liberal party. This man exclaimed vigorously against journalists. 'We are tired,' he said, ' of that indescribably vulgar herd, who, without right or reason, attack, growl, and find fault with everybody and even presume to govern us. To be a soldier, professor, barrister, doctor, aye, even a chemist and druggist, one has to pass an examination, pay fees, and become subject to authority, but journalists who address the public every day of their lives, who advise and excite them, and poison their minds, they can graduate in a dung heap, or a convict settlement, and exercise their dangerous industry without restraint. Surely it is high time we altered all this.' "

In the evening I dined at Princess Mathilde's, where we discussed the President's absolute want of funds at the ·time of the *coup d'état.* " I know it better than anybody," the Princess said, " for when Fleury had to be sent to Africa to bring home Saint-Arnaud and the other officers whose devotion could be relied upon, no one had money enough to pay the expenses of his journey. Fould was asked to lend seven thousand francs and refused point blank. It was Ferdinand Barrot who lent the money."

January 19*th.*—The Emperor of Russia accepts the four propositions of the Western Powers. Peace is making progress, but, all the same, I cannot suppress a doubt which I have great difficulty in keeping to myself. I am afraid that in the forthcoming conference Russia will create difficulties and endeavour once more to deceive France and England. On their side the English press do not seem satisfied with the termination of the conflict. Those who live will see.

On receiving the dispatch which contained the acceptance of the terms by Russia the Emperor could not master his emotion. Doctor Reyer happened to be present, and saw the Emperor change colour. The Emperor said to him: "I am obliged to sit down, doctor; read that and you will not be surprised."

In the evening the Emperor and Empress were at a ball at Princess Mathilde's. The Emperor was radiant. Zébach said to me: "Are you pleased to see me again so soon?" "Certainly," I replied, "since you come like the dove from the ark." This cunning Saxon, who is a relation of Nesselrode's, displayed great tact and judgment in the presence of a hostile assembly.

Yesterday there was a little dance at the Empress's; dress coats and short breeches or pantaloons were to be worn. In consequence of his obesity, Prince Murat begged to be permitted to come in trousers, but the Empress told him that if he could not conform to her rules he might stay at home. During the evening, the Empress arrived on the Duke of Cambridge's arm, the Duke himself wearing trousers.

February 27th.—An armistice until the 31st March has been agreed upon at the first sitting of the Congress. At a concert given by Walewski on

Monday I saw all the plenipotentiaries. Count Orloff is a fine handsome old man, whose face is remarkable for its expression of decision. It is impossible to believe that he is seventy years of age. To-day, Wednesday, the Congress sits for the second time.

On Sunday I saw Alexandre Dumas at Princess Mathilde's. The Princess left quite early for the Tuileries, and I remained with Madame Desprès, the Girauds, and Dumas. I was anxious to be present on an occasion when the great man freely threw off all restraint, and my wish was granted me. The sublime, the magnificent Dumas, reached the extremest limits of vanity. He spoke of the Emperor with a mixture of hatred and superb disdain, and behaved as if he himself were the friend and protector of the family. "Hugo," said he, "has written some magnificent things on Napoleon, but I reserve for him in my memoirs something more bold and striking still." When E. Giraud said something very violent about the Emperor, Dumas muttered through his teeth the word "Scoundrel!" Immediately afterwards he continued : "The comedian had not the courage to avail himself of his position, when during the Strasbourg affair he foolishly allowed himself to be arrested. He ought to have done as I did, and arm himself with a pistol. In 1830 I took the town of Soissons single handed on threatening to blow the commandant's brains out."

For two whole hours Dumas entertained us with an account of how he had refused the membership of the Academy and his son the cross; how the Abbé

Duguerry had gone and asked his son to write a religious drama, in return for which he should have the Cross of the Legion of Honour, and at the end of two years be admitted to the Academy. Dumas the younger replied: "Religion has already been the cause of three great tragedies, which are respectively called 'The massacre of the Albigenses,' 'The massacre of Saint Bartholomew,' and 'The massacre of the Cevennes.' I advise religion to stop there and be content." The Abbé Duguerry is said to have retired with drooping head, speechless, and covered with confusion !

Before the Princess left for the Tuileries Dumas declaimed loudly against the indecorum of the Emperor, who, after witnessing the representation of Benvenuto Cellini, sent a snuff-box to Mélingue as a present. "We no longer live in the days of mendicant poets who received with gratitude the few coins that were thrown to them. People ought to learn respect for artists." I observed to Dumas that snuff-boxes were given to ambassadors, great lords, and persons of the highest eminence. "To an ambassador or a Montmorency very likely," said Dumas, with overweening pomposity; "but artists are of very different calibre, their intelligence merits greater respect." But if I repeated all the impertinencies he gave vent to I should never finish.

March 3rd.—To-day the Emperor opens the Corps Legislatif, but I doubt if he will announce the conclusion of peace. There are feelings of resentment between Russia and Austria of a graver nature than any existing between Russia and England, and this rancour has been greatly increased by the attitude adopted by Austria since the beginning of the war. A few days ago Count Orloff and the Russian mission were at an entertainment at the Foreign Office. The Count and his suite were very courteous in their manners to everyone present, but when they saw Count Buol and the Austrians arrive they put on their hats and assumed a defiant attitude. Count Buol merely shrugged his shoulders.

March 16*th*.—This morning, at three o'clock, the Empress was confined of a son, who, it is said, is to be called " King of Algiers." At six o'clock the guns fired a hundred and one salutes, and the big bell at Notre Dame added its deep notes to their reports. This evening the city will be illuminated. During the whole of yesterday and throughout the night a crowd stood at the Tuileries gates. The Empress was twenty-four hours in labour, and had finally to be delivered with instruments.

I dine at Princess Mathilde's this evening, where, probably, I shall hear little in the Empress's praise. The Princess does not love her, and takes little trouble to hide her dislike. The jealousies and divisions which separate the members of the family are a great misfortune ; self-interest alone ought to make them united.

March 17*th*.—The Emperor is distributing presents most liberally. Yesterday he went to see King Jérôme, who is ill, and on his way was much cheered. The newly-born Prince will bear no other title than that of " Prince Imperial."

Princess Mathilde, contrary to my expectations, expressed herself in very affectionate terms of the Empress and the Prince; she rejoices at the birth of the child as a guarantee for the future of the dynasty, but Prince Napoleon could not hide his bad temper. From the very moment that the sex of the child was known he began to sulk, and has spoken to no one since. He would not be present, as was his duty, at the private christening yesterday morning. The other Princes of the family were not much more amiable, although they did not show the same bad temper. The only one present at the ceremony was Prince Lucien.

The foreign papers will shortly publish a manifesto from the Count de Paris. This young man is about to reveal himself by an act, *proprio motu*, which is a fair example of his stupidity. For a good many years these pretenders have tried to spoil everything.

Monsieur le Comte de Paris is the representative of a pretended right to the throne which rests on no kind of principle whatever, since the revolution which gave Louis-Philippe the crown was in itself a negation of legitimacy. The Proclamation of Royalty in 1830 was brought about by some three hundred and odd votes, but the test of universal suffrage was never appealed to. The Count de Paris, therefore, who represents neither legitimacy on the one hand nor popular opinion on the other, protests against the fusion of Orleanists and Legitimists; he separates himself from his family and wishes to reunite the shreds of his own party. Such an act can only tend to perpetuate divisions; but we pay little heed to such comedies, being occupied with more stirring events for the present. Peace is signed, people say; the pure Orleanists, therefore, can distribute the manifesto of their young Prince if they please; it will have no effect. A fusion will be laughed at which from the first has been described as *" Confusion."*

March 19*th.*—Canrobert and Bosquet have been made marshals, and so has Randon. The Grand Cross of the Legion of Honour has been conferred on Fould and Hamelin. Hamelin well and good, but Fould ! ! I do not know why Princess Mathilde is furious at the promotion of Bosquet, but she is certainly wrong to express her displeasure so openly.

Bosquet and Canrobert were apprised of their promotion in a delicate and charming manner, which aptly illustrates the Emperor's good nature. They were invited to dinner, and on their arrival found themselves alone in the drawing-room. Shortly afterwards the Emperor came in with two or three people, and said to the generals : " I am almost alone to-day, and have asked you to come and share my solitude." The dinner passed off dully enough, they talked about acoustics, but during dessert the Emperor filled his glass, and said : " Gentlemen, let us drink to the health of *Marshals* Canrobert and Bosquet." The two generals, surprised and taken aback, were at first speechless. Bosquet cried like a child, and when he had found words to thank the Emperor he asked permission to forward the good news to his mother, who lives at Pau. The telegraph in the Tuileries Palace was placed at his disposal, and this was the despatch he sent off : " Marshal Bosquet to Widow Bosquet.—My mother, pray to God for the Emperor ! "

I proposed to several influential members of the Imperial Club to get up a subscription amongst ourselves and send twelve thousand francs to the poor of Paris in celebration of the Prince Imperial's birth. Some of the *prudent ones* received my proposition with : " Don't be enthusiastic ; you will not be thanked ; many men will not care to compromise themselves," and so on. Count de Reiset and Baron Heckeren were strongly of those views; they preferred to reserve to themselves their liberty of action, for one is a Diplomatist and the other a Senator.

March 20th.—Princess Mathilde has just left the Louvre, where she has been dining with Nieuwerkerke, St. Marsault and his wife, Count G. de Nieuwerkerke, the everlasting Madame Desprès, and her owl of a daughter. I was also of the party. After dinner the Reisets came to spend the evening.

The Princess told us that her brother Napoleon is still furious about the Prince Imperial's birth, for when the Emperor went to see King Jérôme, who is ill, the Prince, in chorus with Madame de Plancy, the intriguing assistant and Dubarry of the ex-King of Westphalia, exclaimed : " What does the Emperor want here ? Cannot he leave us in peace ? Let him mind his own business, and attend to the government of his Empire. It wants governing badly enough."

The Prince Imperial is strong and doing well.

March 24th.—I met the Girauds at dinner at Princess Mathilde's yesterday. They have just returned from Italy, and are very much impressed with all they have heard there concerning the Emperor. They found the Italians very enthusiastic about him and the French nation. In Italy, the Girauds said they were proud of being Frenchmen of the new Empire, and are beginning to understand the greatness of the man and his work.

I asked, as a matter of historical interest, at what time the Prince Imperial was born. The Princess replied : "I looked at the clock, and it was exactly fourteen minutes past three."

Nieuwerkerke is thinking of resigning his post at the Museum. He has not told me so, for he makes a mystery of everything, but I know it. He wants to wear the Senator's embroidered coat, and mingle with that congregation of fools and traitors. I cannot understand him, as he pretends to love the arts.

If I were ambitious I should be disgusted with ambitious men. No lover suffers more from a capricious mistress than an ambitious man does from the uncertainty of fortune. He is never satisfied, never high enough ; he is pushed here and there by his superiors, and elbowed by his equals. When he has climbed even to the top of the greasy-pole and got the prize, he still looks towards heaven to see if there is no chance of dethroning the Almighty Himself.

March 30th.—Yesterday the Emperor assembled all the great dignitaries of State, and acquainted them with the signature of the treaty of peace. The

Moniteur is silent on the subject this morning, but the guns have been firing at the Invalides in honour of it. It is a big affair, happily accomplished, and Europe is about to enter upon a new era.

April 2nd.—The review yesterday was a magnificent affair, and was favoured by the most beautiful weather imaginable. In the evening the houses were illuminated even in the poorest quarters of the town. For many years I have not witnessed such enthusiasm. On returning to the Louvre about one in the morning I met bands of workmen in the streets and on the boulevards carrying torches and cheering the Emperor and the "Peace." At one o'clock the Place du Carrousel was filled with an enthusiastic mob.

I dined at the Imperial Club with the officers of Orloff's suite, among whom was Count Schouvaloff, Madame de Chelainecourt's grandson. These gentlemen expressed a strong admiration for our army, and with as much good taste as justice, and they described its heroic acts at the battle of the Alma, of which they had themselves been witnesses.

The Emperor ought to be happy and proud of yesterday's doings. France was in truth the "great nation," the pivot on which all Europe turned.

Who would have recognized the France of 1848 in the crowds of people who pressed upon the ranks of the soldiers, in the workmen who applauded the conquerors of Sebastopol, and respectfully saluted the Emperor with their cheers? Who would have thought that France, which in 1848 was placed under the ban of nations, would in so short a time have put herself at their head as their leader and the custodian of European interests ?

Still it is the same country, and these are the same men, but happily we are no longer delivered up to wind-bags under pretence of freedom of speech; licence can no longer disguise itself under the cloak of citizenship, nor have the mob the freedom to rebel. France enjoys well-earned repose, and has conquered for herself the respect of other nations. God grant that we may remain for a long time under Napoleon's guidance.

We are a vain and a talkative people, the prey of the first charlatan who flatters our vanity. For eighteen years we were hated, cursed, and battered about for the amusement of Thiers or Guizot. France was absorbed in the individuality of those two men who, on the 24th February, were found to have delivered their country into the hands of the Socialists.

The divisions of parties must be allowed gradually to die away. It will be a long business, that I know. The middle class, the city merchant, and the tradesman alike, still cry out for reform as they did in 1848. Conceit has made fools of them, and fools they will remain.

April 3rd.—The Legitimist party is showing signs of its existence. There was a grand fancy dress ball at Countess Pozzo di Borgo's yesterday. The Faubourg St. Germain was prodigal in expensive fancy costumes, than which nothing could have been more magnificent.

Feuillet de Conches, the collector of autographs, the ambassadors' chamberlain and their principal protocolist, whose breast is covered with nearly every order under the sun, announced in yesterday's papers that he had stolen the pen with which the plenipotentiaries had signed the treaty of peace, and which was taken from the wing of the eagle in the Zoological Gardens. There's courage for you! Who will say that we have no longer any heroes? In the *Moniteur* of this morning the act of devotion is rewarded, and Feuillet is promoted to the rank of Commander of the Legion of Honour.

At the present moment the Duke of Broglie is being received into the French Academy. Nisard is to reply to his speech. For a month past the Duke has been in the throes of doubt in a matter of grave importance. In the event of his being presented to the Emperor he cannot decide whether he shall have the effigy of Napoleon placed on his star of the Legion of Honour or leave there that of Henry V., surrounded with tricoloured flags. The friends of the Duke are awaiting his decision in great perplexity.

April 8th.—Princess Mathilde gave a charming ball yesterday evening. The Emperor was there, and conversed for a long time with Mons. de Manteuffel.

An event has just happened which I had scarcely dared hope for—the.Princess has dismissed Madame Desprès and her daughter from her service. The decision is irrevocable. This wicked creature, or rather these wicked creatures, have acted their part so well, have gossiped, calumniated, and retailed their scandal to such purpose that the Princess and all the people about her have at length found them out. The insolence of these two women went beyond all bounds, and it was they who reported at the Tuileries, in an exaggerated and coloured form, all that was said and done at the Rue de Courcelles. The Princess told the Emperor and Empress of her intention to dismiss them, whereupon the Empress said to her: "We have hesitated for some time about speaking to you of the injury you have done yourself by keeping these two women in your house, and are very glad to hear they are to be turned away.

April 23rd.—I spent the evening yesterday at Princess Mathilde's after dining at Countess Bolognini's with Prince Porcia and Count and Countess Litta. The last mentioned was afterwards presented to the Princess. She is extremely beautiful, only eighteen years of age, and by no means devoid of wit.

Madame Desprès had been requested not to show herself in the Princess's drawing-room again. She leaves on Saturday for Poitiers, and will be closely watched.

Prince Napoleon was at his sister's. When he had gone and there was nobody left but General Bougenel, Rotomski and his wife, Princess Mathilde spoke unreservedly of her father and brother and all the vile crew of the Palais Royal. The Emperor, it appears, declined to send his cousin to St. Petersburg to represent France at the Czar's coronation. "Let him do foolish things if he will in Paris," he said, "but I do not intend that he should either do

or say them in St. Petersburg in order to discredit us
in the eyes of Russia." The Emperor has shown
the Princess the letters written by Prince Napoleon
from Sebastopol. It is impossible, she tells me, to
read anything more obsequious. In every letter he
avowed that he owed everything to the Emperor,
that he was nothing except by his favour, and that
without his generosity, &c., &c., &c.

As to the Palais Royal, there reigning Sultana and old
Jérôme's favourite is Madame de Plancy, the wife of
the principal equerry. She is thin, unattractive, and
by no means pretty, but full of effrontery. During
the ex-King's illness she always slept in his room. Her
husband remarked at Madame Lehon's three days ago :
" The Prince is better; my wife came home two days
ago. She does not sleep at the Palais Royal any
longer."

April 24th.—General Trochu has just been with me.
For two hours he kept me deeply interested with his
account of the Crimean campaign. He is still lame in
one leg, the calf of which was shot away by a cannon
ball. When he received this injury, which was
during the attack on the Great Redan, he fell, but he
scrambled up and managed to lean upon an Arab who
happened to be near him. On retiring, his progress,
as may be imagined, was slow, and the Russians
kept directing their fire upon the General, who was
conspicuous in his full uniform. In spite of everything, however, even of the wounded man's own en-
treaty, the Arab declined to abandon his General and
take advantage of his better legs. " No, General,"

said he, " I will not leave you wounded and alone. If we must be killed we will die together."

The General is never tired of praising the goodness, courage, and abnegation of the private soldier. That is the subject on which he will allow no contradiction. On the eve of the attack on the Redan, which it was known had no other object or hope than to create a diversion, General Trochu massed his brigade together and, placing himself in the centre, said : " Well, my men, I have some important news for you ; to-morrow we shall make the assault. It is no use disguising the fact that it will be rough work, and that of the men who head the attack very few will live to see the end of the business. Most of them will be left on the field of battle, and, what is more, I can hardly promise that all the survivors will be rewarded. However, I want two hundred volunteers to head the column of attack. I rely upon you, my men, and you know I shall be amongst you." The soldiers replied : " All right ! General," and five hundred offered themselves as volunteers, from whom two hundred were chosen, and out of that number forty only survived ! Out of fifteen hundred men who attacked the Redan eight hundred privates and seventy-four officers were left dead on the field.

General Trochu told me that in the Crimea, on every occasion when the troops went into action, they kept on shouting " Vive l'Empereur ! " just as in ancient and savage times the warriors yelled their war cries. At the Alma, in reforming the lines which had been mowed down by Russian bullets, the men rushed up

the steep hill sides to the cry of " Vive l'Empereur ! "
and so did the Algerian infantry.

General Trochu is young, only 41, brave, intelligent,
and every inch a soldier. He adores the army, and is
filled with admiration for our brave infantry who die
like heroes, but who are as gentle as children with
those who love and appreciate them as they deserve.

April 28*th.*—The Empress is recovering very slowly
from her confinement ; she suffers, it is said, from pains
in the region of the spine ; her health is not very
robust, and requires great care.

May 6*th.*—The treaty of peace, the text of which
appeared in the *Moniteur* a few days ago, contains very
solid guarantees for Europe against the aggressive
policy of Russia. This solution of the Eastern
Question is due in a great measure to the Emperor
Napoleon, and places France at the head of Europe.
She was never before probably held in such high
estimation. Sardinia is endeavouring to enlarge her
power by throwing lighted torches into the European
straw. To free Italy is her watchword, and she
means to attack Naples, Parma, and the States of the
Church and put an end to the French and Austrian
occupations which are obstacles to her design. Piedmont intends to become a great power by possessing
herself of the whole of Italy.

The Powers represented at the Congress of Paris
made a mistake in giving publicity to their deliberations,
in establishing a political platform, and allowing public
attacks more or less well founded to be launched
against the Powers not represented. Another mistake,

according to my idea, was to lend a hand to the ambitious designs of the House of Savoy. The King of Piedmont knows as well as anyone the value of Italian declamation and the patriotism of a people split up into ten nationalities; if he were made King of Italy to-morrow, the day after the Italians would rise against him. We should have a repetition of the spectacle offered by the middle ages, town fighting against town, and rivalries and petty provincial jealousies.

Can it for one moment be pretended that Rome, Naples, Venice, and Milan are inhabited by the same people, by the same race? At what period have those towns been united under the same government? All the public discussions, especially those that are about to take place in the Piedmontese Chamber on the subject of the dispatches and the protests which have emanated from the " Great Cavour," are ridiculous from one point of view, odious from the other. In the midst of peace Piedmont is about to challenge the lives of the different Italian Governments, and to revolutionize Italy, and we allow her to do it, we, who alone saved her from the jaws of Austria.

The Italian lords who are seen here are mere braggart Gascons, for the most part useless beings whom Mazzini would willingly hang if we allowed him a free hand. The lower classes are corrupted with Socialism, and Piedmont, in spite of the fuss designedly made with regard to Cavour and La Marmora, is incapable of making a united Italy, for such a thing has never existed. Moreover, if twenty-five millions of people wanted to be united they would not require anyone to secure their aspirations for them.

That England should coalesce with Piedmontese revolutionists to procure the separation of the States of the Church from the city of Rome seems to me to go beyond the bounds of fair politics. England is Protestant, and there are numbers of Puritans in that country whose only dream is the destruction of the Papal power. If we are to listen to all the Brofferios, the Cavours, and those who think with them, the Pope might as well resign his temporal sovereignty at once. France and Austria should look closer into the matter, for the day the Pope disappears as a temporal sovereign his independence ceases, he becomes simply a machine; Papacy would be at an end and Catholicism in serious jeopardy. It is for France and Austria to say if Catholicism is to be abandoned to Protestantism and the Socialists.

In the absence of Nieuwerkerke I received the King of Wurtemberg at the Louvre yesterday. He appeared to me to be clever and well-informed in matters of art. He spent four hours at the Louvre and was extremely pleasant. We spoke of Italy and the corruption of her population, which the King deplored. "What is to be done?" he said. In a tone of assumed seriousness I replied: "I know but one method, one last resort, your Majesty; it is heroic, but it can alone give peace to Italy, but not having been a member of the Congress I have been unable to give practical effect to my view." "What is it?" said the King. "Transport the Italians into Lapland and the Laplanders into Italy," I replied.

CHAPTER XIII.

1856 (*continued*).

May 9th.—For some time the Emperor has had his eye
upon the speculators, and the *Moniteur* has launched its
diatribes against people who are trying to bamboozle
the public. An Emigration Society has recently published its prospectus, and the names of its Executive
Committee, in the columns of the *Debats*. A certain
Baron de Mortemart-Boisse, who is neither Mortemart

nor Boisse, but a busy schemer, has drawn up the advertisement, in which it is stated that the Company is supported by persons *from the very foot of the throne !* Among the members of the Committee are mentioned : " Monsieur Blanchard, brother of the Colonel of Grenadiers who was killed at the attack on Sebastopol; Prince de Montléar ! ! and General Ricard, principal aide-de-camp to King Jérôme."

This advertisement having been shown to the Emperor by someone in his household, he got very angry, and wrote rather a warm letter to Prince Jérôme, the consequence of which is that the aide-de-camp in question has been deprived of his functions.

This is all very well, but it is remarked that the Emperor's severity is only shown now that it is no longer possible to add to the perquisites of his own familiar and intimate friends. The Mornys, Foulds, Poniatowskis, and Heckerens having satisfied their appetites, others have no right to be hungry.

May 16*th.*—The King of Wurtemberg has made me a Knight of his Order of the Crown.

I dined yesterday at Princess Mathilde's. The Duchess of Albufera came to pay her respects during the evening. This gossip-monger informed the Princess that an amatory intrigue had recently been discovered between Princess Essling, principal lady-in-waiting to the Empress, and Pagol, the son of General Pagol.

On the 2nd June there is to be a sale of autographs, the catalogue of which was sent to me yesterday. On looking through it I found a letter from Prince

Michael Gortchakoff to Prince Jablanowski, which is worth copying.

"Your card-sharping reputation prevents me from accepting your invitation to the rooking entertainment you are preparing for this evening. . . . To-morrow I will pay you a visit, but you must not make me the victim of your skill. I count upon your sharing with me the proceeds of your encounter with the ninnies you are to play against."

The police are redoubling their vigilance against the speculators, and those who are foolish enough to credit their schemes are being warned. It appears that the big promoters are complaining of the injury that is being done them by the smaller ones.

The Empress is asking for more of the Louvre pictures for the St. Cloud Palace. One Murillo has already been taken there, and the public are scandalized.

The Emperor of Austria's brother arrived yesterday. He is staying at St. Cloud, where the Emperor and Empress took up their summer quarters two days ago.

The Italian question is still to the front. Sardinia, supported by England, wishes to lay strong hands on Italy, and Count Cavour, by his speeches and public writings, is doing all in his power to excite a revolution throughout that country. Sardinia presumes to dictate reforms to all the Italian States, and to take away the Pope's dominions under pretence of secularizing them. This is the first time that States assembled in Congress have openly brought accusations against friendly States. Sardinia, who opens her doors to all the enemies of the Pope and Austria, complains of the precautions that are being taken against her.

France would be wrong if she countenanced the ambitious designs of the King of Piedmont; the moment that sovereign succeeds in reuniting Italy under his dominion, England can free herself from our alliance, and form a league with the Italian peninsula, which would be extremely inconvenient to us. England in alliance with the King of Sardinia can very easily hold France and Austria in check; she could augment her influence in the Mediterranean, and place herself at our very gates. In order to bring this about the temporal power of the Pope must be destroyed. Piedmont has put forward a thinly-veiled project, the beginning of a scheme which proposes that there shall be a separate Viceroyalty for the States of the Church. Lord Palmerston has had the audacity to state in the English Parliament that Rome was never better governed than she was by the Revolutionary party of 1848. This little phrase simply infers the condemnation of French policy, which England and her ally, the King of Piedmont, are silently undermining.

All the incendiary proclamations distributed in Sicily, Naples, Lombardy, and Rome for years past have emanated from Malta with the cognizance of England, and are circulated throughout Italy by her agents. The Marquis de Coislin, on this subject, received the confidence of the captain of an English vessel, who happened to be a zealous Tory, and who deplored the orders he had to carry out.

England, although entirely our friend as she appears to be to-day, is taking her precautions against future contingencies by caressing Piedmont with the view of harassing our flank.   English Protestantism plays its part in this important business; holds in reserve a little collection of Revolutionists, which it can let go when it pleases; sheds tears of commiseration over the fate of Italy under the Roman yoke, while she subjects the Catholics of Ireland to harsher serfdom still; and, to sum up, deprives the English of any chance of Sunday amusement.

May 17th.—Count Orloff, who has seen a copy of the catalogue of autographs advertised to be sold on June 2nd, says that the letter of General Gortchakoff is a forgery.   He knows both the General and his correspondent to be honourable men, and much too clever to commit such stupid things to writing.   In the same collection is a letter purporting to be from Count Orloff himself; it is very insignificant in any case, but the Count says it is a forgery in every particular.   The sale will be stopped, and the letters seized.

May 18th.—The brother of the Emperor of Austria, the Archduke Maximilian, came to visit the Louvre yesterday at two o'clock.   As Nieuwerkerke did not come back before three, I received the Prince, who struck me as being amiable, polished, and of cultivated mind.   He has an excellent knowledge of the fine arts, but his appearance is far from attractive; his exaggerated Austrian lip is a great disfigurement.   He intends to pay several visits to the Museum, and to study it in detail.

May 24th.—It is a useful thing to note in the pages of this book any matter that can throw the least light upon the manners, customs, and men of our age. The inner life of an artist, like that of a statesman, is interesting really to know; biographies are too apt to make heroes and martyrs out of very indifferent people. Seen from a distance, the life of an artist receives the reflection of his talent, and is illuminated with the glory which surrounds the personality of the poet, the sculptor, or the painter. The man is sanctified, his faults, his vileness, his crimes disappear, and those who in his day may have condemned him are judged to have been wrong by the tribunal of posterity. In another century we shall be charged with crime for not having adored that good man Béranger, who is the biggest scoundrel in all Christendom; for not having assuaged the sufferings of Musset, who was mad with pride and drink; for not having set in diamonds Mons. Ingres, who builds and then shuts himself up in his own pyramids, is always complaining, always receiving help from every quarter, and whose proceedings are restrained by no feelings of delicacy whatever. Mons. Thiers is astounded that France does not call herself Thiereïde, and Guizot that she does not assume the name of Guizotine.

I have rarely come across a great man who was bearable; they ought all to be born dead. I hold the opinion of the peasant, who proscribed Aristides because he plagued the world with his surname "Just." Aristides must have been a pretentious purist. Chateaubriand was intolerable; his political career is well known, and his private life was one eternal parade. Lamartine, now a beggar, has had since 1848 eighteen hundred thousand francs from his writings. At the present moment he is acting the part of Belisarius, and holds out his hat.

A word as to Paul Delaroche, the great painter, the great man of the Opposition, so dignified and serious, so like Achilles in his virtuous indignation. Well, Paul Delaroche is a tradesman, and much cleverer as a comedian than a painter. Monsieur Benoit Fould, chaperoned by Scheffer, goes to see him in his studio, praises him, tickles his vanity, looks at his sketches, and agrees to purchase a picture of the Girondists, as big as that of the Duke of Guise, for the small sum of thirty thousand francs. The picture was well paid for, very well paid for, but we will say no more about that.

About a month after this contract, Jelabert, Delaroche's factotum, goes to Mons. Benoit Fould and tells him that thirty thousand francs would really not give the artist water to drink. All the Girondists for thirty thousand francs is giving the picture away; the Girondists would be cheap at thirty-five thousand francs.

The picture is then finished; some friends have been to the studio to see it, and Benoit Fould is anxious to hang it in his drawing-room; but wait a moment. The great Jelabert again comes to him, and says that the house of Delaroche cannot allow a picture to leave its premises without payment in advance. Fould thereupon shrugs his shoulders and pays.

June 5th.—I received this morning, through the Austrian ambassador, a gold snuff-box as a present from His Imperial Highness the Archduke Maximilian.

The Emperor left on Sunday for the scene of the frightful inundations caused by the overflow of the Rhone and the Loire, and returned to Paris this morning. He was received in Lyons, Arles, and Avignon with enthusiasm. I have it from the lips of a witness who was on the spot that " nothing can give an idea of the effect his presence produced." At Lyons the Emperor—alone and on horseback, in the middle of a crowd of sixty thousand workmen, their wives and children, all victims of the terrible inundations—was moved to tears and pale with emotion, he distributed, with unrestrained generosity, the gold which he carried in two large bags attached to his saddle-bow. He was the first to bring relief, and he did so with expressions of sympathy and a kindness of manner that went to everybody's heart.

The casualties caused by the inundations are numberless, and many persons have perished.

June 12th.—The marriage of Prince Poniatowski, son of the ex-ambassador of Tuscany, who is now a Senator, with Mdlle. Lehon took place yesterday. The young man is not very intelligent-looking, and has the appearance of unearned fatigue. He has not much to say for himself, and takes very little notice of anything—not even of his wife, who certainly merits attention, as she is most agreeable and clever. There will be some differences in that household, in my opinion, before many years are over.

On Saturday the baptism of the Prince Imperial will take place. The arrangements for the ceremony have been clumsily made, and have given a good deal of dissatisfaction. Prince Jérôme will not go, because he is placed in the same rank as Prince Oscar of Sweden and the Dowager Grand Duchess of Baden, who, with Prince Napoleon, were to occupy one of the carriages. Princess Mathilde is put out at being relegated to a second carriage, along with the Duchess of Hamilton, who is not of Imperial rank, nor a relative of the same degree as herself. She is certainly right, and the masters of the ceremony have blundered.

June 24th.—Dined at the Imperial Club with Toulongeon, the Emperor's orderly officer, from whom I learn that the Duke de Brabant during his stay in Paris last year showed the greatest anxiety to discover any souvenirs of his childhood. The Emperor and he had a friendly conversation, and the former tried to recall to mind any circumstances anterior to 1848. Toulongeon, who was placed near the person of the Duke de Brabant, talked to him without reserve about everything. The Duke wanted to know his opinion about Changarnier and the other generals, such as Bedau and Lamoricière. Toulongeon described to him all Changarnier's artifices, how he tried to ingratiate himself with all parties, and had overwhelmed the Emperor with assurances of devotion ; also how that General had himself frequently suggested a *coup d'état*. In fact, he informed him of much that I have already stated in these memoirs, but there are some truths that the Legitimists and Orleanists are far from wishing to believe.

The Paris correspondent of the " *official Gazette* " of Milan announces the marriage of Mdlle. Lehon in these terms :—" The marriage of Mdlle. Lehon, daughter of Countess Lehon *and Count de Morny*, with the son of Prince Poniatowski, was celebrated yesterday."

July 8th.—For the last twelve months Calvet Rogniat and I have been trying to overcome the opposition of the Academy of Medicine to a discovery that has been made by Mons. Boulomié, the chemist. It has reference to a substitute for sulphate of quinine, which is grown in many parts of Europe, and most abundantly in France. This substitute, which is more efficacious than quinine itself, as has been proved by four years' practical experience in twenty different hospitals, and by a hundred doctors, does not affect the brain, the digestive organs, or the bowels ; it is ten times cheaper than quinine, and is not likely to be affected by maritime wars or the failure of the cinchona tree. But it has enemies in the chemists and druggists, and the doctors who traffic in quinine, especially in the African military druggists, who make a large profit by reselling at Marseilles two-thirds of the sulphate of quinine sent to Africa by the War Minister for the use of fever patients. The Academy of Medicine has taken the side of the quinine, and opposes our discovery.

As the Ministers dare not endow France with this new medicine, the virtues of which have been fully recognized in the reports of a host of medical men, we are forced to take it to foreign countries and get it adopted by our neighbours. The discovery, which is a precious boon to humanity, will probably in a few years come back to us from Germany and Russia. To-morrow Calvet Rogniat, Boulomié, and I have a meeting to decide definitely what steps we shall take. It is very probable that at the end of next month Boulomié and I will go to Holland and offer our discovery to the Government there, and that Calvet Rogniat and Boulomié will subsequently proceed to Russia to make the same offer to the Czar.

Who shall say now that learned bodies are useless, and that the Academy of Medicine is not philanthropic?

July 14th.—I have just come from St. Gratien, where I spent yesterday with Princess Mathilde. I found her in a state of great irritation against the Emperor, and particularly against the Empress. The family council have decided that the eldest son of King Jérôme, born of a marriage which the Emperor does not recognize, may bear the name of Bonaparte, but shall not be allowed the civil rights of affiliation. Two years ago the Princess was allowed to treat this man as her own brother, and often received him and his son at her table, and Nieuwerkerke himself gave him the title of Prince in addressing him.

Now all is changed. He is no longer recognized, and there is great irritation and annoyance in consequence of the concessions that have already been made to him. The Princess goes over to the opposition; her *amour propre* is outraged, and she uses very hostile language.

The Marquis de la Valette, who is also piqued by the want of regard shown him by the Emperor, was at the Princess's. He told us about the debate in the Senate on the subject of the oath which it was desired the Empress should take as Regent; he had wished it to be inserted in the Concordate, accompanied by a promise to respect the separate functions of Church and State. The Government did everything to make him withdraw his amendment, but he declined to do so, and on a division it was only lost by eight votes. Eighteen months ago it was a question of making the religious ceremony obligatory in marriage, and giving it precedence over the civil ceremony. The Empress is ultramontane in her views, and it was thought advisable to provide against her clerical tendencies.

July 15th.—I dined with Germiny and La Valette yesterday at the Imperial Club, and we discussed the relations between Princess Mathilde and Nieuwerkerke, as to which I was able to gather the opinions of society, in many different aspects, from their conversation.

Nieuwerkerke has very few friends, but the Princess has, on the contrary, very many; people sympathize with her, and throw the responsibility of her false position entirely upon Nieuwerkerke. He, by his affectation, grand airs, and self-importance, makes himself disliked, and any disgrace that is in store for him will, I feel assured, cause more satisfaction than pity. I am afraid that his conduct furnishes but too often ample grounds for his discomfiture. The Emperor, and especially the Empress, are very displeased with him. A storm is brewing, and there is already a coolness between the Tuileries and St. Gratien.

The Princess talks too much and with too little reflection, as all her observations, coloured and amplified, are reported; in moments of anger she says whatever comes into her head first, and she speaks before everybody, even her servants. To hear her talk you would take her for the Emperor's bitterest enemy, whereas no one really has a warmer affection for him. The world blames Nieuwerkerke because the Princess does not take the position her exalted rank imposes upon her. She might render important services to the Emperor by bringing over to his policy all the literary and artistic people she influences, and who hold her in the most affectionate regard, but she does not do so. The world accuses Nieuwerkerke of thinking only of himself, of his coveted honours, and the crosses that decorate his breast. This explains the very few friends he has, and yet, incredible as it may seem, he is so blind that he believes he is adored by everybody, even by the Emperor himself.

The Emperor, who is very politic and reserved, has not yet broken silence, but the position occupied by Nieuwerkerke with respect to his cousin annoys and irritates him. He is pained to let foreign princes see the disorder of his Court and of his own family; he divines their thoughts, and almost hears what they say in view of the grave, the public scandal this doubly adulterous connection has given rise to. He does not thank Nieuwerkerke by defying and incessantly braving public opinion. Every day he places to Nieuwerkerke's credit some act which he considers an insult to the dignity of the Imperial throne, and is collecting materials for that individual's ultimate and irrevocable disgrace.

Nieuwerkerke, in his superb disdain, despises all warning, and has done more than would have been elsewhere necessary to justify his dismissal. He stays with the Princess at St. Gratien, where he takes command, assumes the manners of a husband, scolds, orders everybody and everything about, and makes his position as public as he well can. There he keeps his horses, carriages, and servants, and the workmen in the village actually say to him : " We shall do this or that job *at your house* to-morrow."

In Paris he dines, breakfasts, and dresses at the Princess's, and has his things taken there by a porter from the Louvre in the Emperor's livery.

The Emperor knows all this, and I am only astonished at one thing, and that is that he has stood it so long.

On Sunday, when we were dining at Reiset's, Nieuwerkerke, without asking permission of anyone, had a door opened because he was too hot. The Princess, who felt the draught on her shoulders, objected ; thereupon, before us all, La Valette and Benedetti being of the party, he and the Princess had a scene which was anything but agreeable.

Several times since I have taken this book in hand I have wished to defend Nieuwerkerke, whom I like against my better sense, but at the present moment I

feel bound to range myself on the side of the Emperor
and to condemn him. I know that he believes and
says he is my patron, because he procured me the
place at the Museum. That I owe this to him is true,
but for six years past I have, in return, rendered him
important services in his position as Director-General.
Then, I may add, that in a matter in which I made a
hundred and ten thousand francs, as he asked if there
was nothing for him, I made him a present of half.
To free himself from any awkward feeling of obligation,
he remarked : " I accept without restraint, as I have
always stood your friend."

I am, consequently, not in his debt, and my candour
is not ingratitude.

July 16*th.*—Yesterday La Guéronnière, as to whom
it is still a question of appointing him Minister of
Public Instruction, came to the Louvre, accompanied
by Latour Dumoulin, to read me a letter he has
written to Fleury, but which in reality is intended for
the Emperor's eye. The letter, which is admirably
conceived and expressed, places La Guéronnière's
position with regard to public opinion in a very fair
light.

" I do not offer myself as a candidate," he says,
" but I place myself at the Emperor's disposal. I
have given considerable attention to matters coming
within the purview of this particular department, and
I believe I can do useful work in the office committed
to my charge if the Emperor should be disposed to
accept my services." La Guéronnière asked me to
get Nieuwerkerke to write a letter for him to Fleury.

I at once sent off an express to Nieuwerkerke and received from him the following letter, which I am about to forward to Fleury.

"MY DEAR FLEURY,

"Have you any candidate of your own for the post of Minister of Public Instruction? If not, what do you think of La Guéronnière? I believe that he would be an excellent choice in every way, and that we should never have occasion to regret supporting him, as has been the case with regard to someone else. The important point will be for La Guéronnière to obtain an interview with the Emperor before the latter returns from Plombières, which would be easy for you to manage, ostensibly with reference to the last matter the Emperor confided to La Guéronnière (a criticism on the works of Napoleon III.), the first part of which he has completed with remarkable brilliancy, but without any nauseating flattery. You can lead up to this subject, and induce the Emperor to express a wish to see the author. That would help matters forward, for, as you know, La Guéronnière has a capacity for pleasing which has scores of times been usefully employed.

"Anyhow, the names of people who do not belong to 'ours,' and whom it may be as well to checkmate, are being put forward. Old Vaillant, for example, supports his friend Dumas. The Empress, they say, favours Merimée, &c., &c.

"We require in this post, where there is scope for the greatest utility, a man who is devoted, intelligent, and politic. La Guéronnière is all these, and he is our friend besides. Look alive, then, and act accordingly, if your heart so prompts you.

"Good-bye, dear friend; I hope that the little general and his mother are well. Accept the assurance of my sincere and cordial friendship.

"NIEUWERKERKE.

"July 15th, 1856."

Véron has just published a pamphlet on the events that have happened since 1848, and this is what he says with respect to Fould. He is writing about the time of the Presidency, when Véron, be it remembered, reigned in all his glory on the throne of the *Constitutionnel* newspaper. Fould was wavering and uncertain, not knowing where and on whose back he should make his political fortune. He fawned upon Véron, saw him daily, consulted him, and did not even neglect Sophie, the famous Sophie, who in her kitchen has received the homage of more than one Minister.

" Rally, then, cordially, sincerely, and without hesitation to the side of our President," said Véron ; " Louis Napoleon is the man whom France wants; he is the man of the future. Relinquish played out parties and moribund ideas." Fould mentioned the repugnance he felt in attaching himself to the fortunes of a man with whom he had no sympathy. However, one day he is brought into contact with the Prince, and on the following morning, quite early, he repairs to Véron and acquaints him with his interview. " The Prince was charming," he said, " most persuasive, and went

even so far as to tempt me with the offer of a portfolio."
"Accept it," said Véron. "Accept—accept—it is
very easily said," replied Fould, "but he would seize
the opportunity of borrowing twenty-five thousand
francs of me."

Fould at this moment is Minister of State, a
member of the Emperor's household, a Senator, has
the Grand Cross of the Legion of Honour, and a
good deal besides, and has never lent a sou to a soul.

F. Barrot, who speaks from personal knowledge, has
just told me the following anecdote. It is not known
and perhaps never will be :—When Prince Napoleon,
during his incarceration at Ham, learned that his
cousin Princess Mathilde had married Anatole
Demidoff, all the affection, or, rather let us say, all the
love he bore for this fascinating and excellent Princess
was awakened in him ; he cried bitterly, and said to
Barrot : " That is the last and cruellest blow fortune
could have dealt me."

July 20th.—I am too unwell to go to St. Gratien to-
day. Latour-Doumonlin, who has just been to see me,
tells me that Dumas's name has been erased from the
list of candidates for the post of Minister of Public
Instruction and Worship on the ground of his being
a Protestant ; Baroche is doing all he can to procure
the appointment for de Parrieux, an Auvergnat, a man
who is only fitted to be a head clerk, but who holds
strong clerical views.

I am afraid of ultramontanism, which the Empress
so affects, and fear we are on the eve of committing a
grave error, which may God and the Emperor avert.

Doctor Werler de Cesty, late principal medical officer attached to the Ministry of War, who has gone through twenty campaigns in Africa, was talking to me an hour ago about the generals who have recently been made senators or marshals, and he remarked that they did not inspire him with any remarkable feeling of confidence. MacMahon, with whom he was very friendly in Africa, said to him one day in his tent, speaking of the Emperor : " Never as long as that man is in power will I put a foot either in Paris or the Tuileries." Cesty happened to meet him a few days ago and greeted him with " What, you in Paris, General—you, who told me you wouldn't put your foot in Paris during Napoleon's reign ? Why, I am even told that you have been to the Tuileries. How was the Emperor ? " " It is no business of yours," the General replied roughly. " I beg your pardon," said Cesty, " I was not speaking to the General, but to MacMahon." The General assumed a more amiable manner, put his arm through Cesty's, and said, shaking his head : " Don't mention the subject again, doctor."

La Guéronnière, who is full of his candidature for the post of Minister of Public Instruction, has just left me. I have advised him to go to St. Gratien this evening, as this morning I had sent on a letter from Fleury. At the present time there are three influential candidates in the field : Parrieux, La Guéronnière, and Royer, ex-Procureur-General. On leaving me La Guéronnière said : " If I am appointed we will be Ministers of Public Instruction together"—merely courtly politeness on his part, of course.

When La Guéronnière was writing some articles which appeared in the *Moniteur* on the subject of the Eastern campaign the Emperor held long conferences with him and acquainted him with his views. Some time after their publication Fould begged La Guéronnière to go and see him, and said : "The work which you have done for the Emperor is quite exceptional and apart from your duties as Councillor of State, and His Majesty does not wish that so important an undertaking, the value of which he cordially appreciates, should be allowed to go without special remuneration. This I am quite prepared to arrange with you on your own terms." La Guéronnière, surprised and hurt, replied : "You are mistaken in your judgment of me, sir. My particular position and that which the Emperor kindly wished to confer upon me in making me a Councillor of State does not permit me to accept a pecuniary reward. Such a recognition would be repugnant to my feelings, and my antecedents afford no excuse for offering it. If I have rendered some service to the Emperor I am ambitious, I do not deny it, of a more delicate form of recompense. For three years past I have managed the Government newspapers, and their polemics. Had I wished to make a fortune—and I have been often pressingly urged to do so by unprincipled people about me—it was within my reach, but the desire never occurred to me. After three years' service I handed the three papers back without having alienated them, and they still remain friendly to the State. No, sir, I do not accept the proposal you make me, nor do I wish to believe that it emanates from the Emperor himself; such an idea would paralyze my pen if ever in the future he had recourse to my services."

Fould, rather disconcerted, made a clumsy excuse, and La Guéronnière took his departure.

Two days afterwards he received a letter in the Emperor's own handwriting, couched in very gracious and affable terms, and abounding in the most cordial expressions of gratitude. It ended by saying " that the services which La Guéronnière had rendered could only be repaid by the sincerity of his gratitude."

I have this instant been informed by Villain, the Vice-President of the Salvage Association, that a scoundrel, of whom, I believe, I have already had occasion to speak, has just been unmasked. Guérin Laurence—who calls himself Count Guérin de Tencin, who has on a former occasion been brought before the police magistrate on the charge of peculation and dishonest practices, amongst other things for usurping, without authority, the Order of the Legion of Honour, which he subsequently succeeded in getting— having been appointed President of the Salvage Society, has been obliged to send in his resignation. I got Villain to come here three months ago, and I told him all about his president's antecedents. Assisted by Count de Lyonne, a member of the society, he proceeded to make inquiries, and discovered a whole series of dishonest acts, the result being that Guérin Laurence has had to resign.

At the last party given at Villeneuve l'Etang, the Countess de Castiglione and the Emperor managed to lose themselves for some time on a little island in the middle of the lake. When the Countess returned, looking somewhat confused, the Empress showed by her manner the indignation she felt.

I have inquired of several Piedmontese about the means of this Castiglione couple. I find they have only 18,000 francs a year left, and their mode of life necessitates an expenditure of sixty or eighty thousand at least. The Countess has been the King of Piedmont's mistress, and I strongly suspect her of intimacy with Nieuwerkerke.

She wishes to rent for the coming winter 17, Rue de Matignon, a house which at the present moment is occupied by my friends Prince Porcia, Countess Bolognini, and Count and Countess Litta. It has a long narrow garden, the end of which abuts on the Champs Elysées, with a small gate leading to a pretty little arbour, which is very convenient for the introduction of a visitor who does not wish to be seen.

July 31st.—I breakfasted this morning with La Guéronnière, who read me his portrait of de Morny. It will be published in about three weeks' time. His candidature is still going on, and the idea of dividing the Ministry into two departments is relinquished. Parrieux, who is backed by the Bishop of Amiens, is his most redoutable opponent.

The Cabinet is much exercised just now about a pamphlet published in Belgium, of which copies have been sent to each of the principal functionaries and the Emperor. It is directed against Collet Maigret, and exposes a lot of dirty business and trafficking. It is written by a person named Meyer, an old fellow-pupil of Collet's, who has been two or three times convicted of swindling, and is now completely broken. In spite of repeated warnings Collet kept this man about his person, but at last was obliged to get rid of him. Meyer avenges himself by publishing all the secrets he has discovered. I ought not to omit to mention that the reason Collet Maigret himself enjoys so much favour is that his wife is Billault's mistress.

I have seen a letter from de Morny to La Guéron-nière, in which he expresses great satisfaction with the article I saw this morning. He only wishes to have added that before leaving Paris he relinquished all the commercial undertakings in which he was engaged, and that, although much interested in active politics, he particularly dislikes any office entailing endless ceremonials and formalities, and that people are not to be surprised, moreover, if he gives up politics as suddenly as he abandoned other pursuits.

Morny, in point of fact, does not wish to make himself too cheap, or to exhaust his influence. His policy is to keep himself in reserve.

August 10*th.*—Back from St. Gratien, where I met at dinner the Russian Envoy, the Minister of Public Works, and Benedetti. In the morning Princess Mathilde had been to see the Emperor at St. Cloud. She found him looking very well, and delighted with his trip to Plombières. He complained, however, of seeing the Empress look so changed and ill on his return. This poor woman is in a sad state of health, and requires constant medical attention.

The Emperor told Princess Mathilde that the Bonaparte-Pattersons were about to leave France because he would not allow them to call themselves Bonaparte alone, without the Patterson. The son has resigned his cavalry commission, and his resignation has been accepted.

August 14th.—The *Moniteur* announces this morning that Marshal Pelissier has been made Duke de Malakoff, with a pension of one hundred thousand francs, and that Roulland, the Advocate-General, is appointed to the Ministry of Public Instruction.

August 16th.—I have seen La Guéronnière, who has given me the key to the mystery of Roulland's appointment.

On Monday last Fould said to La Guéronnière : " You are virtually our colleague, for you have been accepted by the Emperor and the Council, and your nomination is a mere question of formality." But Fould, who, as Minister of State, could have simplified formalities and presented the nomination for signature, did not hurry himself, as he still hoped to detach from the Ministry of Public Instruction the literary duties of that department in order to incorporate them with his own. Billault and Abbatucci, however, stayed behind after a Council meeting at St. Cloud, got round the Emperor, and, with a little pressure and almost by stealth, procured Roulland's appointment. Some of the Ministers, Mons. Magne amongst others, only learned the news through the columns of the *Moniteur.*

The Emperor has a false notion of the state of parties. He repeats the fatal course adopted after the restoration, when the experiment was tried of endeavouring to promote order with the elements of disorder; to secure the interests of royalty, in fact, with the assistance of the Republicans. The restoration dreamed of conciliating parties by strengthening the Republicans at the expense of the Royalists. Fifteen years were consumed in ridiculing the fidelity of the friends who were thought to be no longer of use, and in strengthening the hands of enemies whom it was hoped to conciliate.

At the present time the Emperor thinks to gain over the Republicans, and to wheedle the Socialists by retaining Mons. Billault in office, but I do not hesitate to say that he deceives himself, for by so doing he alienates all that is honest in the ministerial party, and makes no friends into the bargain. The extreme party can never be relied upon, and the mediation of Billault only gives them additional importance. To place the Ministry of the Interior in Billault's hands and public safety in Collet Maigret's are two grave blunders. Like all sovereigns the Emperor thinks that by travelling about he can judge of the state and disposition of the population, that with agents in the pay and under the authority of the Ministry he can obtain reliable information, that with Mocquard as secretary he will have honesty near his person. The Emperor deceives himself, and is deceived. Fleury is a loyal fellow, who speaks the truth according to his lights, but although intelligent enough he is not in a position to see and hear every-thing.

It is a great misfortune that the Emperor's Court is composed, as it is, half of fools, half of knaves. He wishes to govern through his enemies, and still tem-porizes with that foolish and immoral maxim which has been borrowed from the language of revolution : " All for the people."

One knows what is meant by " the people." What ought to be said, and, above all, what ought to be insisted upon, is : " All for the country."

It is with the aid of intelligence and honesty that one ought to govern. A pick-pocket should not be taken under a ruler's protection in order to pacify the estimable class to which he belongs. Christ hunted the dealers out of the temple, and only left the priests and the communicants. He did not say : " I will be conciliatory by allowing my father's house to become a den of thieves."

Never allow an intelligent nation to mistrust your intelligence and knowledge of mankind. Make fewer restrictions with regard to stock-jobbers and specu-lators, and clean out your own stables. When Fould has been made Minister of State, Mocquard President of the Council, and all the rest of the gang have lined their pockets, is the country to be humbugged into the belief that the government is an honest one ?

August 18*th*.—I have just returned from St. Gratien, whither La Guéronnière and Abbé Coquereau came to spend the evening yesterday. La Guéronnière insists that Roulland's appointment is due to Abbatucci

alone, and that Billault was disagreeably surprised
at it, as he foresees in the new Minister a future
rival for his own office, in proof of which view the
Emperor is said to have remarked to Princess Mathilde
that " Roulland was not yet in his proper place." In
any case, Billault's dismissal has become a matter of
hope in the public mind.

La Rochejaquelein has received a letter from
Billault pressing him to withdraw the resignation of his
membership of the Conseil-Général,* and asking him to
go and see him on the subject at the Ministry of the
Interior.

With that superbly disdainful manner for which
he is celebrated, La Rochejaquelein declined to withdraw his resignation, saying that he could not allow
his freedom of action to be questioned by anybody,
nor his dignity of Senator to be insulted, that he
refused the interview, having no confidence in the
Minister ; that having just returned from the South of
France he found it so justly incensed against him that
he declined to have any dealings with him, and that it
was furthermore his intention to send a copy of his
letter to the Emperor and the President of the Senate.
La Rochejaquelein has since asked the Emperor
for an audience, but it is very doubtful whether he
will obtain it, as His Majesty is in one of his fits of
seclusion, when he is very difficult to approach, and he
may not, after all, attach much importance to the
whole affair.

* A sort of County Board, or Assembly, chosen by the electors to
assist the Préfet in his government.

I am unfortunately obliged to mention two fresh cases of favouritism which are exciting public comment. Two young men who are hardly of age, in spite of existing rights, rules of promotion, or any sense of propriety, have just been appointed special receivers of finance; one of the young men is named Baroche, and the other Magne. Mons. Baroche, the father of one, having a property in the neighbourhood of Mantes, wanted his son made financial administrator in his district. They therefore removed the old receiver, who desired nothing more than to be left where he was, and sent him elsewhere, in order that a vacancy might be made for the young and interesting Baroche, who is a brother of the jackanapes of that name who is a member of the Council of State. The same proceeding happened with regard to young Magne.

If you speak of the old dynasty to people they lose themselves in their abuse of royal favours. But in place of aristocrats, men of birth and position, conspicuous for their tact and good manners, we are now treated to a parcel of blackguards who yesterday still wore the lawyer's gown; an avaricious, middle-class, shuffling race, without energy or courage, eager for the loaves and fishes, and untrue to their trusts.

The Emperor in his former fulminations always criticized unsparingly Governments composed of lawyers, and yet no Administration was ever so full of them, so monopolized by gentlemen of the long-robe, as his own. It is true that under Louis-Philippe barristers occupied too many of the important offices, but the principal

Ministers were always Broglies, Moles, Guizots, or Thierses.   To-day we have descended lower still. Rouher is a barrister, Billault a barrister, Magne a barrister, Abbatucci a barrister, and so on.   A barrister could not be found for the post of War Minister, but the Minister of Foreign Affairs is a Polish Jew, a bastard son of Napoleon I., and the Minister of State a bankrupt Jew, who, through the agency of his son, manages to manipulate all important financial transactions.

CHAPTER XIV.

1856 (*continued*).

August 20th.—The Emperor and Empress left yesterday for Biarritz. England continues her Italian agitation, and the Press is giving her powerful support. The Piedmontese are rubbing their hands with glee, and the King already pictures himself the Sovereign of united Italy, with England as his ally, France in a state of uneasiness, the Papacy abolished (to the joy of all good Protestants), and Austria the laughing stock of Europe.   It will be an unhappy day for us all when English intrigues succeed ; already Italy is full of the elements of trouble.   Mazzini will make profit out of the game England and Piedmont are playing, and France will be forced to intervene, unless, indeed, she abandons for ever the great cause of Catholicism, the work of her Emperor Charlemagne.

The King of Naples has replied to the despatches and insults of England, saying that he does not admit she has more right to interfere with the kingdom of the two Sicilies than he would have to meddle with the affairs of Ireland and India, and that the attempt to coerce him is all the more incredible just at a time when England and France have been engaged in a great war, undertaken for the express purpose of preventing a feeble empire from being intimidated by a powerful one.

The Piedmontese students having expressed· their gratitude to the English papers which have advocated and supported the cause of the Italian revolution, two . hundred self-styled French students, recruited at the Chaumière or some other pot-house, have imitated their example, and thanked the four *good French papers, Le Siècle, La Presse, l'Estafette,* and *La Revue de Paris,* for reproducing the Piedmontese students' address.   Here is an example of the style adopted by these budding Mazzinians :

" We desire, therefore, to respond to our brothers of

Turin, whose intention has not been merely to issue a monarchical and Piedmontese circular, but rather to give expression to patriotic aspirations for national and Italian unity. We are desirous to extend the hand of friendship across Mont-Cenis to a nation with a long and glorious history, which lost its own independence because it became too solicitous for the welfare of the universe, and which now only seeks to recover its freedom in order that in conjunction with ourselves it may labour for the fraternal alliance of all European peoples."

Such is the thinly-veiled language of these young Socialists, who only yesterday left school and their mothers' apron strings to study medicine and law, and now set themselves up as the arbiters of the universe. A respectable authority, indeed, to follow !

The Universal Republicans of New York have just resolved, under date of August 6th, that a meeting shall be held on the 10th to take into consideration the instant departure of those of its members who desire to repair to whatever country first sounds the tocsin of revolution.

All this is nectar to England, who begins to find France too powerful by half. Italy must be set in commotion in order to give the French something to do and to think about, and to satisfy the cravings of the Puritanical party in old England, who calmly demand the expropriation of the Pope for the sake of the public weal.

September 3rd.—I have been ill, and my black book has been closed in consequence, but I am now recovered,

and must open it again, as I have a bit of scandal to
inscribe upon its pages.

Madame de Silveyra (Mdlle. de Menneval that was),
the wife of a member of the Portuguese Embassy, a
gambler without visible means of existence, who is
principally remarkable for having hitherto evaded social
ostracism, has just eloped with a certain young gentleman named de Louvencourt. Madame de Silveyra
is a leader of fashion, rather coquettish in her manner
and lax in her morals. She once remarked in my
hearing, with the only touch of simplicity I ever
observed in her: " I only care for gold." She is the
sister of Madame Murat, who for a long time has lived
publicly with Prince de la Moskowa, and her brother,
the little Baron de Menneval, is the Emperor's orderly
officer.

I am told that Moskowa, who has already had three
attacks of apoplexy, is given over by his doctors.

Mons. Bonaparte-Patterson took me aside when I
met him at the Imperial Club yesterday and assured me
that Princess Mathilde was incorrect in her statement
that he had resigned his commission in the French
cavalry. Why have started such a story ? What is
the object of such misleading rumours ? I know not.

September 7th.—The working classes throughout
the towns of Normandy and Picardy are violently
excited about the proposed reduction in the Customs
tariffs, and there will probably be some danger just
now in touching the protective dues.

September 11th.—Many people are living in a fool's
paradise. After every revolutionary crisis, there are

persons who, believing that all danger is over, and that there is nothing more to fear, allow themselves, in defiance of all experience, to be lulled into a feeling of false security.

The different political parties, which were for a moment the victims of fright, are now regaining confidence and resuming their old quarrels. Those who call themselves the party of order say : " It is for the Government to protect society," and, as soon as their terror is allayed, they revert to their internal divisions, leaving the authorities to combat single-handed with the anarchists and others who do not allow their objects to be frustrated, or their cause to be weakened by foolish dissensions.

What a fright they were in, in what abject terror, in 1848 and again on December 2nd, were these fine gentlemen, who have now resumed their old Legitimist and Orleanist conspiracies, these ridiculous, vain, middle-class politicians who always side with the Opposition and Irreconcilables when once their courage is restored.

For some time an extensive conspiracy, under an economic disguise, has been on foot against the Government. The Orleanists are assisting the movement through their organ the *Debats*, and the rest of the imbeciles are joining in chorus. It has reference to the lowering of the duties, and France is divided into two camps, consisting of Protectionists and Freetraders. A lively agitation has resulted, and the question is being threshed out by the Conseils Généraux.

If the protection of French industry is given up

and free-trade is established a terrible crisis will follow ; the minds of the working classes are so excited on the subject that a revolution may take place at any moment.

Letting alone the discontent of the manufacturers, one of the effects of free-trade will be the lowering of wages, and the working man, who is already scarcely able to exist with the present price of labour, will be reduced to penury. Wherever the railways penetrate food and lodging become dearer, without any corresponding increase in wages ; this has already given the Conseils Généraux cause for uneasiness, and their anxiety will be alarmingly augmented by the advent of free-trade.

A Government which is consolidating its position and requires peace should not introduce so radical a measure into its economical system. It is not wise to smoke over a barrel of gunpowder.

The gentlemen of the *Debats* are urging Messieurs Chevalier and Kœchlin to inaugurate free-trade, they even go so far as to praise the Emperor and promise him all their support in the hope that he will fall into the snare ! How they would rub their hands if he did so, for their only dream is of the Count de Paris, and that good and zealous Protestant the Duchess d'Orleans, for whose edification two or three excellent Catholic prelates are every day roasted alive.

They cheer free-trade at the top of their voices, and blow their political trumpets, but it simply means after all : "Revolutions are our game, they will clear the atmosphere, and enable us to settle down under the energizing influence of parliamentary government, with the Count de Paris, his august mother, and the illustrious Ministers, Thiers and Guizot, at the head of it.

Old jugglers of the parliamentary arena, how absolutely you resemble the irreconcilables of 1815. You have learned nothing and forgotten nothing !

Another very disquieting sign in France is that there is scarcely anyone left who takes the least heed of the public interest; things are allowed to drift. People are becoming rather like the Gauls of the fifth century, who made their offerings to the Muses, and then shut themselves up in their " villas," not wishing to hear the approach of the barbarians whose invasion became daily more imminent.

The public functionaries are either timid, venal, or incapable, and the Magistracy, under the direction of Abbatucci, is distinctly hostile.

Quite recently the advocate Crémieux went to conduct a case at Limoges, where the Bench received him with a kind of ovation. He dined with the President of the Court and the Judges, and during dessert greatly amused those worthies with some rather doubtful anecdotes about the Emperor and Empress. The party was most hilarious.

Crémieux said to one of the Judges who had failed in an application he had made to Abbatucci : "Why the devil did you allow yourself to be recommended by the Right Honourable the Count de la Guéronnière ? a man who calls himself Count and places the prefix ' de' before his name. Abbatucci, my dear Judge, is a true Republican of the olden time; he detests, as I do, all titles of nobility. We are the best friends in the world, and I could have arranged the matter for you without difficulty had you come to me." Such language as this requires no comment.

September 26*th.*—We are about to receive an embassy from the King of Burmah. The ambassador-in-chief, General d'Orgoni, probably arrived in Paris this morning. Before 1830 he was a non-commissioned officer in the Mounted Chasseurs of the Guard, and was then called Girandeau. In 1832 he took part, during the Brittany War, with the Royalists, after which he served under Marshal Bourmont in Don Miguel's army, where he gained the rank of Captain. After Don Miguel's defeat Girandeau spent some time in Italy, and then went to the island of Bourbon. There he started a riding-school, and married an old Rear-Admiral's daughter, who died and left him a widower after eighteen months of married bliss. The year following he married another of the Rear-Admiral's daughters, but there seemed to be a fatality connected with these marriages, for in a very short time she died also. Finally, in 1847, his resources having come to an end, and being hard pressed by his creditors, Girandeau changed his name to Orgoni, which was a family patronymic, set sail for India, and, after many changes of fortune, became General-in-Chief of the Burmese army. D'Orgoni detests the English, and is entirely devoted to French interests.

September 29*th.*—The *Cologne Gazette* has given publicity during the last few days to a circular issued from the Russian Chancellor's Office. It has been copied into all the papers, and is, in my opinion, an important document. It has reference to the pressure which the Powers, more especially France and England, are bringing to bear upon the kingdoms of Naples and Greece.

In principle, and according to strict equity, Russia is perfectly right, when in dignified and moderate language she says that she fails to understand how, after proclaiming and sustaining by force of arms the equality of sovereigns and the respect due to weak Powers from strong ones, it can now be thought consistent to put pressure upon an inferior nation in regard to the administration and government of its own internal affairs. Russia, furthermore, says that she cannot ally herself with such a policy, and instructs her agents to protest against any acts consequent upon it.

As far as regards Naples, Russia is entirely in the right; but with respect to Greece her position is not so logical.

It must not be forgotten that the Grecian Kingdom is the work of Europe, the joint achievement of the Powers. She is, therefore, under their tutelage, supported by their influence and purse, and still in their debt. That being so, the Powers have a right to intervene in her affairs, and to interest themselves in a country in which they are in a sense conjoint partners.

But in Naples there is no such right of intervention; the King owes nothing to the Powers, and he is not their debtor. Without their assistance he suppressed the Revolution of 1848, which was, moreover, largely due to interference on the part of England.

The despatch of the fleets is a hostile demonstration against the Neapolitan King, and a further source of delight to the revolutionary party, while the co-operation of the Sardinian war-vessels, few as they may be, is an act of monstrosity.

Sardinia is the centre of all Italian agitation, and the place of refuge for revolutionists from every part of the peninsula. Under the guidance of Monsieur de Cavour, that kingdom aspires to the dominion of the whole of Italy, and France allows her to come and parade herself under the very shadow of her flag in the Bay of Naples.

England pushes forward Sardinia, whom she wishes to see paramount in Italy, because in that case she weakens Austria, and creates future embarrassment for France, also because, as a Protestant Power, she foresees that the success of her project will sooner or later lead to the abolition of the Papal authority.

All this is an extremely grave matter, and exhibits our diplomatists in a very poor light. Persigny, in London, is a mockery; and Bourquency, in Vienna, a simple farce.

I veritably believe that the end of the world is approaching, for governments and nations alike are becoming insane.

Whenever a revolution triumphs, never mind how monstrous it may be, England cries out " No intervention !" but when royalty is in the ascendant, then, forsooth, she proclaims a crusade.

October 12th.—A matter which is of serious importance to Walewski, serious, indeed, from all points of view, is now being publicly talked about. Although actually Minister of Foreign Affairs, Walewski has been speculating on the Bourse and lost his money. Manuel, his stockbroker, has applied to him for considerable sums due for differences. He has offered to pay a part of his debt, but Manuel says : " No, it is either owed me, or it is not. I can consent to no compromise ; you shall pay me the whole amount or petition the Courts to adjudge it a debt of honour." In order to avoid a scandal the Emperor has paid the money.

This happened at the time the Congress was sitting in Paris.

It is to be noted, therefore, that a Minister can speculate in the public funds, render himself amenable to the law, and get off scot free with the Grand Cross of the Legion of Honour as his reward !

La Guéronnière told me yesterday that he was talking with Fould about the financial crisis that has depleted so many fortunes, and of the evils inseparable from the passion for speculation, and that Fould had emphatically remarked : " Yes, all this proves the more conclusively that work is the only and the surest road to fortune ! "

October 13th.—Have returned from St. Gratien, which I found in a state of faction and gossip. Princess Mathilde's little court is curiously composed, no one seems to live on good terms there with his neighbour. The Princess is very capricious in her friendships, and frequently changes her favourites both male and female. But the Reisets and the two Girauds still reign, and Nieuwerkerke still governs.

Madame de Serlay has grown jealous, and has treated Madame Reiset with scant courtesy. Explanations have been demanded, and the Princess and General Bougenel have had to interfere; everything, in fact, is as fish-wife in tone as it can well be.

The Empress, Prince Jérôme, and his son paid a visit to St. Gratien on Saturday.

October 14th.—Important news reached us from Spain yesterday. Marshal O'Donnel and the Ministry have resigned, and Marshal Narvaez has been charged to form a Government. Ever since the last Spanish revolution began I have constantly predicted that directly Marshal Narvaez set his foot in Spain he would make short work of such revolutionary leaders as O'Donnel and Prim. I defended this opinion yesterday at the Imperial Club against the Marquis de Benalua, an old Spanish diplomatist; he is a keen-scented politician, and, generally speaking, a very good judge of events, but he attributes in this instance too much importance to Prim and O'Donnel.

What will happen now? Neither I nor anyone else can foresee. For my part I do not wish to know what Narvaez's programme is to be. I care little for programmes. All I want to know is how he will act, and what course he will adopt in order to rid Spain of her Esparteros, O'Donnels and Prims.

There is nothing fresh from Naples.

The big wigs of our Court are very much exercised just now. The Emperor has commanded that during the residence of the Court at Compiègne the wearers of the " button " are to dine in hunting coats, white breeches, silk stockings, and patent-leather shoes, a decree which, strange to relate, has at present drawn forth no protest from the European Powers !

Three extraordinary marriages have recently taken place. E. de Girardin espouses the reigning beauty of Paris during the past winter, Mdlle. de Tiffembach, a delightful blonde, very elegant, and a great coquette. She is said to be the natural daughter of the Duke of Nassau, but, whether that be so or not, it is well known that her mother was the Duke's mistress.

The Duchess de Mouchy has married Mons. Pinel, late Secretary General to the Prefecture of Police, who is allied to the Noailles through a left-handed marriage.

Lastly, Louis de Noailles, the younger brother of the late Duke de Mouchy, is married to the daughter of an old soldier pensioner at the Hôtel des Invalides. For some time past he has been paying his addresses to the young person, taking his glass with her father, and playing piquet of an evening with her mother, who sells salad at the Gros Caillou. The Noailles are an unfortunate family.

October 21*st.*—A paragraph in the *Moniteur* of yesterday announces the breaking off of diplomatic relations between France and England and the kingdom of Naples. The ambassadors have left the country, but the fleets will not take possession of the

Bay of Naples. In the paragraph in question it is stated that the King of Naples has not yielded to the friendly representations of France and England as Belgium and Greece have done, and that the system of coercion adopted by the King of Naples being a constant menace to the peace of Europe, the allied Great Powers have thought it their duty to break off diplomatic relations without, at the same time, having recourse to actively hostile measures. Europe at the present moment is far from being in a normal or tranquil state, for, besides the Neapolitan business and the financial crisis, the affairs of the Danubian Principalities, the navigation of the Danube, and the misunderstanding between England and Persia, are all matters of serious moment.

The Duchess of Genoa having formed an imprudent intimacy with a captain in the Piedmontese army, she confided her condition to her brother-in-law, the King of Piedmont, who did everything in his power to keep the matter a profound secret, but in this he reckoned without the Duchess's confessor, the Bishop of Turin. This prelate would not allow so admirable an opportunity of showing his spite to the King of Piedmont to pass, ill-feeling being admittedly as strong in the Church as in politics. One morning, therefore, without previous warning or formality of any kind, the King learns that his sister-in-law has just been married by the Bishop to the aforesaid captain.

The Duchess of Genoa, who was a Saxon Princess, is sent back to her country, the custody of her children

is taken from her, and her husband is deprived of his
commission for having married without the King's
consent.

October 22nd.—After the review of troops, which
took place at Vincennes a few days ago, and when the
Emperor was returning to Paris by the Faubourg St.
Antoine, some workmen placed themselves in his way
and cried, " Vive la Republique! " They were immediately arrested.

If I ever required proof that Paris is the most gossiping place in the world I have now got it. At the
present moment I am building on some land close to
the Bois de Boulogne, and in the avenue leading to the
Porte des Princes, a little house, half stone, half brick,
in the style of Louis XIII. The whole of the ground,
garden included, is about 750 yards square, and the
land and building will cost me 28,000 francs. To fill
the house I have a lot of old furniture, porcelain, and
odd follies that I have been collecting for some time,
curious in their way, but nothing more. Well, the
news has got about, how I know not, that I am
building and furnishing a sumptuous palace, and that
I have made an enormous fortune by speculations, &c.,
&c. How I shall be lionized this winter!

The gathering at Compiègne is a curious one; the
Court is really not very happy in its selection.
Literature is represented by Count Alfred de Vigny,
a sort of musical Dorat, who tries to wear his hair like
Bernardin de Saint-Pierre, plasters his face, and
touches up his lips to make them pink; in fact, he
resembles an old woman dressed in man's attire

contrary to police regulations. De Vigny has been clever in his fashion, but now has nothing left but affectation; he simpers, screws up his mouth to make some remark which is generally inaudible, and affects little roguish ways. He has the very greatest respect for his own person, and considers himself so inimitable that he even watches his own shadow with affectionate interest. He has ceased to write any more, however, for fear of making a hash of it.

October 23rd.—We will not pursue the biography of the Compiègne guests any further; it might tempt us too far. Prince Beauvau, who is one of the party, is one of the greatest bores I know. Prince de Bauffremont is a nonentity wrapped up in the skin of an old *beau*. Count de Caumont la Force is an old *roué* with questionable manners, whose wife was assassinated less than a year ago. The Marquis de Caulaincourt is a plucky fellow, who lost his sight in the army, but he is by no means bright. Count Frederick de Lagrange adds to a bad reputation an inordinate vanity. Baron Hallez Claparède is as tiring as autumn rain. Baron de Rothschild will, perhaps, amuse the assembly with some financial calculations. Aubert and Meyerbeer will talk music with Verdi, and Horace Vernet and Isabey will distribute their puns. The Marquis of Hertford is very clever and amusing, but Ossuna, Sclafani, and the Prince de Croye are outsiders.

Fill up the background of this picture with Ministers, Generals, and officials, with Madames Magne, Hamelin, Roulland, Troplong, Baroche, and Magnan, and if you do not admit that the society is a very pretty and select assortment you are really too difficult to please.

October 24th.—The following paragraph, which appears to-day in the unofficial part of the *Moniteur*, is not without significance :—

"Paris, October 23rd.

"For some time past certain English newspapers have endeavoured to spread calumnious reports concerning the French Government, which are the more safely indulged in since, being of anonymous origin, they can only be replied to with contempt. We are aware of the great respect accorded to the Press in England and the freedom it enjoys, so much so that in calling attention to its misdeeds we only wish to appeal to the good sense and loyalty of the English people, and to warn them against the dangers of a system which, while diminishing the good feeling between the two Governments, may also tend to destroy the friendship of two nations whose continued alliance is the surest guarantee of the peace of the world."

The English alliance will soon be what I have always thought it would become, an alliance the duration of which is assured so long as all the advantages are on the side of England.

This nation urges us on in the Neapolitan affair, and desires that we should be more energetic. The fact is, she wants to possess herself of Sicily and the sulphur mines of Naples. A great deal too complimentary to France during the Crimean war, where her own army made a very poor figure, and during the expedition to the Baltic, which her fleet did not succeed in Anglicizing, she now resumes her arrogant tone. Our expedition to the Crimea will have been made simply for the purpose of facilitating her designs against Persia, and in acknowledgment of our assistance she proceeds to upset Italy, and place on our flank, strengthened in influence and power, her ally the King of Piedmont.

October 31*st.*—Some of the English papers approve of the paragraph in the *Moniteur*, but others continue their aggressive tone. In point of fact, we are not in agreement with England either as regards the Danubian Principalities or the Neapolitan question. Matters are very strained.

On the other hand, the Orleanists and Socialists are bent on agitation, in which they are seconded by the dearness of food and lodging, the commercial and financial depression, and the state of affairs on the Bourse.

The Court is at Compiègne, and will move from there to Fontainbleau. It has just come from Biarritz, after previously spending a month at Plombières. These holidays are thought to be a good deal too protracted. Considerable dissatisfaction is also felt with the diplomatic *rôle* we are playing in Europe. Nothing can be more abject than two-thirds of our diplomatic agents. It is time that the Emperor awoke to the situation.

November 7*th.*—The position of affairs gives cause for anxiety. It seems certain that England and Austria have come to an understanding with regard to Turkey. These two Powers have agreed to prolong the occupation of the Black Sea and the Danubian Principalities. It is also said that England thinks of occupying with her troops some place in Sicily as a set-off against the presence of the French in Rome, and of the Austrians in the States of the Church. But England forgets that France and Austria were appealed to by the Roman Government because it was unable to defend itself alone against the revolution by which it was menaced.

For a month past the English Press has been unrestrained in its violence against the French Government; the alliance, indeed, is at an end, and the Congress, which was to have held further sittings in Paris, will not meet again, because, as the Austrian papers put it, in the present condition of distrust and irritation between the European Cabinets a meeting would be fraught with more danger than utility. Besides, adds the Austrian Press, England will know how to defend the Treaty of Paris!

The Turkish Ministry which demanded the evacuation of the Principalities and the withdrawal of the English fleet has been superseded.

Our diplomacy is defeated everywhere and at all points, owing to the incapacity of our agents, during which time the Court is amusing itself at Compiègne at a cost of " thirty-five thousand francs a day."

The English ambassador and the Marquis of Hertford are the only two persons of distinction who are invited to stay the whole of the time the Court is there.

November 14*th.*—The Emperor's reply to the address

presented to him by the Russian ambassador, Count de Kisselef, is the subject of general conversation. It is held to be very friendly to Russia, and people see in it a confirmation of the understanding which gives so much umbrage to England.

I do not believe, as all the enemies of the Government do, that we have altogether burnt the writings, but we do not see things in the same light. We are particularly averse, after acting as the ally of England in a matter of general European interest, to become her tool in a cause in which her own interest alone is involved. We do not wish to engage in war afresh merely to add to her preponderance.

England separates from us and allies herself with Austria in the affair of the Principalities and the Black Sea, a different cause altogether from that with which we went to the Crimea. Let her by all means, if she wishes to, only let it be a lesson to us in the future not to allow ourselves to be hoodwinked by English friendship.

Our marriage with England was one of prudence. The moment that common-sense ceases to confirm the conditions of the alliance, let the Divorce Court intervene. Russia and Prussia are drawing closer to us. Austria coquettes with England, and her ambassador, it is stated this morning, is the only foreign diplomatist invited by the Emperor of Austria to accompany him during his journey to Italy.

I dined alone with Marshal Canrobert yesterday. He is a very agreeable man, a little conscious of his own dignity, perhaps, but this is noticeable rather in his manner and attitude than in his speech. He talks well on the subject of the war, and without ostentation.

Walewski will probably leave the Ministry, and Billault, they say, is to be replaced by Roulland. The dismissal of the former will be no loss, that of the latter will be much to the Emperor's credit.

November 17*th.*—The English alliance is still rather shaky, and the *Times* remarks that if it is not consolidated before the meeting of Parliament there is great risk of a rupture. England is exercising all her influence, and wishes to frighten us into joining in her aggressive policy. She pretends, too, that we are to participate in the advantages accruing from all her enterprises. To be agreeable to her, therefore, we have declined to receive the embassy Persia proposed to send to us, and have snubbed General d'Orgoni, who came to arrange a very desirable commercial treaty with the King of Burmah. Poor General d'Orgoni is really too badly treated, he is barely listened to, can get no answer to his proposals, and the Foreign Minister scarcely condescends to receive him.

The sole object of the English alliance is to range us among her satellites, and make us in a sort of manner her police constable. The interests of France should lead us in another direction. It is contrary to all sane policy to support England's ambitious views with regard to Sicily, and to facilitate her complete absorption of India. She has raised the cry of " Stop thief " against Russia in order to mask her own dishonest projects; no one has even the right to look at

India, and to facilitate the defence of that immense colony, consisting of whole kingdoms under the subjection and sway of a company of London merchants; she now wishes to get a footing in some Persian province. Persia's point of attack, be it noted, is not so much India as Herat, which is a sort of half-way-house.

What England does in India she wishes to do in Italy, and that ostentatious sympathy with the poor Italians is only a piece of acting in which she is seconded by the King of Piedmont. Manin, who is in Paris, said a day or two ago : " France and England want to best the Italians, and it is for that reason that I will not allow myself to be taken in with all this fuss about Naples. England wants to dominate Italy with her onerous protection, while France wants to force some Murat or other upon the throne of the two Sicilies. We, who are real Italians, do not wish for all this humbug ; we look forward to a united Italy, either in the form of a Kingdom or a Republic, and as for the new dynasty they wish to plant upon us, we after all much prefer the race of Neapolitan Bourbons, who have become naturalized, and whom we can respect."

The *Presse* and the *Indépendence* have published within the last few days a letter from Louis-Philippe to the King of Naples, in which the monarch of the Revolution counsels his nephew to make concessions, and avail himself of the example afforded by France. The King of Naples, in his reply, which is also published, says that he does not wish to suffer either the fate of Louis XVI. or of Charles X., that he intends to remain King to the end of the chapter, and that it is his business to think and act for his people, to whom he wishes to secure peace and a good and honest administration, and that, moreover, he does not intend to take his example from French politics, which have been the horror and scandal of Europe.

Louis-Philippe, with his policy of concession, lost his throne; the King of Naples, with his policy of resistance, still retains his; moreover it is not revolution that will depose him, but probably the active assistance France and England will give to his enemies. England was not very concerned about the massacres of the priests which took place in 1848, and was on sufficiently good terms with the Ledru-Rollins and Louis Blancs when they attempted to ruin France and oppress the sanest portion of her population. She covenants with all rebels, and naturally enough, therefore, sides against a King who takes his precautions against the emissaries of revolution.

What the devil does France want to mix herself up in this mess for? Is it on account of Murat and his connection Chassiron? That would, indeed, be an excellent joke!

Our Ministry forgets that to be on good terms with England you must make yourself respected. She must be bullied. She is like those women who adore husbands who beat them. Look at America. America insults England, scoffs at her, hunts her Minister out of the country, and violates her treaties, and yet England stands it all, no expression on her physiognomy betrays the pain she suffers from the kicks she receives behind.

December 4th.—England has at length succeeded in exciting a revolution in Sicily. It is not yet known what the gravity of the crisis is, but the Neapolitan army is very much distracted with revolutionary proclamations. The English fleet in the Black Sea is augmented by a number of vessels. England doubtless hopes by means of the Neapolitan and Neuchâtel business to blind Europe as to her designs in the East.

Our alliance with England is compromised because we will not act the part of her very humble servants. There is no abuse of us too gross for the English newspapers, and I shall not be at all surprised if before very long the refugees enjoying English protection do not excite some troubles in France. Walweski and Morny are above all the objects of the bitterest attacks of the English Press, but the Emperor himself comes in for his share of abuse.

The *Times* tells him "that the restoration in France collapsed a very few months after the coolness which arose with England on account of the expedition to Algiers, and that Louis-Philippe's fall dated from the disagreement about the Spanish marriages."

This comes in the form of a little friendly advice, but it is, at the same time, a documentary statement, which is not without importance, as throwing light upon the existing causes of our two last revolutions.

The Crown Prince of Prussia has just paid his second visit to the Museum. He was here at nine o'clock. Nieuwerkerke having gone shooting I had the honour of escorting the Prince through the Gallery of Antiquities. He is a young man with distinguished presence and an agreeable face, courteous, intelligent, and extremely fond of art, of which he speaks with the knowledge of a connoisseur.

The *Moniteur* of this morning contains a very important announcement with regard to the Neuchâtel affair. The Government therein says that all its conciliatory endeavours have failed through the obstinacy of the Swiss and the advice given to them by incendiary leaders, and that the Swiss will now only have themselves to thank if rigorous measures are adopted.

England fans the beginning of every conflagration in order to free her hand in Persia.

That selfish people, that country of egotism called England, wishes to set up as law that no one has the right to interfere with India or the kings she dethrones there, the Empires she overthrows, the dynasties she strangles, while she herself is everywhere else to have a finger in the pie. She raises a hue and cry against Russian designs in the East, and excites a tempest against France on account of Algeria. England is the old Rome of the Emperors, and all the rest of the world is composed of tributary kingdoms!

December 19th.—There was a little dance at the Tuileries yesterday, at which some Egyptian Highness was the most notable person present.

On Wednesday I dined at Princess Mathilde's with Vimercati, aide-de-camp to the King of Sardinia, and La Guéronnière. The affairs of Italy were the principal topic of conversation. Benedetti came in after dinner. The Princess, as usual, was very revolutionary in her language about Italy, and spoke in a most deplorable manner of the clergy. Vimercati also indulged in

Utopianism, according to the order of the day in
Turin : "the papacy ousted from Rome," &c., &c., and
then always the same ill-disguised : "Yes, we have
been masters of the world."

I answered him : "You are no more ancient Romans
than the Turks are Greeks of the Byzantine Empire.
You Lombards were a northern race of invaders. You
were intruders just as the Germans are intruders at
the present day. And, besides, what is the record of
your history from the time of the middle ages until
now ? A succession of internecine struggles, wars
waged to determine what foreign Prince should hold
the Duchy of Milan. If to-day the freedom of Italy
were proclaimed, to-morrow we should see this town
holding that one by the throat. Pope Pius IX. endeavoured to govern by constitutional methods, and
how has he been rewarded ? They assassinated his
Minister, a man of mark, on the steps of the Constituent Assembly, and when the members of the house
were informed of the horrible deed they agreed to
proceed with the previous question. The bust of
the murderer was crowned with flowers, and carried
from *café* to *café*, and the Pope's palace was attacked
by armed men. Again, during the reign of the Roman
convention priests were massacred at Saint Firmin.

"Italy is menaced by mad passions, which England
and Sardinia are too prone to foment; honest
Utopians like yourself, my dear Vimercati, will be
among the first victims of the coming revolution."

END OF VOL. I.